Stephen Moore

2008

Beyond
Yonder

Beyond Yonder

Stephen Morris

The Public Press

Randolph   Caspar

Requests for permission to make copies of any part of this book
should be mailed to

Permissions Department
The Public Press
100 Gilead Brook Road
Randolph, Vermont 05060.

Library of Congress Cataloging-in-Publication Data
Morris, Stephen
Beyond Yonder.
I. Title.
ISBN 0-9764520-3-0

Maps by Barbara W. Carter
Book design by Michael Potts
for The Public Press

contents:

Preface:
North Country Dominion

Newcomers migrate north from the megalopolis, lured by the perceived simplicity of rural life. They soon discover that settings are more easily changed than habits. Having purchased their piece of sylvan paradise, ex-suburbanites want to lock the gate behind them. For many the first action following the closing of a sale is posting the "No Trespassing" and "No Hunting" signs.

It comes as no surprise that tensions arise between these invaders and a native population that has no perception of the novelty factor in their setting. The North Country is where they live. This is the world. What's the big deal?

Because the human species has a constant need for stimulation, the groups focus on each other. This is a melting pot with only two ingredients. In the suburbs, stimulation may be achieved via shopping malls, traffic jams, and amusement parks. In the North Country, people-watching takes the place of all three. Once in a while there is time to talk about the weather.

Each group thinks it has a divine right to the North Country. The recent arrivals bought their way in, and because this is America, they now own it. They combat adversity with money and technology. The natives use different weapons, such as experience and expectations, but they are not above using guns.

Beyond Yonder is yet another view of the continuing struggle for North Country dominion. The world becomes divided into Flatlanders and Chucks, the cultural demarcations maintained as diligently as the farmer's fences. The groups align only when equally threatened by a neutral third party, such as the Elements. The story has been written a hundred times before, usually by Flatlanders more proficient with pens than guns. It is comforting to know that the story will be written a hundred times more, because this is a struggle not unlike the World Series. Any team can be champion for a while, but no one holds the crown for long. The concept of an ultimate winner would remove all interest from the struggle.

In the real world there are few purebred Chucks or Flatlanders, but rather flesh-and-blood people who straddle the fence, a little more to one side than the other. Several have been very helpful in the creation of this book and deserve my sincere thanks.

Maryjane Kennedy (10% Flatlander, 90% Chuck) and Stephen Reid (30/70) guided the manuscript in its most formative stages and kept me from making many statements that would have betrayed my own Down Country roots. Jack Rowell, whose Chuck pedigree is unquestioned, provided the original photo illustrations, and Barbara Carter (40/60) the illustrations. For anyone who cares, I rate a perfect 50/50 on the Flatlander/Chuck scale, the only person in Vermont to be able to make that claim.

The greatest debt is owed to the people of central Vermont, specifically the Randolph to West Brookfield corridor, who provided models for the characters. They will be able to glimpse a nose here, a forehead there, an incident everywhere. Because the characters in the book are intended to amuse, rather than portray, I caution against application of names and faces in the book to counterparts in real life.

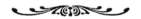

Over and Beyond

Part One
Upper Granville B.F.

(Before Flatlanders)

Over Yonder Hill

The valley runs north and south for almost four miles. Hills rise on all sides, Granville Ridge to the east, Bear Hill to the west, Bailey's Peak to the north, obscure and unnamed mounds to the south. Tomar Brook is the primary watershed, originating as a series of rivulets in the surrounding hills and emptying into the Fifth Branch of the White River. This stream, in turn, cuts through Granville "Gulf" (the Vermonter's term for the narrow ravine between two sharply angled hills) and flows eventually into the Connecticut River.

The topography is distinctly Green Mountain, formed by creeping glaciers at the onset of the last interstadial. Nothing spectacular, but beauty at every turn. It is a world of small scale where all horizons are within throwing distance. Visitors feel exposed because they cannot see enemies approaching; conversely, natives feel protected because enemies cannot see them. The ever-present trees enhance the feeling of seclusion. Vermont is squarely in the midst of one of the world's few remaining hardwood forests. Despite the penchant of the natives to insert pieces of this forest into cast iron stoves with great regularity from September through May, the forest is expanding.

The winters are long, but livable. Upper Granville catches the north wind "dead nuts on," in the words of locals like Emil Dummerston Weed, but is otherwise protected from winter's iciest blasts. The town's elevation means that it frequently gets snow when Granville gets rain. As much as thirty inches more will fall in the high valley than in neighboring towns.

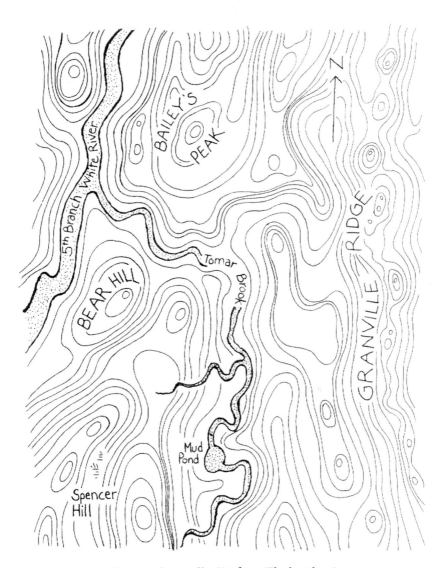

Upper Granville (Before Flatlanders)

January is the coldest month, although the third week produces a spiteful thaw that ruins the roads and skiing. February is the bleakest, as nature spews forth the most vile of its venom. March is ridiculous, kisses of springtime interspersed with frigid slaps. The roads thaw each day only to freeze at night. Everyone spends at least some time in a ditch.

April is the cruelest month; the flippancy of March goes to extremes just when the human psyche is least able to resist. Cabin fever and the flu run hand in hand. Kids play baseball in the snow, and trout season opens on frozen ponds. Suicides reach their annual peak. The most fanatical dig through the snow to put in peas. May explodes. The unmistakable first spring day, then the last patch of snow, then KABOOM ... an electric green world combines limey soil with photosynthesis to create a color so vivid it is outshone only by dandelions that pop out like flashbulbs, until the Holsteins get them.

June is ecstatic. July sublime. Then in August the first cool days remind of what is approaching. Although it has been barely six weeks since the last frost, the summer had seemed immortal, winter eternally conquered. Everyone in the state gets depressed. Then the reprieve. September is irrepressible, with warm bright days that harken to July. October sees the summer die in a finale not seen since the Fourth of July fireworks.

November brings the first freeze (if October has not), the first snow, and the precipice of December, beyond which stretches the abyss. The days become anorexic. Despair. There will be no end to this winter.

The valley of Upper Granville and the surrounding hillsides were cleared in the mid-1800s, leaving room for about a dozen small farms. Most of the community's existing homes date from this period of prosperity. Life barely changed through the turn of the century, the First World War, and the Depression. World War II took its toll, however. A total of eight community residents went off to war and not one returned. No one was killed, but the exposure to the outside world was too dazzling. Thereafter, Upper Granville had difficulty keeping its youth. One by one the family farms withered and consolidated, until only the Blanchards remained to earn a living from the land. The Blanchards retained the bottom land and sold the houses to whatever Flatlander wanted them. The hillsides returned to forest, giving the valley the sense of snugness that now overwhelms the first-time visitor.

The first settlers of Upper Granville might have been Abanaki Indians, but no one knows. The tribal name was spelled "Abanaki" in Alton Blanchard's epic history of Upper Granville, *Over Yonder Hill*, written in 1955 and privately published. Elsewhere it is spelled "Abnaki," "Ebanqui," or "Abbanak," with as many variations in pronunciation. The tribe's mark on civilization is faint at present and might disappear entirely but for the diligent scholarship of men like Alton. The same might be said for the entire history of Upper Granville.

The territory was granted to an English noble, Lord Granville, whose holdings were so vast that he never bothered to visit, not even to see the foliage. For a short period both New York and New Hampshire lay claim to the land, but the arrogant heroics of Ethan Allen soon established the independence of the Green Mountains. Vermont's first son is described by Alton Blanchard as "a first class lout, so vain that he strutted about in a uniform of his own design, a drunkard, a braggart, a bully." Allen's only virtue in Blanchard's eyes was that he was slightly less despicable than the Yorkers to the west of Lake Champlain. The evident disdain for the Yorkers of colonial times is mirrored today in the mutterings of natives that accompany each busload of fall foliage leaf peepers. Today they are called Flatlanders.

The first settlers to Upper Granville came in the late 1700s, part of the northward and westward sprawl continuing to this day in America. By 1839 there was enough of a community to warrant a church that still dominates the town. Other commercial enterprises were a sawmill, general store, stagecoach stop, and tavern. Eighteen thirty-nine was also the first year that a Blanchard came to town. Hiram Blanchard moved to Upper Granville by way of Baddeck, Nova Scotia, and Plymouth, England. Little more than a century later, his descendants man the lone remaining valley farm.

Other significant events since the publication of *Over Yonder Hill* have shaped the character of Upper Granville. In 1964 the community fought a bitter struggle to eliminate a Granville exit on the newly constructed interstate passing five miles to the east.

Then in 1968 at the Granville Town Meeting the funds to pave the connecting road between Upper Granville and Route 100 were denied. This was the citizens' expression that Upper Granville was in its death throes, unworthy of more than minimal maintenance.

The school closed the next year, and parishioners in the church voted to hold winter services in the heated comfort of the First Baptist in Granville. The sawmill and tavern were already dim memories of more prosperous times, but now Oakley McBean closed down his tiny store and relocated to the paved road leading into Granville proper. Residents had to go to town for even basic commodities. Upper Granville seemed destined for the same fate as the Abanakis. Obscurity and oblivion. A backwater. The little agricultural hamlet that had a brief flourishing was on the verge of disappearing from the map.

Alton was a black sheep Blanchard who made the odd decision not to go into farming, instead remaining in Upper Granville to perform odd jobs and write poetry. Depending on who describes him, he was either "the village idiot," "touched in the head," or "a charming and brilliant fellow who freed himself from the shackles of the family farm to pursue a calling of a higher sort" (from a review of *Over Yonder Hill*, in the Granville Clarion). To his fellow Blanchards, Alton was like a purple birthmark, a blotch of genetic aberration. That *Over Yonder Hill* was an unabashed immortalization of the Blanchard clan was his sole redeeming grace.

According to Alton, Blanchards are born, they grow up, they marry, they acquire more land, they farm, they die. An occasional one goes off to war or decides to live in town, but mostly they follow the prescribed family pattern. Hiram begat Eben, who begat Jonah, who begat Simon, who begat seven girls before begetting Alton and his brother, Hoyt, who is the current patriarch of the family farm. A lot of other begetting took place as well, with the result that there are presently six operating Blanchard dairy farms in central Vermont, twelve families carrying the surname in the Greater Granville phone directory, and countless cousins spread throughout the state. In the manner of hardscrabble Yankees, however, it is not a close family so much as a collection of fierce independents, united only by their isolation. The idea of a family reunion, or even cooperating on farm-related ventures, would strike the Blanchards as odd.

Alton never assumed the stewardship of the farm, leaving the honor instead to his younger brother, Hoyt, born in 1909. Alton never married, he never begat. He even burned all his poetry just before taking his own life in 1977. The family never speaks of him. *Over Yonder Hill* remains as his legacy. Alton despaired over what he saw as the impending demise of the beloved community he had immortalized in print. Had he hung on for a few more years, he would have been heartened to see a renaissance in the valley, a continuation of the history of Upper Granville, and his own literary effort inspire a sequel that would see its birth on a day a strong-willed character named B. J. Bosco came to town.

B. J. Bosco Comes to Town

By January 23 in the Northland, the days grow long enough that the natives have their first impulse of spring. The woodpiles are barely half-exhausted, and winter still holds countless hearty blasts. But for the first time since the Fourth of July, there is no longer the hopelessness of funneling ever downward into the cold, dark spiral of the season.

Walt Gunion's beige Oldsmobile 98 hammered up the washboard road to Upper Granville on this January 23. The year was 1980, the dawn of a new decade. Beside him was a woman in her late twenties, a blonde with telltale streaks of a previous life on Florida beaches, with a toughness around the eyes that suggested a total lack of fear. She was B. J. Bosco, and she was many miles from her native Fort Lauderdale. Her thoughts at the moment were of the quality of light, and of infinite shades of gray that develop whenever afternoon shadows spread over a snow-covered landscape. She was reminded of the Emily Dickinson poem she had memorized in her freshman year at Radcliffe light-years ago. "There's a certain slant of light, on winter afternoons ... somethingorother, somethingorother" She was glad she had brought her camera with her.

Gunion was talking, and being ignored, but like many realtors he was undeterred by even a total lack of response. His subject of the moment was "washboard," the rippled surface condition endemic to dirt roads. Walt did not know what caused washboard, or where it came from, but only that it described the road condition perfectly. It was a hobby of his to ask people about the origins of washboard, and he claimed never to have heard the same explanation twice. Washboard on the Upper Granville road was not too bad at the moment, but just wait until spring, he told B.J. Yes, some day he would write a book on the subject. She answered, "I hope you're a better writer than you are a realtor."

Walt Gunion had spent a fair amount of time with B.J. over the past few months, trying to find the house that he knew did not exist. He had listened patiently the day she had first come into the small office he maintained in downtown Granville. "Old farmhouse, some land, outbuildings enough to keep a few animals, end of a town road, needs some work, preferably owner financed, around forty thousand dollars or so." He nodded dutifully and said he knew exactly what she wanted. He then took her out to see the available properties, a group that consisted of a few flimsy A-frames, Appalachian wrecks, and a selection of doublewides. After the requisite falling out when B.J.'s vision confronted reality, they recommenced the painstaking task of trying to find a home suitable to her identity. After all, she had not left a damn good job with a Boston advertising agency to become art director for a Vermont wood stove company just to live in a cramped single room of a decrepit rooming house in Granville, Vermont.

The object of today's search was a schoolhouse, a rental with no land or outbuildings which had come on the market suddenly when the prior tenant left in the midst of a cold spell that had frozen solid every tap and toilet. In fact, this was the schoolhouse, the one around which the rest of the Upper Granville village revolved, the schoolhouse in which Stella Blanchard had taught for forty-five years, the schoolhouse in which Bennett and Hoyt Blanchard and Oakley McBean had been educated, and, ahem, the schoolhouse now owned by Walt Gunion. Walt's instincts told him there was a potential match, so while B.J. studied the slants of light, he extolled the virtues of Upper Granville: "This is your picture perfect Vermont hamlet, the kind you'd see on a calendar or in *Vermont Life*. In fact I think it was in the *Vermont Life* calendar one year. Is that the one I have in the office? No, I think it must have been last year. It was sometime. But the good thing about this town is the Blanchards. They've lived here for centuries, and as long as they're here, it will be protected. And there are lots of young people in the community. Very interesting young people." Walt was thinking about a particularly fetching young lady named Francoise when he made the statement.

The heat in Gunion's car was too high. Like many proud new car owners, he demonstrated every feature to excess. Between the soft suspension, Gunion's rambling, and ninety-degree heat, B.J. was tempted to slip into sleep. Just then, however, they crested the hill that opens into the narrow valley of Upper Granville.

Gunion had the good sense to stop the car and let his client overview the scene. He also had enough timing to let the visuals speak for themselves. The village was, indeed, perfect. Half a dozen homes, flanked by steep hills, were nestled around a triangular common and a white clapboard church. The symmetry combined with the light to create a unity of man and the cosmos.

"The fields belong to the Blanchards," began Gunion as B.J. clicked away madly with her camera. "So does the sugarbush. That's why this valley is so well protected. They're still making a go of dairy farming. The schoolhouse is just at the left corner of the green. See it there? See the bell tower. The bell is still in it. You can ring it on your birthday, or whenever."

B.J. was enraptured. The dirt road, the snow, the afternoon light, the panorama of the high valley. The house was a long way from B.J.'s ideal, but at last, she felt, she had discovered Vermont, and Brigadoon.

"Pretty town." said Gunion, shifting his land yacht back into gear. "Used to be full of Blanchards, but now there's Hoyt and Stella, and, of course, their son, Bennett, and his wife, Teresa. Old Hoyt's quite a guy. Typical farmer and a real Vermonter. Stella taught at the schoolhouse for years, until they closed it, oh, six or seven years back. Emil Dummerston Weed, he's the Blanchards' farmhand, he'll put up your wood or do your plowing for a few bucks. In fact Emil'll do anything for a few bucks."

B.J. leveled an icy stare at Gunion to let him know that comments about the helplessness of females were not appreciated. It was a wasted gesture, however. Gunion was impervious to any social innovations of the last century. B.J. reminded herself that this was not Boston.

"There's old Emil now;' he said. Emil was plowing the schoolhouse driveway with a rusty, four-wheel-drive International truck that had seen lots of backwoods use. Emil was hardly old, looking to be in his mid-thirties, but with a stubbly, through-the-mill look that suggested too many sixteen-hour workdays followed by three six-pack nights. From a distance there was a Clint Eastwood quality to him, but that evaporated upon closer inspection when his smile revealed a yellowed and neglect-ridden toothy display, a shocking contrast to B.J.'s carefully sculpted, beach-girl-perfect collection.

Gunion pushed the button to lower the passenger side window as he pulled alongside the pickup. Emil's window was already open. There was an awkward moment of semisilence, marred only by the static whine of a distant country and western station on the pickup's radio as the men stared at each other across B.J.s body. When it became obvious that Emil could hold his stuporous pose at least for the rest of his life, Gunion spoke: "Hi." It was a brilliant beginning, B.J. had to admit. Emil nodded imperceptibly. It seemed to her that his stare was the kind normally reserved for aliens from another planet. Gunion finally mustered another utterance: "Howsa boy?"

Emil nodded again, and another impasse seemed at hand. But no, Emil spoke: "Whatcha get for mileage on your new hog, Walt?"

" 'Bout thirteen."

"Guess you don't worry much about that or you wouldn't buy one."

"Well, I always say you've got to drive a nice car if you're serious about the real estate business. No one wants to buy a house from someone who looks like he doesn't have a pot to piss in. No sir, a Ninety-eight gives you a lot of things, but great mileage ain't one. Seems that's all people care about these days." B.J. took note of his use of "ain't." Walt had undoubtedly lapsed into a good ol' boy mode.

"I get about eight on my truck," said Emil. "About eight driveways, that is." The men thought this hysterically funny. B.J. managed a polite smile.

"Hey Walt," continued Emil, revving his engine a few times to keep it from stalling, "didja hear about the farmer over to South Granville who got married, then found out his wife was a virgin?"

Walt shook his head, the perfect straight man. B.J. realized Emil was now playing to her.

"Yuh, well he divorced her right away, soon's he found out. He said 'any girl not good enough for her own kin's not good enough for me'" He dissolved into yelps of hilarity at his own cleverness. Gunion seemed to find the story equally humorous, although he mercifully turned the conversation back to business.

"That's a good one, Emil. The house ready?"

Emil swallowed the last of his laughs. "Eyup. Just 'bout" With another rev of the engine, he put the truck in gear and plunged back into the snowy driveway.

"Nice guy," said Gunion rolling up the window. "Hope you don't mind a little saltiness, because Emil's not the most refined guy in the world."

"I hadn't noticed. Who does this place belong to?"

"Oh, someone local." Walt had decided not to reveal his real estate holdings unless B.J. indicated some real interest. He remembered this technique from a sales success seminar he had taken. The rationale, however, eluded him, and he was not entirely comfortable with the ruse.

"Flatlander?"

"How did you know? He lives in that beautiful, contemporary chalet just up on that ridge." Gunion pointed off to the north. "He dabbles in real estate and different ventures, but there's lots of talk that her family comes from money." Gunion dug himself in deeper each time he opened his mouth. He wished he could remember why it was that it was smart to keep the seller's identity from the buyer.

B.J. excused herself to walk around. Walt, not surprisingly, opted to remain in his land yacht, where he could listen to a scratchy station on the FM and bask in ninety-degree heat.

Outside it was cold and still. B.J. loved the scrunching sound her feet made in the snow. The schoolhouse, she had already decided, was perfect. In describing her priorities to Gunion, the one thing she had been unable to put across had been the importance of harmony in her living situation. She could no more live in a chalet pasted onto a hillside than in a mobile home. She would prefer a teepee to either. But this—this was perfect. She got down on one knee to click off a shot that contrasted the clean symmetry of the clapboards with the barren chaos of hardwoods on the hillside.

Emil finished a last swath on the driveway and killed the engine on his truck after one final, mighty roar. He got out and approached B.J. "You moving in here?"

"I don't know. I need to know a few particulars first."

"Yeah," laughed Emil, showing his yellow teeth, "like about the pipes. Now it don't make no sense to me why anyone would rent out a place when they know the pipes'll freeze every time it goes to ten below. Then again, I don't understand a lot of things Flatlanders do."

A moment of silence was followed by Emil sucking in a sip of air, making a slight sound of "yip." B.J. soon learned that this often signaled the impending end of conversation for Vermonters. Emil finished: "Got to hustle. Walt said he wants this place to look lived in. I'm supposed to put a pot of soup cooking on the stove to give it a homey smell. Seems somewhat strange for you two to be waitin' out here so's you can smell soup when you walk inside. Is that how you folks do business down in the Flatlands?"

"Forget the soup," said B.J. authoritatively. "Walt's taken too many Dale Carnegie courses." She paused, realizing that the Dale Carnegie reference was probably beyond Emil's ken.

He shook his head. "Don't know 'im."

"Never mind. Tell me about the pipes, and who is this Flatlander who owns the place?"

Emil looked confused. "It's Walt, didn't he tell you?"

"No, does he live in that chalet up on the hill?"

Emil sucked in an affirmative "yip."

"This gets weirder by the minute."

"Might interest you," said Emil conspiratorially, "to know that the last tenant was paying two hundred and twenty-five dollars a month rent."

As B.J. murmured thanks to Emil, a striking couple wearing expensive, matching sheepskin coats walked up and asked if anyone had seen Townshend Clarke, explaining that his sheep were loose in the road. Emil shook his head, and B.J. said she was here to look at the schoolhouse. The woman, who spoke with a French accent nearly as fashionable as her wardrobe, called Walt a "scumbag" for renting a place with inferior plumbing to an unsuspecting Flatlander.

B.J. turned to Emil. "Why wouldn't he tell me that he owned it? I'd find out eventually."

Emil shrugged. "Only God can explain the ways of Nature and Flatlanders. Why's he want me to put a can of soup on the stove? Why's Townshend Clarke not keep his fences mended?"

Walt extracted his amorphous frame from the Ninety-eight to see what the group was talking about.

"Walt!" said the as yet unintroduced man, who was, in fact, Bruce Liebermann, a.k.a. Nathaniel Hale Winship, a.k.a. the Stowe Stallion. "This is an incredibly sleazy scam you're trying to pull off."

"Scumbag," hissed Francoise, giving the world equal parts charm and venom, and functioning as a Greek chorus for her husband, who was now working up to a fever of righteousness.

"This is a nice person here, obviously the type of sapient being we want here in Upper Granville. If you try to rip her off, she'll end up stiffing you like all those tenants you go through in the Cowdrey Place."

"Dirtball!" murmured the chorus, but the smile betrayed her.

The Stallion approached the overmatched Gunion and grasped him by the shoulders, as one would to get the attention of a child. "Walt. Walt! Just make the plumbing right, and this nice person will take the place."

"The plumbing's fine!" blustered Gunion. "And this is none of your business."

As if on cue, a panel van with "Pisano's Plumbing and Heating" on its side drove up and was flagged by a shout of "Hey Joe." A sloe-eyed man with dark, friendly features got out and was prevailed upon to give an instant, independent assessment of the plumbing. Gunion protested but was totally ignored. A silver Saab Turbo pulled up, and its occupant, a wiry man in his mid-thirties with blond, wavy hair, bounded out. "Great news, everyone. I've been visited by the Divine Muse."

"We don't care," said Gunion, his frustration more apparent with each intrusion. "We're trying to conduct some business here."

"Really? I love business. Can I watch?"

"No." Gunion's voice was lost among the chorus of affirmatives.

Darwin Hunter reached back into the Saab and pulled out a shopping bag. "Great. Wait'll I tell you this. It's a million-dollar idea for sure. I even bought a few six-packs of Molson Golden to celebrate. So what's the business? Walt trying to foist the school-house onto another unsuspecting Flatlander?"

"This is not a party, Darwin" stammered Gunion, but the Stallion and Pisano's were already heading toward a bulkhead to examine the pipes, while Darwin was popping open beers and circulating them. Each person had a suggestion for dealing with poor Walt Gunion, who at least had enough sense to drown his sorrow in one of the proffered beers.

"B.J., whatever he asks," said Darwin, now properly introduced and informed of the reason for the gathering, "offer fifty dollars less."

Townshend and Sue Clarke arrived and were given the message about their sheep, but stopped to join the party for a while before going home. Sammi Burger-Hunter observed the commotion from her home across the street and could not resist giving in to her curiosity. The only sour note was Bennett Blanchard, who drove up on his John Deere to remind Emil that there was work to do, and who only grunted inhospitably when offered a beer by Darwin.

The Stallion and Joe Pisano returned with an assessment, an estimate, and an appointment for the next day. Gunion had lost his ability to function, so the Stallion took command: "Here's what we do. You take this lovely lady on a tour of the place, and do your negotiating in private."

"Right," seconded Darwin. "The rest of us will just wait out here and kill these beers. Don't hurry for us, but if you take more than five minutes, we're coming in." Then, in an aside to B.J., he added, "I've got the perfect housewarming present. I'll be right back." He dashed to the house across the street.

The negotiations were easy. After a tour, Walt Gunion revealed the rent to be $325. B.J. offered $250, stipulating that the pipes be weatherproofed by Joe Pisano. Then she told Gunion the offer was good for sixty seconds.

Walt whimpered. Walt whined. He whined about increasing real estate taxes, about property values, about Pisano's rates, about what he had promised his wife he would charge for rent. But when his sixty seconds were up, he accepted.

"Terrific;' said B.J., shaking his hand. "You drive a tough bargain, Walt. It's impossible to get the better of a deal with a shrewd master like you. Say, is there still a bell in this schoolhouse?"

"Sure is." Gunion had been buoyed by the reference to himself as shrewd. Now he wanted to be as helpful as possible. "Cementing the sale" was what they called it in his sales seminar. He took her to the attic where the rope still hung from the days when the bell called the valley children to Stella Blanchard's classes. B.J. pulled it with gusto, a beacon of sound pealing across a cold, silent valley settling into dusk. Outside, the crowd burst into cheers.

B.J. and Walt walked out to heroes' welcomes. Darwin Hunter handed B.J. a package hastily wrapped in some leftover Christmas paper. Despite the apparent spontaneity, there was a ceremonial flourish to the presentation.

"On behalf of the residents of Upper Granville, even those you haven't yet met, or may never want to, I officially welcome you to Upper Granville, Vermont."

"The hippest burgh in Appalachia," added the Stallion.

"Where men are men, and women are glad of it," said Joe.

"Where the greatest sin is to chill Beaujolais Nouveau," said Francoise.

"And where the cows still need to be milked," said a dour Bennett Blanchard, who had stayed on to observe the excitement despite protestations of disinterest.

B.J. unwrapped her package. It was a book. She intoned the title: *"Over Yonder Hill."*

Emil gestured to the west with his chin. "That there's *Yonder Hill*. Book was wrote by Bennett's uncle."

"It's the history of Upper Granville," explained Walt Gunion.

"I'm overwhelmed," sputtered B.J., rarely at a loss for words. The Stowe Stallion punctuated the moment by grasping her face with both hands and kissing each cheek.

"I have an announcement," said Darwin, taking advantage of the silence that followed the Stallion's kisses. "I've found my calling in life. The Divine Muse visited me in my den last night and suggested that I write a sequel to *Over Yonder Hill*. I'm going to be a famous author"

Bennett Blanchard nearly fell off the seat of his John Deere.

"It figures," he gasped between spasms of hilarity. "Alton didn't have all his bolts tightened, either."

Emil Dummerston Weed was more serious. "Took more'n two centuries of things happening in Upper Granville for Alton to come up with 'nuff stuff to fill up a book. Ain't much happened since nineteen fifty-five."

Darwin used his belt buckle to pry the cap off another Molson Golden. "This is a different book. This isn't a history, but a snapshot, a portrait, a slice of contemporary life in a metaphysical hamlet that provides an allegory for the timeless themes of life. You know, Life, Art, Man, the Cosmos, the relationships of Art and Man, Life and Art, Man and the Cosmos. You know what I'm saying?"

A smirking Emil answered by muttering, "All I know is I agree with Bennett."

Darwin was undeterred, obviously in his element and enjoying every hyperbolic moment of it. He began gesturing, his voice soaring, carrying his imagination to new flights of fancy: "This is the book that tells what life is like in our little paradise. It gets beneath the veneer of sylvan bliss to reveal the seamy underside of Upper Granville. It's all there, the warts, the pimples, the petty squabbling, the gossip, the incest, the bigotry, the back-stabbing that simmers beneath the surface. The walls of this valley are the walls of a very sordid world."

Darwin paused for a breath. "I thought I should tell you about the book," he continued, "because you might notice a change in me. At social gatherings, for instance, while the rest of you are carousing, gossiping, and overindulging, I will be quietly observing. Then I'll make those of you who are significant part of my book."

"Hah," snorted Darwin's wife, Sammi. "That will be a change, because you're the biggest gossip in town, and certainly the only person with a drinking problem."

"I don't have a drinking problem," sniffed Darwin.

Townshend Clarke brought the conversation back outside the domestic arena: "What are you going to call this book, Darwin? *Over Yonder Hill*, Part Two?"

"How about *Over Yonder Hill*, and Then Back Again."

"I like *The Final Chapter*."

"I've got it" screamed the Stallion. "*Son of Over*."

"No, no, no." Darwin smiled and shook his head. "You guys are messing with my book. I tell you, this is serious. I'm already hard at work. I am poised."

"So what do you call it?" asked Francoise.

Darwin took his time. His face had the pleasant look of a man who had achieved peace at long last. "That's easy," he said, "It's called *Beyond Yonder*." The ensuing silence, he knew, connoted approval.

B.J. was next to speak. " '*Beyond Yonder*, by Darwin Hunter: It has a nice ring. How about 'by Darwin Hunter, with photographs by B. J. Bosco?' "

Darwin turned his attention to the town's newest resident, taking only a second to consider the offer. "You're on," he said.

"When do we start?" asked B.J., holding her camera up to her face and snapping a close-up of Darwin.

"Today, now, maintenant! Oil your camera, or whatever you do, B.J., because I'm absorbing every nuance, inflection, and quirk. Focused by the lens of your camera and filtered by the cobwebs of my mind, we'll turn the mundane happenings of this little town into Art. We'll make 'em remember the day B. J. Bosco came to town."

Beyond Yonder

Introduction

There are thirteen structures in Upper Granville, not counting outbuildings or the remains of a trailer complex established by a group of misguided Canadians in 1981 and demolished in 1983. The dominant edifice is the church, built by community artisans in 1839, the year of Hiram Blanchard's arrival. It is a solid structure, lacking the inspirational accent of a towering spire, but majestic enough to comment appropriately on the relationship of man and the cosmos in this rural setting.

Five houses predate the church. Four are standard capes, probably built by the same man in quick succession during the first influx of settlers. Although the years have given these structures individual personalities, they still bear the imprint of the same craftsman's hand. The other early building is the two-story, brick colonial built originally as a tavern. For more than a hundred and fifty years this place has set the standard for style and elegance in the community, and its respective owners have maintained it with careful pride.

The second wave of building came during the late 1800s. The schoolhouse and the Blanchards' two farmhouses, undistinguished but functionally well-suited structures, still stand. The schoolhouse is a one-room classic now converted to a residence. The Blanchard farmhouses are large with hodgepodge additions and extensions that tell of days when houses grew along with families.

The Blanchards' farmhand, Emil Dummerston Weed, lives in a house one step above a migrant worker's, but comfortable enough for his simple tastes. Oakley McBean, of Granville General Store fame, has a similarly modest domicile. Both are held together by tar paper and plastic, and are fronted by grounds cluttered with unfinished repair and fix-it projects. Between the two they have five snow machines, four truck caps, three tractors, two balers, three mowers, and nine cars, all in a state of advanced decay. Despite the frailty of their homes, Emil and Oakley never complain about the rigors of winter. Emil complains only when someone pronounces his name "A-meel," as if he was a goldurn Canuck. For both men, as long as there is enough wood for the stove and their feet stay dry, there is no test of the Elements that cannot be met.

By 1977, the year Alton Blanchard despaired, six houses in Upper Granville were vacant, and grass grew in the middle of the dirt road surrounding the valley. At just this nadir, with the community on the brink of extinction, the pendulum reversed its arc and gained momentum in the opposite direction. Real estate prices were very depressed, attracting young couples of limited means and high ideals. Within a short period, families named Clarke, Pisano, and Liebermann moved to town, a generation of hardscrabble-by-choice pioneers. All came from hardcore suburban backgrounds, seeking the same qualities of life as had Hiram Blanchard back in 1839. The new couples worked hard on their decaying farmhouses. For the most part they kept their distance from the natives, a mutually acceptable arrangement, although conducive to the creation of needless suspicions.

The next year Walt and Martha Gunion bought a contemporary abomination started, then abandoned, by a doctor with more money than sense. A retired realtor from Short Hills, New Jersey, Gunion quickly acquired the schoolhouse and one of the old capes know as the Cowdrey Place, thus establishing himself as the only rival to the Blanchards in terms of possession of the valley. It was a couple known as Darwin and Sammi Burger-Hunter, however, who put Upper Granville officially on the road to viability by purchasing the brick tavern that provides the community with its physical focal point. And when B. J. Bosco finally came to town, the balance of power, for the first time since the Abanakis had been chased up north, tipped to the newcomers.

The balance of power." Here was a theme of Darwinesque proportions. As he first scratched the phrase onto a yellow legal pad with his blue Bic pen, he knew he had touched on the central theme of *Beyond Yonder*. This was not a folksy tale of rural quaintness, but rather an expose of a continuing, universal struggle. Within the intimate setting of their upper valley stage were played the small dramas that took on significance beyond apparent meanings. This was the charge of Darwin Hunter, to isolate and to remove the everyday events of rural life, then to magnify them, demonstrating the epic struggle for dominance, a timeless confrontation with roots stretching back to the origins of Man, the battle of the Flatlander and Chuck.

A Cast of Characters

D arwin remembered the first time he had heard the term "Chuck." It was just after he and Sammi moved to Upper Granville. In an immediate display of Midwestern gregariousness, the Hunters invited the neighborhood for a barbeque.

Everyone was there, exchanging pleasantries and making small talk about the weather. Despite sharing a tiny valley, there had been, to date, little social interaction within the community, since the residents apparently preferred the isolation of Yankee independence. The last arrivals were the Stallion and Francoise. He wore leather breeches and a ruffled shirt, right out of the colonial era. Francoise looked ready for a lawn party on the Hamptons, perfect as usual, and a complete contrast to the blue jeans and peasant shirts of the other women. An immediate blanket of tension spread over the gathering. Accustomed to such an impact, the Stallion took the lead by establishing his architectural credentials. "This house used to be a tavern, you know."

"Really?" questioned the Hunters. Sammi asked where he got his information.

"I didn't get my information anywhere," he responded, registering about 8 on the haughtiness scale. "I just know. I know from the roofline, from the corner detail, from the tie rings for the horses, and from the position relative to the road. And I've never been inside, but I can tell you about the floor plan, the woodwork, the attic beams, and the nails in the floor-boards, that is, if some Chuck hasn't put linoleum over them."

"What's a Chuck?" asked Sammi Burger-Hunter innocently. The rest of the mixed group had taken a deep breath and cringed.

The Stallion reared and whinnied: "A Chuck is a person with no taste whatsoever."

"I have 'no taste whatsoever,'" piped in Darwin. "Am I a Chuck?" The Stallion had not yet met his host, but had seen the pink flamingos that Darwin had placed in the front yard.

"There's a difference between "no taste" and "bad taste." You happen to have the latter, which is worse than being a Chuck. Now, this guy's a Chuck." He gestured to Emil Dummerston

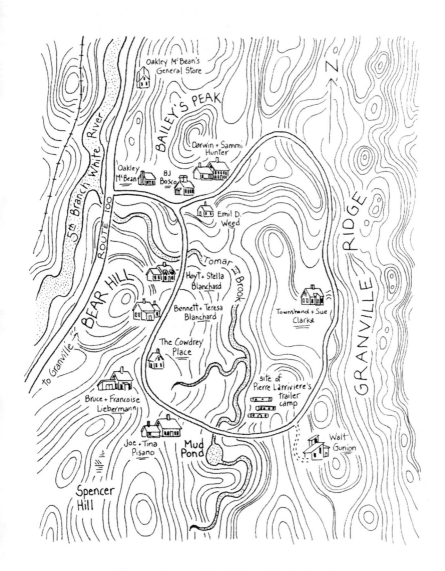

Upper Granville (After Flatlanders)

Weed, who had a toothpick wedged between his yellow teeth. The Stallion continued, first shaking Emil's hand with a murmured "howyadoin'?" "This guy, guaranteed, drives a pickup with a rifle mounted in the rear window. His favorite time of year is deer hunting season and his favorite sport is snowmobiling."

"Guess I'm a Chuck, then," drawled Emil, " 'cuz I'm all of them things."

Bennett Blanchard entered the fray. "Guess I'm a Chuck, too. But even though I'd be the last person in the world to accuse Emil of having good taste, I can tell you that when it comes to outright bad taste, there's nothing to compare to a Flatlander."

The gauntlet had been tendered, and now the crowd waited to see if it would be picked up. The Stallion picked it up, but handed it back with a laugh. "That's for sure. Look at Walt's house up on the hillside. No one but a Flatlander could combine a total lack of taste with a total lack of good sense to come up with that monstrosity." The Stallion put his arm around Walt, whose pudgy face was screwed into quizzical perplexion.

"Old Walt here was shrewd enough to pick it up for pennies on the dollar." The Stallion gave Walt his conspiratorial "sly dog" expression. "That place must have a quarter-million in materials in it. You stole that place, didn't you?" His pride salvaged, Walt smiled beatifically.

The Stallion turned back to Sammi, who had asked the original question. "So Chucks are people with no taste whatsoever, but they're not the only people with no taste whatsoever. And then, there's a separate category for people like your husband."

"So," probed Sammi, "is this group divided into Chucks and Flatlanders?"

The Stallion sidestepped deftly and parried with an infectious laugh, "The whole world's divided into Chucks and Flats. It's not racial, geographic, or genetic. It's a state of mind. Anyone who would cover beautiful wide, pine flooring with linoleum is a Chuck. Anyone who sees beauty in pink plastic flamingos is a Flatlander. The question is, 'Who stands where?'"

The Chucks

Depending on whose perspective is represented, Chucks are

either salt of the earth or scum of the earth. In either case, their territorial claim is indisputable. They are the rightful owners of Vermont, the keepers of the land. The term "Chuck" derives from either "woodchuck," the generally useless animal that native Vermonters like to shoot from the windows of their pickups on the first warm days of spring, or "woodchuckers" in reference to the prodigious amounts of wood that have to be chucked into a stove to keep a body from freezing during the endless winters.

The extreme Chuck is a person of low intelligence and even lower ambition who ekes out a living by cutting wood, boiling sap, and bilking tourists. His favorite food is jacked deer, his hobbies range from bondo sculpture to recreational welding, and he collects anything with a motor and puts it upside down in the side yard to rust. As can be seen from the very real people, there is just enough truth in the stereotype to cause trouble.

It is easiest to describe the origins of the Upper Granville Chucks by starting at the center and working out. Hoyt Blanchard and Oakley McBean were born in the houses in which they presently reside. Hoyt has never spent more than a single night away from home, except when he had a kidney infection and the doctors, with his wife, Stella's, help, kept him in the hospital for a week. Both men fit any conceivable definition of "native Vermonter," although by nature they could not be more different. Hoyt, like every Blanchard since Hiram, is built low to the ground with the barrel chest and massive forearms designed to make short work of arduous tasks. The broad, low forehead has withstood the onslaught of pounding sun and driving sleet with no ill effects. Most people cannot believe that Hoyt is in his eighth decade. His only concession to age is that the glint in his steely blue eyes has softened to a twinkle since his son, Bennett, is clearly prepared for the next generation. He loafs through mere twelve-hour days, feeling as sinfully lazy as if he were spending his retirement in the trailer park in Sarasota.

Oakley, in contrast, has as many lines and wrinkles on his face as there are ridges and gulfs in the Green Mountains. He is tall, thin, and spare, like a nail that has been used too many times. He has the stoop of a farmer — not surprising, since the McBeans were the last family to sell their bottom land to the Blanchards.

That was ten years ago. Oakley's wife, Clara, gave him three lovely daughters, each of whom grew up and married a professional type up in Burlington. This was the upward mobility Oakley had always hoped for, but once achieved, immediately regretted. Then Clara died, and with no son to carry on, Oakley became the shop-keeper, first in Upper Granville, then down on the paved road leading into town. Although his wit and wisdom endear him to all, there is a lingering reticence of one who has abandoned his land and whose daughters have abandoned him.

The family that gave up farming just before the McBeans was the Bennetts, whose family name was carried by Hoyt Blanchard's son. Without tracing the genealogies exactly, suffice it to say that in an isolated community such as Upper Granville, anyone who lives there long enough ends up with a little Bennett, Blanchard, and McBean blood.

Born in Hoyt's house, Bennett now lives with his own family one hundred yards up the road. He will move into "the big house" once his father dies. It is Bennett upon whose thick shoulders now rests the mantle of the family farm. His eyes carry the glint of purposefulness, his visage the determined set of destiny, as if nothing in the world is so important as the daily milking of cows. He will carry the load until his own son takes over, when he can allow his own glint to soften to a twinkle. Between now and then, however, there is lots of milking to be done.

Thanks to the liberal influence of his mother, Bennett has broader horizons than most Vermont dairy farmers, having been to 4-H gatherings all over the country, as far away as Oklahoma. His mother, Stella, even influenced her son to go off to college, unheard of in most farm families and the source of the only real arguments she ever had with Hoyt. Alas, the territorial roots proved too deep, and Bennett's college career lasted less than a semester. His grades were fine, but he was unable to establish any connection between what he was learning and what he felt he needed to know to run the farm that was to become his world. Stella was disappointed, yet accepting. One could not see Bennett and Hoyt, their matching bodies and matching eyes, and deny the tide of destiny.

Bennett married Teresa shortly after his return from college.

They were sweethearts at Granville Union Regional High School. Their pairing seemed as natural as the annual greening of the meadows. The only complication was her maiden name — Bennett — which ensured fertile material for anyone predisposed to hold incestuous stereotypes of rural life. The Bennetts, like the Blanchards, have spread their family tree throughout central Vermont. No one would have given a second thought to their marriage if it hadn't been for Hoyt and Stella's lack of foresight in giving their son the name of their longtime valley neighbors. The matter is complicated by the fact that there is an unmistakable resemblance between Bennett and Teresa. Put a blond wig on him and a couple of grapefruit down his shirt, and ... uh, change the subject.

Like Teresa, Emil Dummerston Weed is from the town of Granville. The two went through high school together, several years behind Bennett. Emil dropped out of school in the eleventh grade to join the Army. This was during the early stages of the Vietnam War, and in the circles that Emil traveled, bagging a gook ranked up there with bagging a seven-point buck as fun and challenge. Whether he achieved his goal no one knows, but when he came back from Vietnam, a lot of the happy-go-lucky was gone, replaced with a smirk. He received decorations for valor, yet the man who returned to Vermont was content to scratch out an existence performing menial jobs in the middle of nowhere. Emil has worked for Bennett off and on for eight years, a casual but mutually satisfactory arrangement. Emil is content with life's simplest pleasures: a quart of cheap beer, a scratchy portable radio, a thunderous fart. He neither requires much from, nor contributes much to, life. Although theoretically still in the prime of life, he has a frayed look of squandered youth, his lanky frame showing early traces of the classic farmer's stoop. Just remember, it's "A-mull," not "A-meel."

Stella Blanchard, Hoyt's wife, personifies the noble farm wife. She came to Upper Granville in 1933 from Wallingford, Vermont, just south of Rutland. Stella is a slim, erudite woman, taut as a piano wire and just as high-strung; it is hard to imagine her exiled to the rural hinterlands at a tender age. She taught at the schoolhouse for ten years before Hoyt generated the nerve to ask for her hand, then for thirty-five years thereafter. Although she can bake pies, quilt up a storm, thaw pipes, and jump start a car with the best of them, she also has an active mind and combative nature, as anyone who has seen her in action at a town meeting can testify. She will take on land developers, town fathers, or even the farming community to support whatever she thinks is right. Stella has earned universal respect, with the exception of her daughter-in-law and rival for her son's heart, Teresa. She has never understood her son's selection of a big-boobed, bleached blonde whose idea of a good book is *People* magazine and whose idea of paradise would be to be living in the world of soap operas. Not surprisingly, some of the great pitched battles of the Western world take place between the Blanchard women, Stella and Teresa.

The Flatlanders

Then there is the Flatlander, a creature so helpless he cannot even drive in the snow. The Flatlander is governed by personal greed and social guilt, making him unworthy of voting privileges in what used to be a democratic society. On the scale of mammalian order, the Chuck ranks the Flatlander as above porcupine, equal to skunk, and below coyote. His intelligence is frequently compared to the domestic turkey, a creature known to drown by looking up during a rainstorm.

The Hunters: Dr. Darwin and Sammi

A veteran of Woodstock, every political rally between 1968 and 1972, four rock and roll bands, and Dartmouth, Darwin Hunter became an ophthalmologist less from desire to help humanity than a need for a high paying career not requiring undue ambition. His partnership affords respect and a good income with flexibility to pursue myriad hobbies and athletic activities, while letting him live in sylvan bliss. It has worked out just as he planned. Darwin is free to enjoy what he enjoys most — the simple combination of good company and intoxicants of all manner and form.

"Doctor Darwin," or simply "Doc," is secure to the point of smugness. (Sue "the Shrew" Clarke is always quick to point out

35

that an ophthalmologist is not really a doctor.) His native Midwestern affability is counterbalanced by Ivy League cynicism, expressed spontaneously without fear of consequences. With a wisecrack for every occasion, Darwin is reliable only in that he can be counted on to be the last one to leave the party.

Darwin spent six months of his college years plotting out the rest of his life. While his classmates were guzzling beer and carousing, Darwin was planning a career that would allow him to spend the rest of his life guzzling beer and carousing with a minimum of effort. He factored real estate prices, average salaries, inflation, market demand, and myriad other variables into the ultimate decision to become an ophthalmologist with a practice in Montpelier, Vermont. If everything worked to plan, Darwin would find himself in a permanent state of semi-retirement, able to live in relative luxury, with ample time to diddle around on his guitar and ample money to not have to worry.

The plan worked like a charm. At the age of thirty Darwin found himself with a prosperous private practice that allowed him to live in the Upper Granville town mansion, drive a Saab Turbo, and keep a keg of Miller Lite on tap in his basement. On busy weeks he works four days. Twice a year he goes to conventions in southern climes. He has every toy he can think of. He is beholden to no one.

Darwin's sense of humor has always kept him separate from the masses. What kind of man buys a beautiful brick home in rural Vermont, then immediately adorns the front yard with a brace of plastic flamingos, flanked by two blue glare balls, a Madonna in a half-buried bathtub, and enough flapping wooden ducks to cause more than one person to think he was in the tacky lawn decoration business?

Equally confusing are the neon signs in the upstairs windows, "Eat" and "Good Food." Darwin's most prized possession is his collection of dead rock and roll star memorabilia. He has twelve biographies of Elvis, a lamp with Jim Hendrix's image, a velvet wall hanging commemorating Janis Joplin, and a piece of metal reportedly from the fuselage of the plane in which Buddy Holly was killed. His den is both a mausoleum and a party palace, with an awesome stereo that can be heard throughout the valley. The den also contains Darwin's roll-top desk, his collection of single malt scotch, and his guitar, a beat up Gibson that he bought second-hand back in 1962.

Whenever asked why his humor is so aberrant, Darwin always is quick to blame it on his career in rock and roll. "It's the drugs." he'll say. "My gray matter is gone. The neocortex is as smooth as a baby's bottom."

Sammi Burger-Hunter has become accustomed to mock expressions of sympathy over her ability to put up with Darwin's warped perspective and insipid music. She shrugs and explains that of the many things that Darwin is, "dull" is not one.

Marrying Sammi was also part of Darwin's master plan. Born Samantha Burger in Cincinnati, Ohio, of a Jewish father and Italian mother, she is equal parts of the most fiery of each. When an older brother was seriously wounded in a fire fight near Da Nang, Sammi's Midwestern foundation cracked. The demure University of Cincinnati coed major became an apple pie radical, protesting everything from the bombing of Cambodia to the work conditions of the cafeteria help. Darwin Hunter, as a two-bit musician always plotting to find the easy way out, personified every quality her father found reprehensible. Even his subsequent successes academically and professionally failed to dispel her family's image of Darwin as a slothful ne'er-do-well.

Sammi's immense energy finds outlets in her home, her children, and social activism organizations ranging from the National Organization for Women to the Vermont Natural Resources Commission. Even then there is energy left over. She will rest only when the world is at peace, all its children fed, and women are given equal pay for equal work.

The Hunters, by living in the old tavern and through their generous and gregarious natures, have provided Upper Granville with a social epicenter.

The Clarkes: Townshend IV & Sue the Shrew

Townshend Clarke's roots go deep into the beach houses and country clubs of Rhode Island. His father owns a junk jewelry factory that employs wetback labor to produce atrocious baubles for other wetbacks to buy with meager wages earned in sweatshops like the one owned by his father. When Townshend IV made this cosmic realization during an acid trip in 1968, he sunk into a cesspool of guilt from which he has not yet been able to emerge. Renouncing materialism was the only response he could muster.

Townshend led a normal youth, if one calls formal tea dances and being sent off to Mount Hermon to "prep" at age twelve "normal." His academic career was undistinguished, but not disastrous, aside from the fact that he refused to play basketball even though he was the tallest boy in school.

In the summer of 1968, Townshend consumed vast quantities of hallucinogens, smashed up the family Volvo, and tried to bomb the Mashpaug, Rhode Island, Country Club just prior to the annual Father-Son Match Play Championship. It was intended to be a revolutionary act, but Townshend underestimated the strength of the upper crust network. The family shrugged and made sure nothing got in the papers. His father even praised him for finally showing some initiative. Townshend responded by volunteering for Special Forces. He injured his back in boot camp, however, and spent the war stooped over a typewriter in Saigon dispatching form letters to next of kin. The stoop never left.

Upon his return, Townshend nursed his fractured ego while attending college. He married Susan LaFollette, a common sort of girl whose outstanding feature was an ability to find an infinite number of faults in Townshend. He was sure his parents would disapprove.

The day after graduating from college, Townshend sold his graduation present, an Oldsmobile Cutlass, and used the money as a down payment on a ten-acre woodlot near Upper Granville, Vermont. The plan was to build a geodesic dome atop an octagonal log cabin built from trees on the land. Mercifully, it was never built.

Townshend thrives on the simplicity of hardscrabble life; his wife, Sue, less so. He has worked as a carpenter, farmhand, assistant pressman, prefab building salesman, and roof shoveler, never earning more than seven thousand dollars in any calendar year. Along the way he has acquired enough carpentry skills to get by, although he is far from the fine cabinetmaker he considers himself.

On his thirtieth birthday, Townshend gained access to a trust fund worth close to one million dollars. To the chagrin of his wife, he cannot bring himself to spend any, preferring the ascetic astringency of life without running water or electricity. His stubbornness, in turn, makes Sue more ill-tempered. A familiar sight is his gangly frame stooped under a torrent of abuse, his hangdog face wincing from the blows as Sue the Shrew tells him how he has failed again. Shave your beard, cut off that ridiculous ponytail, get rid of that disgusting headband. Townshend can never seem to get it right.

The Pisanos: Joe & Tina

The Pisanos hail from Secaucus, New Jersey, a malodorous sliver of the New York megalopolis. Joe was the heir apparent to a family plumbing and heating business founded by his grandfather. Although hardly a grand empire, it promised a secure future. As a teenager he fell in love with Tina diGiacomo, a shy only child doted on by her father, a prosperous local restaurateur. He wanted nothing but the best for his baby, and Joe was too much like himself to represent that. The diGiacomos tried to discourage the romance by sending Tina away to college, then Europe. But love prevailed, and Tina and Joe eloped and moved to an unwired, unheated love nest in rural Vermont.

Joe worked like a slave to fix up the old cape, scrounging odd jobs to meet mortgage payments. The family rift melted with the coming of the first child, a boy. Both families embraced the next generation warmly, as well as bestowing blessing on the once-thwarted courtship.

The Pisanos now have one of the greatest extended families anywhere. They arrive en masse each summer, each set of grandparents with their own travel trailer, to whack nails, paint barns, prepare feasts, and drink homemade wine. Along the way they have made the Pisano's home more than a functional shack and provided the financing and support for Joe to establish the northern branch of Pisano's Plumbing and Heating.

The Gunions: Walt & Martha

Walt Gunion presents himself as a successful retired realtor from Short Hills, New Jersey, so successful that he could retire at a relatively young age to shuttle between homes in Vermont and Florida while dabbling in properties in both places. The truth is that after a succession of forgettable jobs and marriages, he was working as the camera department manager at the Short Hills K mart when he met Martha Penn Ambercrombie.

The Ambercrombies are among New Jersey's first families, abounding in money and social status. Despite massive injections of finishing schools, riding lessons, and trips abroad, Martha never lived up to family expectations. She was persistently middle class, a plain and unpretentious person more at ease in the discount store than the country club.

Martha and Walt met in the solid entrenchment of middle age. He knew nothing about her family or wealth. Suddenly they were married, and even his little piece of the Ambercrombie pie made the continuation of his career at the K mart ludicrous. They bought the doctor's hillside abomination in Upper Granville and named it "Shangri-la." To keep himself purposeful, Walt earned his real estate license and dabbled in local properties. In his mind he was a wheeler and dealer, a mover and shaker who could talk big numbers at the local Chamber of Commerce and Kiwanis gatherings. To Martha he was whatever he wanted to be. To everyone else he was just Walt, a comfortable old shoe of a guy with a big mouth, a fat wallet, and small ideas.

The Liebermanns: Bruce (the Stowe Stallion) & Francoise

Vermonters are, by nature, suspicious of outsiders. Make an outsider a Flatlander, from New York City, no less; Jewish; tall; strikingly handsome, with an Afro-like explosion of black, kinky hair. Put at least two broken marriages in his past. Accent him with an earring; accompany him with a Garboesque blonde who speaks with a French accent; dress him in Madison Avenue's version of country chic; give him the confidence, make that arrogance, of someone coming off recent stints as Big Man on Campus and Stud of the Slopes; and finally, give him the completely rigid attitude that Vermont's natural beauty is ruined equally by greedy Flatlanders and ignorant Woodchucks—and you have someone able to offend, then charm, every person in the world within five minutes of acquaintance. This is Bruce Liebermann.

Francoise (Delacroix) Liebermann is able to get by on her ravishing looks in most situations. She claims a professional background in "retailing," but what she really means is that she was paid money to look gorgeous wearing fabulous clothes. Born in Nantes, France, she was drawn to Paris as a teenager. She moved in with an up-and-coming fashion designer who used her as a model for his creations. Through him she met a man she refers to only as "Harry," a wealthy American importer, thirty years her senior. They married and moved to Manhattan, where he kept Francoise swaddled in luxury, the better to showcase her exquisite looks.

She met the Stallion on a weekend trip to Stowe, where Harry was looking to buy a condominium. Bruce, under his professional pseudonym of Nathaniel Hale Winship, was already started in the restoration business, trying to generate interest in a small development of second homes based on the styles prevalent in Vermont at the time of the American Revolution. Ten investors, including Harry, were convinced to put up more than a hundred thousand each, with the promise of a second home near the ski areas, as well as tax credits for their historic structures.

Construction took place over a two-year period, during which the investors were not allowed to visit the site. There were, however, periodic progress reports over ripened Brie and champagne. The one exception to the no visitation rule was Francoise, who began commuting from New York on an almost weekly basis to "help."

A gala affair marked the opening of Cold Hollow Gore, as the development was named. A fife and drum band, marching militiamen, and a demonstration of colonial crafts, including candle making, quilting, and weaving, contributed to a festive, authentic atmosphere, a mood that was further enhanced by the serving of grog, foaming flips, West Indies rum, and claret. Francoise was at her fetching best in a corseted white lace dress cut so low that sneaking a glimpse of her nipples was irresistible. The Stallion was resplendent in a tailored uniform ostensibly patterned after the garb of Ethan Allen, but in reality of his own design.

The mood was euphoric. Plenty of reporters from local newspapers had been recruited for the occasion, as well as representatives from the broadcast media. The Stallion even hired his own video crew of nebulous affiliation to make sure that all owners were interviewed at least once. With cameras pointed into their faces and reporters immortalizing every word, the proud owners waxed eloquent about the significance of Cold Hollow Gore, their personal commitments to historical preservation, and the selfless devotion of Nathaniel Hale Winship, who made this all possible. As dusk settled they found themselves pumping the Stallion's hand in gratitude for allowing them to be part of this venture.

Later—as they discovered that the reconstructions they had purchased were, in fact, true reproductions of the muddy little hovels that people lived in during revolutionary times—their feelings were less charitable. The floors were packed dirt, the windows translucent grease paper. The furnishings were spare and crude, the environment dark and damp. There was no electricity, no running water, no indoor plumbing. Moreover, the residents soon found their requests for amenities and services met with hoots of derision from the haughty Stallion. The mood turned ugly.

"Garbage removal?" he would say in disbelief. "You better worry about surviving twenty below, not about who is going to haul away your Perrier bottles."

Matters were not helped by Francoise's abandoning Harry to move in with the Stallion. In fact it was Harry who eventually rallied his fellow purchasers of log and mud huts to file a class-action suit against the feckless developer, who now openly ridiculed the people who had paid so much to get something they did not really want. It came out in court that comparable structures could be created for one-tenth the cost charged at Cold Hollow Gore. The Stallion countered with testimony from experts as to the authenticity of the project. It had cost him a fortune, he claimed, to recreate the primitiveness of Vermont's roots.

The Stallion won the suit. He had defrauded no one and had misled people only in that he executed an unbelievable plan literally. Flatlander-on-Flatlander crime in Vermont is not a serious offense. Nevertheless, his prospects in Stowe were limited. He and Francoise set out to find an unspoiled Vermont town that could provide a platform for future ambitions. As soon as they came down the hill into Upper Granville, they knew they had found their new home.

The Cowdrey Place

For many years there lived in Upper Granville a merchant marine captain named Elijah Cowdrey. He was a silent man who nodded and waved, spoke hardly a word, and kept to himself. Eventually the locals showed their acceptance by referring to his house as the Cowdrey Place, an accolade that connotes acceptance in the North. Walt Gunion acquired the house as his first real estate deal, intending to keep it as an income property. He then rented it to a succession of characters united by the fact that they stayed no more than a single winter and stuck Walt with at least the final month's rent. Each player stayed long enough to leave a footprint in the valley soil and to gain an immortal niche in Darwin Hunter's Beyond Yonder. Among the occupants of the Cowdrey Place:

• Foster and Jenna Welland, a well-heeled couple from Fort Worth, Texas. They arrived in a Jaguar and left in a Subaru, their vehicular decline a mirror of personal disintegration. The Wellands had it all—youth, money, looks, possessions. By the end of their first winter, they had simply had it. The couple destined to become king and queen of Upper Granville were humbled by their humble abode.

• Moira Chappee, a prep school refugee who provided the community with its juiciest moments of gossip. The neighborhood men developed a collective teenage crush on her as soon as she moved to town. She was, as Darwin confessed to the Stallion one day, "the roaringest piece of ass ever seen in this valley." Even from the separation of fifty years and a different culture, Hoyt Blanchard could spot her as "quite a riggin'."

She looked very much the girl next door, with sandy hair, blue eyes, and a terrific figure that teetered between a girl's and a woman's. Moira was friendly, laid-back, and feminine; not too bright but never offensive. She was as wholesome as a Cortland apple, with just enough of a suggestion of kinkiness, such as the tiny jeweled stud she wore on her left nostril, to walk both sides of the fence. She loved parties and carousing. She could dance with the power of a chain saw and the grace of a diving swallow. During the time she lived in town, there was not a riotous gathering that she missed.

When she left the Cowdrey Place, it was not to leave town but to move into the schoolhouse, where she consorted with the aforementioned Ms. Bosco. The saga of Moira Chappee had only begun.

• Benny Malone, a live-for-the-moment Chuck whose specialty was finding ditches during winter. An illogical, yet appropriate, successor for Moira in the Cowdrey Place, Benny went through cars as dexterously as Darwin could a six-pack. His specialty was the American land yacht, rear-wheel drive, no muffler, all body rot and bondo, but with a vestigial veneer of luxury appropriate for someone whose forearm bore a tattoo reading "Born to Boogie."

Benny earned a semblance of a living as a photographer for the Granville Clarion, but never quite enough to make ends meet. He could be heard coming for miles, the roar of his V-8 accompanied by a lurching cloud of blue smoke. The assault on the serenity of the valley was redeemed only by the genuine enthusiasm with which Benny called out his trademark greeting of "Hey-hey-hey"

The valley residents could only shake their heads, fan the dust and smoke from their faces, and agree with the Stallion's observation that "there goes the son Walt and Martha always wanted?'

The players were in place. The setting was set. All that remained was for Darwin Hunter to transcend reality and to lift them onto the pages of Beyond Yonder. Toward that end, he poured himself another drink and set about his task.

Awaiting the Muse

The introduction to *Beyond Yonder* was written in a spasm of creative frenzy the night of the very day that B. J. Bosco came to town. Satisfied that the writing process would be simple, Darwin then devoted himself to the establishment of a proper creative environment.

His first step was the acquisition of a roll-top desk in need of refinishing and repair. After reading a book on the subject, picking the Stallion's brain, and enlisting Townshend Clarke to demonstrate techniques, Darwin created a worthy platform for the ancient Underwood that he purchased from Stella Blanchard. This was the same machine on which she had converted the hand-scribbled notes of Alton Blanchard into *Over Yonder Hill*. Darwin was overwhelmed by his good fortune.

Desk complete, Darwin bribed Emil with free beer to overhaul the Underwood. For weeks the parts were spread out and labeled on the floor of the Hunters' den. Darwin observed each operation intently, his functional role limited to the procurement of more beer. He would get an hour of useful work from Emil before his motor capabilities became impaired. Then there would be another hour of creating, then undoing, mistakes. Amazingly, although Emil had never worked on anything smaller than a Volkswagen, the Underwood was resurrected, clicking out letters with the snap and precision of a West Point drill team.

"All you need is words now," said a deservedly proud Emil.

"Words are the easy part for me," said Darwin. "Machines are my downfall."

Now, with the desk and typewriter, Darwin obviously needed something to sit on. He and Sammi started hitting the antique shops and yard sales, finally finding a suitable piece at an auction. His refinishing experience now paid a dividend, as Darwin created a handsome repository for the bottom of the man destined to become the next chronicler of Upper Granville.

What's a roll-top without a collection of single malt scotch atop it? Darwin considered flying to Edinburgh, but settled instead for trips to Cambridge, Massachusetts, and New York City to come up with an even dozen smoky elixirs. "I'm no fool," said Darwin to anyone who came into his den. "I've read enough Hemingway, Fitzgerald, and Mailer to know that alcohol is indispensable to the creative process."

The physical environment was now set, leaving Darwin free to tackle the big issues. How would this book be organized? He brooded long and hard over the question, spending night after night in troubled rumination. He went through three bottles of scotch, and still the proper megastructure eluded him. As had already become his custom, he turned to Alton Blanchard for inspiration. Alton, once described by his brother, Hoyt, as "creative as the sole of my shoe," had organized *Over Yonder Hill* alphabetically into chapters from `Apples" to "Zithering Zephyrs."

So pure, so simple, so completely appropriate Again, Alton was the beacon that guided Darwin through the clouds and chaos. His book, too, would utilize the simple ordering of his predecessor's. *Beyond Yonder* would have contemporary subjects from "Act 250" to "Zucchini," a sensible, yet Yankee hardscrabble, approach to life's complexities.

A set of hanging files for the expected subjects was quickly established. Into these folders would be inserted the notes, photos, and insightful observations that would become the raw material of *Beyond Yonder*.

"Poised," said Darwin, admiring his hanging files. "I am a cat stalking its prey, a hungry hawk circling. The next motion will be a blur of action. I am poised." So pleased was he with his progress that he took several months off to recharge his creative batteries. Although not a word had been written, Darwin was the picture of confidence, unconcerned that by this time nearly two years had passed since B. J. Bosco had come to town.

Part Two

From the Collected Notes of Darwin Hunter

Act 250

> "A man should be free to make a fool of himself
> on his own land."
> — ALTON BLANCHARD,
> from *Over Yonder Hill*

> "The State of Vermont is prejudiced against fools,
> especially greedy ones."
> — DARWIN HUNTER,
> from *Beyond Yonder*

Act 250 is the rarest of legislative acts, one that protects all factions of the citizenry by inconveniencing them equally. In the war between the Chucks and the Flatlanders, each side feels that Act 250 was created to protect them from the other group. The Blanchards feel that this law protects them from the unscrupulous transients of the world, the Walt Gunions and Bruce Liebermanns, for instance, who are forever trying to figure out a way to package chunks of Vermont for sale to other Flatlanders.

There is a paradox to the thinking. The Flatlander moves to Vermont to escape the city. Once he has a secure deed to his piece of paradise, he wants to lock the door behind him so that no one else can get in. He posts his land with ugly fluorescent signs that make it off-limits to those who have hunted and fished upon it, perhaps for generations. After several years the Flatlander happens upon the irresistible deal. Some poor dairy farmer has fallen on hard times and has to dispose of the family farm at a fire sale price. The Flatlander rubs his palms together and dips into the trust fund to buy it. Soon he is engulfed in blueprints and marketing plans to package his little bits of paradise to other Flatlanders. Ironically, the imagined fortunes are to allow him luxuries such as shopping sprees in Boston or New York, the bastions of humanity whence he originally escaped.

Act 250 comes to the rescue in the form of avalanches of paperwork and bureaucratic gobbledygook that cool the ardor of even the most enthusiastic entrepreneur. After blowing thousands of dollars on septic surveys and perc tests, the would-be developer sees the futility of his efforts and puts the land up for sale, expecting to find another Flatlander stupider than himself. After two frustrating years, the price is lowered to a level 20 percent less than what the purchaser originally paid. The land is bought back by the original farmer, who has regrouped to give dairy farming another shot. The difference is that now he is debt-free and driving a new four-wheel-drive truck purchased with the profits from the original sale to the Flatlander. Act 250 has saved Vermont again, making it safe for Holsteins and woodchucks.

The corollary occurs when farmer Hiram decides that the lower forty would make the ideal site for a trailer park. He starts bulldozing and laying cable until a local selectman, tipped off by a friendly neighbor, drops by to inform the farmer of the filing requirements of Act 250, making it seem as routine as a crop subsidy application. Hundreds of dollars and mountains of paper later, the landowner realizes how much better off he was with the lower forty under corn than a bunch of trailers. Act 250 is the hero again, this time making the countryside safe for Volvos and Flatlanders.

The irony of Act 250 is that natives think it exists to protect them, but that they are exempt. When Walt Gunion proposed converting his monstrously ill-designed home into a cross-country ski lodge, the first people to scream "Act 250" were the Blanchards. Bennett proved encyclopedic in his knowledge of the bureaucratic nuances that doomed the plan to failure. And yet, when it came time for the Blanchards to add an equipment shed onto their dairy complex, they launched into construction with scarcely an acknowledgment of obligation to society. There was quite a shouting match in the middle of the road when the state inspector showed up. It got even worse when it turned out they had located the building two feet closer to the road than was allowable.

Bennett and Hoyt blustered like nor'easters, but in the end they took the building down, filled out the necessary paperwork, and started again two feet back. Bennett speculated openly and bitterly that the source of his aggravation was that self-appointed guardian of the town's architectural purity, Bruce Nathaniel Hale Winship Liebermann. But the Stallion, who indeed considered every unblessed home improvement project a personal affront, maintained his innocence while stating emphatically that he would never knowingly miss an opportunity to turn Bennett over to state authorities. The culprit revealed herself only two years after the original incident. Her motivation was neither vindictiveness nor revenge, but rather a desire to see the laws of the state administered fairly to all residents.

It was Stella Blanchard.

Act 250, however, is powerless to protect anyone against poor taste. Darwin Hunter, for instance, thinks it hilarious to have a collection of tacky lawn paraphernalia in front of his brick colonial. The Stowe Stallion is physically pained by the pink flamingos, blue glare balls, and flapping wooden ducks. He says Darwin has no taste. Darwin says he has no sense of humor. They're both right.

Architecture

> "The early homes were simple sturdy structures,
> reflecting the character of their creators."
> — ALTON BLANCHARD,
> from *Over Yonder Hill*

> "Perhaps no social sin carried more stigma than to be
> deemed 'architecturally inappropriate.'"
> — DARWIN HUNTER,
> from *Beyond Yonder*

Whereas most newcomers to Upper Granville assimilate quietly, enduring a probation period of up to forty years where contact is limited to noncommittal waves, everyone knew of the Stowe Stallion within forty-eight hours of his arrival. Within this period he introduced himself to, and offended, most town residents.

The Blanchards he offended by his appearance, neither Hoyt nor Bennett fully comprehending why a grown man would need a diamond stud in his left ear. To their complete surprise, however, Bruce held his own in a discussion on the merits of milk price supports. This did not sound like your average Flatlander. Then he obliterated his newfound credibility by asking Hoyt if he was the Ben Cartwright of Upper Granville.

"Ben Cartwright? Don't know 'im."

"You know," said the Stallion offhandedly. He had a way of making you feel stupid if you were not exactly on his wavelength. "The big cheese on the Ponderosa. I figure you guys are alike because you both own all the land as far as you can see."

"Dairy farmer?" asked Hoyt.

Bennett's instincts told him he was being ridiculed. "You mean the TV show?"

"Very good, Little Joe. You're not exactly the Big Hoss type, if you know what I mean. Actually, you're not the Little Joe type, either. Not good-looking enough. But you're probably smarter than Hoss. Who knows? Well, I've got to boogie. Nice meeting you, neighbor. Ciao"

The Gunions were next. Walt proudly showed the newcomer around the construction site of their half-finished dream house, at that time barely improved from when abandoned by the Connecticut podiatrist. The Stallion responded with repeated murmurs of "interesting concept." A load of lumber arrived, and the Stallion pitched in to off-load the truck. Some of the two-by-fours were slightly warped, and, although Walt was willing to accept them, the Stallion took it upon himself to excoriate the driver, finally insisting that the lumber be taken back and replaced. Afterward, Walt offered him a beer, a Budweiser that Bruce eyed disdainfully between sips. Finally, he put down the unfinished bottle, pausing to look at the house one final time, and delivered a summary pronouncement: "I am in awe. I don't know how you found this place, but it's perfect, absolutely perfect. There is not one, I mean not one, not a single solitary piece of this entire project that gives the tiniest indication of anyone knowing what they were doing, except for spending tons of money. Then some shrewd devil like you comes along and picks it up for a song. Hey, thanks again for the beer. I'm a Beck's guy, myself, but hey, it was wet. Have a good one."

The Clarkes and Pisanos came next. The Stallion and Francoise stopped at each homestead, ostensibly to inform the occupants of their good fortune to live in fabulous, unspoiled, early American homes. "And I should know," he said to each of them. "I'm the expert." The statement was accompanied by a flourish and the presentation of a business card reading "Winship-Adams Associates, Restoration Consultants, Nathaniel Hale Winship, President"

"I use the Nathaniel Hale Winship name professionally," explained the Stallion to the Clarkes. "No one wants to think they're buying Americana from a Jew." Francoise tempered his brashness with her beauty. Whenever she could sense a Stallion victim becoming too befuddled, she would simply derail the conversation with a smile and simple inquisition of "Vot do you theenk?"

In the course of praising his neighbors' structures, however, the Stallion undermined their modest efforts to make their homes more comfortable. Townshend Clarke, who took such pride in his self-taught craftsmanship, was devastated by the accusation of "chain saw carpentry." Bruce rubbed salt in the wound by offering, in all sincerity, to loan him a level the next time he tried to put in a door, and, even better, to teach him how to use it first. He then complimented Sue on the lovely kitchen, making a point of saying that it was wonderful that they did not have to spend a lot of time and effort ripping out someone else's bad taste. In fact, said Bruce, the only complete abomination was the kitchen floor.

When they left, Sue broke into tears; she and Townshend had just finished the kitchen floor the previous week.

At the Pisanos', the Stallion offered to help Joe remove the clear plastic in which he had just swaddled the house in preparation for winter. Joe explained that the plastic helped them keep warm by serving as a substitute for storm windows.

"But," protested the Stallion, "you can burn more wood to keep warm. I'll even help you put up the wood. But to take a nice old home like this and put it in a Baggie is architecturally inappropriate. It's such a Chuck thing to do."

"Maybe," admitted Joe. "But I'd rather be warm than `architecturally appropriate: If they had had plastic back in the 1800s, they would have used it."

The Stallion took Joe's statement whimsically. "At least you haven't done anything completely atrocious, like ... ," he paused for dramatic effect, "skylights." Joe fidgeted, hoping the newcomer would not see the boxed skylights from Sears in the shed. Bruce bade his farewell, pausing to gaze once more at Joe's plastic handicraft. "Someday," he said, a note of eternal hope in his voice, "there will be a law against selling beautiful, old houses to people with no money or no taste."

Auctions

"But life was hard. More than one settler just gave up
and disappeared off to the South."
— ALTON BLANCHARD,
from *Over Yonder Hill*

"In an environment of stimulus deprivation, even the
simple transaction of selling a used lawn mower gen-
erates community interest."
— DARWIN HUNTER,
from *Beyond Yonder*

Foster Welland seemed like a world beater when he arrived in Upper Granville. Driving a green Jaguar with Texas plates, he swept through the valley like a summer storm, introducing himself with a hearty handshake and exaggerated drawl to everyone from Hoyt Blanchard to B. J. Bosco. Not since the Stowe Stallion had a newcomer made his presence felt so quickly. Foster was a hired gun, brought in by the Green Mountain Stove Company, B.J.'s employer, to launch them into the next stratosphere of development. He was a man with big plans and all the answers. The native Vermonters hated him.

"Won't last the winter," predicted Oakley McBean to any patrons of the Granville General Store who cared to listen.

Foster immediately rented the Cowdrey Place, Walt Gunion's ill-fated house of many tenants, ostensibly as a temporary abode. "Just a place to roost," said Foster, "until we can start building in the spring." The Cowdrey Place suited him well, because he planned to purchase the top of Bailey's Peak from Walt Gunion and construct a magnificent spread.

Everything with Foster happened at an accelerated pace. He brought "the little woman" up from his native Fort Worth. Jenna Welland was a fine-boned, pampered beauty, a southwestern translation of Francoise Liebermann. Naturally the two hated each other, although their big-thinking husbands became fast friends. Guided by the Stallion, the Wellands' future home on the hill quickly took the shape of a magnificent restoration project masterminded by Nathaniel Hale Winship of Winship-Adams Associates.

Foster and Jenna flung themselves into the community. When Atlas Van Lines arrived from the South with the Wellands' possessions, the first thing Foster unloaded was his pit-style barbeque, an elaborate Texas size contraption from Neiman Marcus never seen before in Upper Granville. Except for the food, he had all the elements of a terrific barbeque, including three cases of Lone Star Beer that he had had the foresight to pack onto the van. The neighbors were quickly convinced to supply the food, and instantly a party was in progress. For the afternoon and into the evening, the group ogled the parade of finery. The Cowdrey Place had never been so well-appointed. Foster and Jenna were a couple accustomed to and comfortable with an environment of opulence.

Foster's big plans steamed through the fall. The house on the hill evolved to the blueprint and Planning Commission stages. Jenna added to their already jammed house by spending most of her time seeking treasures at antique shops. The Stallion began disassembling buildings around the state for eventual reconstruction on Abanaki Acres, the chosen name for the future complex. Walt Gunion busied himself with perc tests and building permits. This would be his biggest deal ever.

The first hiccup was right after Thanksgiving when Foster's Jag found first an icy spot, then a ditch. Jenna got the flu and could not seem to shake it. Their pipes froze because Foster forgot to turn on the electric heat tapes; then there was a chimney fire that nearly ended the checkered history of the Cowdrey Place. A trip back to Texas made matters worse. January brought a return of the miseries. Foster continued to drive his car off the road, until in disgust he traded it for a used Subaru four-wheel drive wagon. Jenna caught a cold that became bronchitis, and ice dams during the January thaw caused so much leaking that the plaster on their bedroom ceiling fell down.

Foster's ebullience darkened. Jenna coughed, hacked, and sputtered through another month. He complained bitterly to Walt Gunion about the Cowdrey Place's lack of amenities and began withholding monthly rent checks. Jenna took two weeks in the Caribbean, then announced upon her return that she was leaving Foster for her scuba diving instructor in Barbados. The check Foster gave the Stallion for blueprints bounced. His professional career disintegrated with equal rapidity. Early in March, just as the sap was beginning to flow, B.J. revealed that Foster's big plans for the stove company had matched the disasters of his personal life and that he had been sacked. Thereafter, he became a shadowy figure, unwilling to wave a greeting to a passing car.

"I can't blame him," said Darwin. "He's come down a long way in a short time."

"Never thought he'd make it this long," said a vindicated Oakley McBean.

"The bastard owes me seven hundred dollars," hissed the Stallion.

"Does this mean that the Abanaki Acres plan is dead?" moaned Walt.

`Any fool'd drive a car like that up here's gonna wind up in a ditch," added Emil.

"Poor bugger," said B.J.

"Good riddance," said Bennett.

Everyone had a thought or judgment on Foster Welland. Then, in the last week of April, an excited Sue Clarke called Sammi Burger-Hunter.

"Did you read the *Clarion*?"

"Not yet. Why?"

"There's going to be an auction at the Wellands' on Saturday. All that great stuff is going to be sold."

"Ooo-o-o," squealed Sammi. "I want the sideboard."

"I want the sideboard" countered Sue. "How are we going to get in there before the auction? Maybe we can snake off the good stuff before Saturday."

Over the protests of Darwin, who advised them to leave Foster alone and take their chances on Saturday with everyone else, Sammi and Sue hatched a plan. They would call Foster to invite him to dinner, a farewell supper. Then they would broach the subject of an early attack on the goods. His phone had been disconnected, so they went over to proffer the invitation in person.

A sullen Foster let them in. Sammi chitchatted, making a pretense of interest in Foster's well-being. Sue, however, could not contain herself, going from room to room, sizing up the merchandise and asking pointed questions about the source and value of desirable items. When the dinner invitation was finally issued, Foster just grunted and showed them the door: "Get out of here, you hypocrites. First that Blanchard bitch and now you. You're just vultures, coming over to pick the bones from the carcass. Pretty soon you'll be fighting about who gets to peck out my eyes. You can just come on Saturday like everyone else. Just bring money, okay?"

Sue sputtered with indignant rage as they walked away. First she said that she would boycott the auction. Then she blasted the outrageous tackiness of Teresa Blanchard for having the nerve to beat them to the punch.

By Saturday, however, the incident was forgotten, swallowed up in an overall mood of springtime, festivity, and the greedy anticipation of bargains. A tent was set up in the front yard, lending a colorful accent. Sammi, Sue, and Teresa arrived on the dot of nine o'clock for the preview period. They eyed each other warily, trying to guess the competition for individual items.

By the first bidding at ten, a trail of parked cars stretched for several hundred yards in either direction from the Cowdrey Place. The auctioneer, a colorful man with a booming voice and big cigar, kept the crowd spellbound with witty descriptions of each item. The three women sat together, knitting, needlepointing, and drinking coffee, but mostly making sure that one did not outbid the other for a particularly juicy item. There were bargains enough for everyone, however, so by midmorning competitiveness settled into a benign coalition with each woman complimenting and congratulating the other after a successful bidding.

Everyone got something. Sue got the Queen Anne sideboard by agreeing not to bid against Sammi on the porcelain umbrella stand. Teresa concentrated on the appliances, and Stella bought Hoyt a leatherette StratoLounger for Sunday afternoon dozing. Oakley bought cases of magazines and old books. Emil became the proud new owner of Foster's Abercrombie and Fitch hunting boots.

Darwin and B.J. wandered over late in the day. The man with the big cigar was pushing out merchandise as fast as bidders could raise their hands. They encountered Foster loading a few personal items into his Subaru wagon and a tiny U-Haul trailer. They offered to help.

"I don't need help," came the snapped reply. "The fewer obligations I leave this burgh with, the better." He paused to look over the valley. The Cowdrey Place was set nicely on the south-facing hillside. Although there were still patches of snow and the road was a quagmire, a hint of green was beginning to blush the grass of the Blanchards' pasture. A big laugh came from the auction crowd. Undoubtedly the auctioneer had found something humorous about a small aspect of Foster Welland's life. B.J. and Darwin were silent. Foster took a deep breath. When he spoke again, the edge was gone from his voice, and in its place, serenity. "I hate this place. I never want to see it or any of you ever again. When today is over I want the entire experience to be summed up in one number, the dollar amount that the asshole with the big cigar writes on the check. I'm never going to haul another piece of wood. I'm never going to worry about how my water gets into the bathtub. I'm never going to have another woman tell me that she's been cold since the Fourth of July."

"Where are you going?" asked B.J.

Foster answered with a rueful laugh, "I'm not going anywhere. I'm just going."

Darwin and B.J. left him to his misery and wandered back to the auction, where they encountered a bubbling and excited Sammi.

"Darwin You won't believe this," she giggled conspiratorially. "I just bought Foster's pit-style barbeque for, are you ready for this, twenty-two bucks. It's worth hundreds"

Beach, The

'As opposed to the tedium of winter, summertime allowed residents to devote themselves fully to their livelihoods. There was no time to idle."
— ALTON BLANCHARD,
from *Over Yonder Hill*

"Summertime ends enslavement to the wood stove and thus is a time of idyll and leisure."
— DARWIN HUNTER,
from *Beyond Yonder*

To Vermonters "the beach" is either the swimming hole, a bend in the stream where if you contort just right you can immerse your body up to the shoulders, or the pond, a euphemism for a scum-covered hole in a field hiding leeches, hornpout, and tadpoles. The trick is to stay afloat with a modified breaststroke, brushing aside floating algae and avoiding contact with bottom. Typically, the pond bottom consists of six inches of feathery, decomposed organic matter, beneath which is a slimy muck that slithers between the toes, enveloping the feet and sucking them into a primal death grip. You stand there, muck creeping to knee level, and gaze at the slimy surface. As black flies swarm about your head, thoughts turn to the invigorating astringency of the

ocean. Ah, the North Atlantic, wave upon endless wave of thera-
peutic salt water crashing upon grainy beaches of polished sand.
Your body scrubbed to the pore by the combination of sun, sand,
and wind; your soul renewed by contact with the timeless immen-
sity of the sea. By comparison, at the pond the experience is anemic.

For aquatic recreation, Upper Granville possesses Tomar
Brook and the Gunions' pond. The brook rages for most of the
spring because the runoff from mountain snows keeps it brim-
ming with icy froth. In July the water warms as the level drops.
There is a period of about a week when it is a passable swimming
hole, then it dwindles to just another lazy farm stream struggling
to maintain its existence. Besides the neighborhood kids who find
the stream a never-ending source of entertainment, the principal
user is B. J. Bosco, who, whenever she works up a sweat, will
spontaneously strip to the altogether and wallow amid the gurgles
and boulders. Large, unbelievably pale, and distinctly immodest,
her imitations of beached whales have electrified the community.
Teresa Bennett Blanchard spews about indignantly, using the
word "tramp" twice in every sentence. Bennett, Hoyt, and Emil
agree, yet always find ample excuse to drive by in the tractor every
thirty seconds, looking away suddenly whenever B.J. waves or
stands up. If they are out jogging, Darwin and the Stallion will
stop by for a casual chat. Sue Clarke, meanwhile, forbids
Townshend to go outside during B.J.'s exhibitions.

The Gunions' pond is a different experience. Each summer
they schedule a pond party that in their minds is a Gatsbyesque
affair of elegant food, beautiful people, and witty conversation.
For most Upper Granvillites, it is one of the more dreaded affairs
on the summer social calendar. The weather rarely cooperates, the
bugs are rampant, and Walt spends the afternoon endlessly
exhorting everyone to take a dip in his slime hole. To underscore
his point, he periodically undrapes his pear-shaped body and wad-
dle-sprints from the picnic area to the pond, belly flopping in a
lime green flourish punctuated by a bloodcurdling "yahoo." The
others watch, cringe, and think up new excuses why they cannot
join him. Darwin always defers demurely by claiming it is "that
time of month." The best year was when the event ended early

because B.J. ran over one of the Gunions' toy poodles, sending Martha into a swoon and ending the ordeal. The next year Darwin, Joe, and the Stallion offered her fifty dollars to do it again.

And it came to pass one winter that several residents of the Flatlander Valley were lamenting Vermont's total lack of an acceptable beach. Sue Clarke said that it would be great if they had a beach like the one at Mashpaug, a tiny private community in southern Rhode Island where Townshend's parents owned a huge rambling, turn-of-the-century beach cottage.

The Stallion homed in immediately: "Townie, you've been holding back on us. A beach house? A private community? Sounds like the ideal place for a summer community outing."

Townshend was reluctant. "I haven't really gone there since I was a teenager. It's really kind of a stodgy place. And I don't know if my parents could cope with an invasion of all of us."

"We'll just kick them out for the weekend," countered the Stallion, instantly galvanizing the group to action. "How much room is there?"

Before Townshend could muster another protest, Sue had undermined his position by revealing that there was plenty of room and that Townshend's parents were constantly issuing invitations for them to come down and would likely be receptive to such a proposition. Within an hour the event had been fully planned, Townshend having been peer- and spouse- pressured into calling his parents and even setting the date some six months hence.

So on the first weekend of August three vehicles set forth from Upper Granville for what was to become the first annual weekend at the shore. The kids were packed into one car, driven by Darwin wearing a Sony Walkman, while the adults cruised in opulent comfort, listening to William Ackerman and George Winston, all the while powering down soft cheeses and white wines with flowery labels. The Clarkes' summer residence was revealed to be more mansion than cottage, forever blowing Townshend's cover as a hardscrabble, Yankee goat farmer. The elder Clarkes were gracious, even solicitous of their son's friends. The accommodations were lavish, each couple having a private bedroom with ocean view, and the kids sequestered in a large dormitory room where they could create mayhem with impunity. The adults set about all manner of beachiness. The Stallion, Joe, Darwin, and B.J. played killer volleyball, touch football, and other rituals of male competition. Sammi, Francoise, and Tina oiled their bodies and took the intensive course in two-day tanning, while Sue found ample outlet for her maternal impulses, turning the Clarke kitchen into a nonstop orgy of summer savories. Only Townshend remained immune to the group frenzy, spending most of his time cursing and muttering over a hopelessly snarled fishing reel.

The novel setting propelled the normally high levels of group interaction into the stratosphere. A spectacular sunset over Long Island Sound provided the backdrop for a cookout of boiled lobster, grilled bluefish, steamers, corn on the cob, and local tomatoes. Following cleanup, the group sat in the warm womb of a perfect summer night, watching mists form and roll in over the hedgerows of rose hips while conversation and wine consumption kept pace in perfect proportion. Still, Townshend remained aloof from the group, spending most of the time fussbudgeting in the kitchen.

The group sat in the creaking wicker rockers on the back porch debating such topics as whether rape was possible within the confines of a marriage. The splits were along fairly predictable lines with the "yea's" consisting of Sammi, B.J., and Tina, and the "nay's" the Stallion (and his darling), Sue, and Joe. Townshend did not participate, and Darwin assumed his normal role of instigating trouble in whichever quarter seemed most inflammable. The highlight came when Sammi called the Stallion a "sexist cocksucker," which Darwin pointed out was a contradiction in terms, whereupon B.J. told him to shut his pig mouth or have his voice raised an octave. The Stallion was equal to the situation by stating categorically that he had intimately known scores of bleeding-heart females of the Sammi/B.J./Tina ilk, and that their positions of feminism were hypocritical manifestations of never having been serviced by an appropriately endowed male. This brought all three out of their respective chairs spewing indignant protests and countercharges.

Before long, however, the same group was matching wits in an impromptu game of Trivial Pursuit, without board, cards, or structure. Darwin amazed all by knowing the five members of the original Animals, Joe Pisano proved unstumpable on state capitals and presidents, and Sue Clarke recited the prologue to the Canterbury Tales in Olde English. Soon it was one o'clock in the morning, and everyone reluctantly agreed that at least a little sleep was in order before commencing another day at the shore.

The men went for a brief walk on the beach before turning in. Townshend led the way down a dark path through the rose hips and across a small boardwalk until they were crunching through the soft sand. Distant lights and the sound of a band drifted over the rhythmic surf.

"Someone's still partying," said Darwin.

"That's the country club," replied Townshend matter-of-factly.

"You know what we should do?" said the Stallion. "We should look into getting a community place down here. I'll bet if we got four or five couples involved we could afford it."

Townshend continued staring at the lights of the country club as if the Stallion had never spoken. "I once tried to blow up that place."

The Stallion, meanwhile, continued unfazed: "We could form some kind of community association, might even have some tax advantages."

"Townshend," said Darwin, "what do you mean? This place is fabulous. You tried to blow it up?"

"I didn't succeed," replied Townshend in the same depressed tone that had characterized him all weekend. "In fact it was a pretty botched job. But I meant it." No one responded. No one wanted to be part of his pain.

"Well, let's go to bed," said Townshend, and he turned to lead them back through the bushes. The band finished the last few bars. The music faded over the water and into the sand. All that was left was the hiss and roar of the surf.

Beer

> "Brewing was a common household practice Every occasion, social or official, was bonded by the toast of an appropriate libation."
>
> — ALTON BLANCHARD,
> from *Over Yonder Hill*

> "Despite a wave of temperance in the mid-1980s, beer drinking was common at every valley function."
>
> — DARWIN HUNTER,
> from *Beyond Yonder*

Beer is the ultimate male-bonding beverage. This is as true for Upper Granville, Vermont, as for San Antonio, Texas, or for that matter Heidelberg, Germany. Beer is the beverage that crosses boundaries, sexes, generations, and cultures. Beer is also a badge, not of courage but of identity, worn by the male of the species to make a single but complete statement on Life.

The Flatlander side of the valley favors Canadian beers such as Molson, LaBatt's, and Moosehead. These are full-flavored, well-brewed products with a reputation for quality without pretension. How can a moose be considered pretentious? These are the safe beers for all occasions, although one must remember to carry an opener, since the slick marketers behind the moose is loose want you to believe that the twist-off cap has not yet made it north of the border.

B. J. Bosco drinks Molson Golden exclusively. She can remove a cap with her belt buckle, her knife, a chain link fence, the door handle on a car, or her teeth. She can also snap bottle caps at frightening speeds and with unerring accuracy for distances up to fifty feet. She can out drink any man in Upper Granville, and she thoroughly disgusts the Martha Gunions of the world. No one messes with B.J. She has her own techniques for crossing cultural and generational gaps.

Emil Dummerston Weed sticks to Genesee, brewed in Rochester, New York. He buys sixteen-ounce bottles ("pounders") or quarts, whichever is cheaper. Emil is a man of no airs and little cash. Fluid per dollar is his primary criterion for brand selection. On warm summer evenings he will sit on the front porch of his little house with his transistor radio tuned to Granville's country and western station, hitting on a Genny quart. More than once, B.J. has joined him and they pass the bottle back and forth, then another after that. One night it was a few more than two. Around midnight B.J. made the type of comment that can be made only when one is sharing the camaraderie of brew: "Emil, this really isn't bad beer, but how can you drink something with such low-rent graphics?"

Emil had an able response: "I drunk more of these than Carter's has little liver pills, and I ain't tasted the label yet. I tasted near anything that can be put into the mouth. I tasted dust; I tasted blood; I tasted shit; but I ain't tasted a label yet."

The Stallion has been offered a hit off of Emil's Genesee more than once, but has politely refused, mentally retching at the thought of the germs that made Emil's teeth yellow somehow entering the temple that he calls his body. His own preferred brew is St. Pauli Girl, with Beck's, Heineken, or anything else costing six dollars a six-pack acceptable. Emil once bet him a case of beer that he could not tell the difference between Genesee and one of his "foil-wrapped jobs" in a blind taste test. The Stallion insisted that he could, yet steadfastly refused to take the test even after considerable group pressure. Emil, meanwhile, has told the story a hundred times as evidence of the hypocrisy of Flatlanders.

Dr. Darwin Hunter will drink anything, anytime. He refers to himself as an "equal opportunity drinker." He has no favorite brand, although he has gone to the trouble of converting a refrigerator in his basement to a beer cooler where he maintains a quarter keg of Miller Lite on tap. Darwin freely admits to this brand being a wimpy substitute for beer, but he buys the idea of a low calorie beer being less filling, thereby enabling him to drink more of it. He loves it.

Bennett Blanchard does not drink beer much, but when he does, the choice is Budweiser. Ask him why, and he will tell you that it is because he likes to go first class. Bennett likes his drink, but he cannot resolve his enjoyment of it with the notion that drink is somehow the devil's work. He adapts by interspersing long months of abstention with interludes of excess.

Bennett's father, Hoyt, is much the same way. Before the spring of 1985 he had gone nine years with no more than an occasional sip of wine. Somehow the topic of beer came up on Christmas Eve, just after the service, when the community was gathered in the back of the church sipping nonalcoholic eggnog. Hoyt related a wonderfully rich story about how his father brewed his own beer. Hoyt's first taste came at the age of twelve in the sugar house where he and his dad would while away countless hours boiling down the sap. It was a touching story, combining the timelessness of beer's generation-spanning capabilities with a uniquely Vermont setting. Hoyt was plainly enjoying the revived memory of his own father, and the rest of the group was spellbound. At the end of the story, B. J. Bosco asked if he still had the recipe.

"For the beer? I sure do. Dad wasn't a fool. He taught me and Mother to brew so's he could concentrate on the drinking."

"You ought to try it again," suggested B.J.

"I might. I just might," said Hoyt enthusiastically.

No one gave it another thought. Months passed, and it was April. Patches of snow were separated by puddles and islands of ground peeking skyward for the first time since November. It was classic Mud Season, the days promising spring and nights reminding of winter. The sap was gushing, and the steam was billowing out of the Blanchard sugar house like a huge cumulus cloud trying to escape. The Stallion and Joe Pisano were waiting in their hats, gloves, and running suits for Darwin when he came home from work.

"Hurry up, get your stuff," said Joe.

"It's too muddy to run." protested Darwin.

"Don't you wimp out on us," warned the Stallion. "We waited for you."

"Wear some old shoes," suggested Joe.

The trio splattered forth through the puddles and ooze, satisfying some primal instinct. On their return they were greeted outside the sugar house by a waving Hoyt Blanchard.

"Ho, boys. Care to try a little of the real stuff?" He was obviously in good spirits. Usually Hoyt regarded joggers as minor nuisances from another planet. The runners were disconcerted by the sudden joviality. B.J. brought the situation into focus by emerging from the sugar house carrying a beer mug.

"Hi guys. He did it He made the beer. His father's recipe. Just like he said he was going to. Good stuff, too. Come on, try some."

"Avec pleasure," exclaimed Darwin, ever debonair. The others followed. Inside, the sugar house was warm and wet, lit by a single dangling bulb and more akin to a womb than a steambath. A radio had a baseball game on.

"Is today opening day?" asked the Stallion.

"Sox are up by two," answered Hoyt. "Rice has two homers. Wait'll you take a taste of this." He went over to a ceramic crock with a wooden lid, lifted off the top, and ladled the beer into coffee cups to pass around. "When I was ten years old my father took me down to Boston to see the Red Sox. We took the train and stayed overnight with some cousins in West Roxbury. I remember it like it was yesterday. Nineteen nineteen It was the only time I ever remember my father taking days off from the farm. The Red Sox had this big left-handed pitcher who could hit the ball so far —"

"Babe Ruth," interjected the Stallion.

"Babe Ruth," concurred Hoyt. "We got to Fenway two hours before game time so we could watch batting practice. That Babe Ruth hit these towering drives that had all of us in the stands with our mouths open. Say, what do you think of the beer?"

Darwin responded by holding his cup out for a refill. Joe Pisano described the taste as halfway between apple cider and molasses. The Stallion, the beer snob of snobs, said the taste was faintly reminiscent of Bass Ale and asked for a second cup as well. His first baseball game had been at the Polo Grounds with his Cub Scout troop. His father traveled extensively and hadn't much interest in baseball, although the Stallion himself was quite the fanatic and had an almost encyclopedic knowledge of obscure statistics. Joe had gone to a Yankee game and remembered that his favorite player, Mickey Mantle, struck out three times. Darwin's father had taken him to see the Reds play the Giants specifically so he could see Willie Mays, but the player who impressed Darwin the most was Ted Kluzewski, the Reds' muscle bound first baseman who wore a sleeveless uniform that exposed his bulging biceps. B.J. started attending Red Sox games in college. She and her friends would smoke dope in the bleachers on warm summer nights and cheer wildly whenever Bill Lee, the Spaceman, made an appearance.

The sound of a tractor was heard, and Hoyt commandeered Emil to come in and try his beer. By now the top was being left off the crock and the individuals were simply dipping their cups in rather than waiting for Hoyt to ladle out a serving.

Emil, it turns out, had never been to a baseball game. Joe Pisano ran back to the Hunters' to tell Sammi where Darwin was and to call Francoise and Tina. He came back with a bag of potato chips and another of pretzels. The Stallion was helping Hoyt keep the fire stoked and the pans boiling. B.J. had an abundance of questions about the sugaring process, specifically the weather conditions that caused the sap run to be good or bad. Hoyt and Emil were filled with homilies about the sap. Hard rain after snow, the sap runs slow, that sort of thing. As evening settled over Upper Granville, the Blanchard sugar house took on the rosy hue and hum of a neighborhood pub.

The joy was brought to a screeching halt by the appearance of Bennett at the doorway. Everyone was fairly well lit by this point and inclined to drop cultural hostilities.

"Bennett," said the Stallion, "your father's beer is fabulous. Why don't you join us for a wee dram?"

Bennett looked through him, not so much with hostility, but with the purposefulness of someone with something more important to do. The mantle of the family farm hung heavily on his shoulders.

"Come on, Emil, cows to be milked." Emil glanced at Hoyt, appealing for clemency, but received only a sympathetic shake of the head.

"Ten minutes," pleaded B.J. "Take ten minutes and join us for a cup, Bennett." Bennett never even answered her. He kept his steady stare on Emil.

"Cows don't wait, Emil."

Emil followed Bennett out into the mud. The party was clearly over. The Flatlanders offered profuse thanks and took the cue to leave. Only B.J. lingered behind.

"Weren't you just like him at his age?" she asked.

"I was," nodded Hoyt. "There was days I felt running this farm was more responsibility than a man could hardly stand. But then there comes a day when you realize that it's just a farm like a million other farms."

Hoyt looked up at B.J. "And Bennett ain't recognized that yet."

Boots

"Clothing was homemade and a young man's first
sign of prosperity was the purchase
of store-bought boots."
— ALTON BLANCHARD,
from *Over Yonder Hill*

"Footwear could be the subject of great debate.
Which shoe for instance was better
for winter jogging, Adidas Terra Trainers
or Reebok LX 8500's?"
— DARWIN HUNTER,
from *Beyond Yonder*

Oakley McBean, as close to a sage as there is in central Vermont, always claimed that you could tell a man by his boots. The reason Oakley spent so much time leaning on the cash register of the Granville General Store, sucking pensively on his pipe, was that it gave him a direct angle for foot gazing and, therefore, great insight into the human condition. Just as all nerves in the body have termination points in the feet, so do the strands of the personality. Age, social class, sex, and ethnic heritage can be revealed as well as the innermost secrets of the individual. All it takes is an experience in foot-gazing.

While buying the Sunday paper one day, Oakley took the time to explain the tricks of his trade to B. J. Bosco: "Now take your shoes," he said. "You're wearin' them joggin' shoes, though you ain't no jogger as demonstrated by the fact that no serious jogger would wear shoes with holes in 'em. Also, they're them Adidases, which cost a lot. So right away I know you're a Flatlander, 'cause local people buy their shoes up to Harry's House of Discount or K mart. But you're not a rich Flatlander or you wouldn't wear such raggy shoes. Or maybe you're just lazy and frugal like a good Scotsman. In any case, you don't care about style."

B.J. agreed that Oakley had nailed her accurately with his shoe analysis. There were no other customers, and B.J. had nowhere to go, so she listened as Oakley continued his footwear analysis.

" 'Course it tells me somethin' that you're wearing sneakers with holes in 'em, and it must be about zero degrees out, don't you know? Tells me you're a Flatlander or a fool, because if your car broke down on your trip down here, your feet would turn to sticks before you could get here for help. So you wear sensible shoes, but you don't wear them at sensible times. Tells me that you're young, 'cuz young folk tend not to be too sensible."

"So what would a real Vermonter wear, Sorels?"

"Hell no, the only people who wear Sorels are Flatlanders who want to pretend they're real Vermonters. Now if the Sorels look like they've been handed down from generation to generation and had the wool liners changed about a hundred times, then maybe it would be a real Vermonter, but chances are he bought them at a yard sale from a Flatlander. Vermonters don't wear hiking boots, either. Hiking boots are the surest sign of an out-of-stater there can be. Snow and mud gets caught up in that fancy tread, don't you know, and you track it all over the house. You won't find a Vermonter in cowboy boots either. Damndest thing in the world, people wearing boots with high heels and pointy toes that come up to their knees to protect them from rattlesnake bites. The only rattlesnakes in Vermont are the politicians and ski area operators Whenever I see a pair of cowboy boots in here, I shudder. Mostly see 'em during leaf season when all the fools come to Vermont."

"So what do the real Vermonters wear?" B.J. persisted.

"Rubber"

"Rubbers?"

"No. Rubber boots. Black ones with an orange stripe at the top. Sold 'em for years in this store for six ninety-eight a pair. Now they cost three times that."

"I paid seventy bucks for these running shoes and they wore out in a year."

"You won't get too many years out of a pair of rubber boots, unless you know what you're doin: You can wear 'em in the barn, tromp through the cow plop, hose 'em down, and walk in the house. Put on a few extra pair of socks and they're good for winter. Wear the old ones with holes in 'em in the summer, that's how you make 'em last. They get good traction without trackin' up the living room. They're God's gift to the foot."

B.J. gathered her Sunday paper and prepared to leave. She had reached the maximum dose of wisdom for the day. "Rubber boots are so versatile," she returned to Oakley. "You can go running in them, take them dancing, even wear them to church on Sunday, don't you know"

Oakley gave B.J. a long glance, knew he was having his leg pulled, but was equal to the task: "Eyuh, but what sensible man would want to do any of those things?"

Boundaries

"Settlers clearly marked properties to avoid
disputes. Boundaries were then recorded
on permanent deeds."
— ALTON BLANCHARD,
from *Over Yonder Hill*

"Anyone who has ever bought property in Vermont
knows that deeds are useless. Property lines are
marked by trees that have died, stone fences that
have moved, and streams that have disappeared. The
situation is a mess. At some point the serious buyer
swallows hard and takes a chance."
— DARWIN HUNTER,
from *Beyond Yonder*

When the Pisanos moved into their house, they thought it quaint and unique that one of the outbuildings was once the Upper Granville granary. History and personality were connected with their new home, a refreshing change from the faceless New Jersey suburbia whence they came. In the summer of their first year, they watched proudly as Bennett and Hoyt Blanchard drove their herd of milkers to pasture through the narrow roadway between their house and granary. Although overgrown and no longer maintained by the town, the path was still officially a town road, and the Blanchards had been using it for access since Hoyt was a boy.

The cattle drive gave Tina and Joe a sense of belonging to the community. Whenever they had friends or relatives visiting from New Jersey in the summer, they would gather on the front porch in the evening to sip gin and tonics, wave to Hoyt and Bennett, and imitate the calls of "HAH" that directed the beasts.

Misgivings started when the Pisanos' two-year-old became mobile. Not that they feared his being trampled by the Blanchard cows; they disliked the strip of cowpies running through the center of their property. Joe talked first to Bennett, then Hoyt, explaining how he wanted to avoid any possibility of a health hazard and respectfully requested that they no longer move their cattle across this segment of the Pisano property. He offered as an alternative an access fifty yards north of the current pathway. Bennett and Hoyt promised to think about it, but continued to drive the cows between the house and granary twice a day. After several weeks Joe questioned them again. They replied that they had talked it over, but had decided to maintain the status quo. Although rerouting the cows would cost little in time, aggravation, or money, they saw no benefit in accommodating the Pisano request.

Joe appealed to the town selectmen to have the road reclassed, but was discouraged to learn that any protest by the Blanchards would be upheld, allowing them to move the cows as they had for generations. This revolting development provoked Joe into his Jersey mentality, a combination of survival of the fittest, every man for himself, and fuck them before they fuck you.

Tina stood squarely behind him, ready to fight.

Joe's first move was to post the property. Next he put out large fluorescent stakes to make his boundary lines. Bennett, realizing that battle lines were being drawn, countered by uprooting those boundary markers and throwing them ceremoniously on the Pisanos' porch one evening while they were sitting peacefully with Tina's parents. Then, while Joe and Tina were on a vacation in Nova Scotia, he hired trucks to dump several loads of gravel that transformed the right-of-way into a superhighway.

The Pisanos were horror-struck by the arrogant implementation of construction and enlisted the services of Larry Lipschitz, a Montpelier lawyer renowned for his willingness to use obnoxious tactics to achieve results. Joe began to gloat. Now they were getting onto his turf, street fighting, and, to Joe, there was no difference between a superhighway and a gravel path.

Alas, after five hundred dollars' worth of investigating the deed and the town bylaws, Lipschitz told the Pisanos that their legal recourse was limited. Unless they could get the town of Granville to change the status of the path, Bennett Blanchard had every legal right to drive his cows between their house and granary. The best he could offer were suggestions for obnoxious, but legal, behavior that might harass the Blanchards into a more reasonable stance.

Joe and Tina listened carefully to Lipschitz and formed a battle plan. Their first attack took place on a sleepy August morning when summer was in its full, but waning, glory. It was a languid day, perfect for a cup of coffee on the front porch. The tinkle of cowbells signaled pastoral harmony, as Bennett and Hoyt, accompanied by the usual retinue of wives and children, drove the herd to the pasture. As the cows sauntered onto the pathway, Joe and Tina emerged from the front door wearing the grim, determined expressions of terrorists. Each carried an air horn, the type carried on boats. With not a glimmer of emotion they pointed the horns at the herd and let fly with the ear-piercing wail. Bedlam came instantly as the poor, dumb beasts scattered randomly, oblivious to the shouts and gestures of the farmers. Ironically, the Pisanos fared poorly in the chaos: the heifers trashed the flower garden, into which Tina had put many loving hours that spring and which was just now reaching full flower.

The farmers devoted their efforts fully to the cows, waving and shouting until all were safely inside the pasture. Then they charged the Pisano front lawn where Joe and Tina were standing, braced for the assault. Bennett slapped the air horn out of Joe's hand, picked it up, and threw it across the street, whereupon Tina took point-blank aim with hers and let it wail about six inches from Bennett's head. He grabbed for the can, Joe interceded, and a brief tussle ensued. Bennett succeeded in throwing the can after the first.

"You're trespassing, Blanchard" said Joe, straining to keep his composure, but showing obvious effects of his emotional turmoil. "And now you're guilty of assault."

"If you think that's assault, try it again, and I'll shove the horn down your throat."

"Oh, so now you're threatening us, too? You're playing right into our hands. I'm going to sue you for all you're worth. I'm going to own the farm."

The blood flushed to Bennett's face, and the veins on his neck popped out like those on a Holstein's udder. "Not before I kick your ass back to Short Hairs" he screamed.

Hoyt caught up to the group. He was huffing from exertion, with a look of agitation rarely seen in the face of a dairy farmer. Joe avoided his gaze. He considered the dispute to be between himself and Bennett.

"Damn fools," Hoyt sputtered. "What if one of them cows ran down one of the kids? Or tore its bag on a fence?"

"You might have a right to use the path." snarled Tina using a tone of voice and body posture she had picked up from the Dairy Queen in Secaucus, New Jersey, "but you can't control what we do on our own property."

`And if you trespass," added Joe, "be prepared for the worst."

Bennett started toward Joe, but Hoyt restrained him. "Don't bother," he told his son. "There's no use dealing with these people." They stalked down the road. A momentary peace had returned to the Upper Granville valley. Both parties wasted no time in notifying the authorities. The Pisanos called Chief Magoun, head of the modest Granville force, and the Blanchards went directly to the state police. Magoun arrived an hour later. He parked his cruiser in front of the Pisanos' and met with them on the porch. Very calmly and rationally they explained the situation, how their health, safety, and property were routinely threatened by arrogant, malicious, uncaring dairy farmers who thought that the entire world existed to support their farm.

After they finished, Magoun said, "I suspect there's another version to this story," and he called Hoyt Blanchard to ask him to come over. The Blanchards came as a clan, with everyone—from Stella to nine-month old Bennett junior—present. Stella, surprisingly, acted as the Blanchard spokesperson and told the saga of law-abiding, peaceful countryfolk whose access to their own fields was hindered by newcomers unconcerned with the needs of the farm and the rights of the farmer.

"It's not as if we didn't offer an alternative," broke in Joe. "We told you that if you just walked fifty yards further up the road, you could access, but you wouldn't budge."

"Why should we change anything?" said Bennett. "We've already got our right-of-way."

"Because we wouldn't have all this trouble if you had shown a trace of human decency."

"We're not the one who stampeded the cows"

'And we're going to —"

"Hold it, hold it, hold it" shouted Chief Magoun. "Let's not get into it again." By this time one could feel emotions gathering momentum. Moreover, several of the neighbors, attracted by the commotion and the police car, had joined the group.

"Chief Magoun's right," chimed in Sammi Burger-Hunter. "Yelling and shouting won't solve a thing. If we —"

At last Bennett and Joe found something to be united about. They both jumped down Sammi's throat, telling her to mind her own business. Luckily this tangent was ended by the arrival of a state police car. An officer with a properly authoritative military bearing, spitshine and epaulettes, got out, put on his flat-brimmed hat, and strolled over to the group. His presence was that of complete authority, and the crowd was instantly poised to accept his will as law. He nodded to Chief Magoun, and they engaged in a brief, whispered conference. Then the trooper addressed the group.

"I understand someone here has been blowing an air horn at cows on a legal right-of-way"

"It's not quite that cut-and-dried, officer," said Joe, who stepped forward, prepared to point out the nuances of the situation. He never had the chance, because he was cut short by the clipped response from the trooper.

"Thank you, sir. And which of you is the farmer accused of trespassing and assault whose cows were stampeded?"

Bennett answered in the affirmative. The trooper faced him directly like a drill instructor at a platoon inspection. "Mister, don't go on this man's land again. If he pulls a stunt like that again, just shoot him and you can borrow my gun. Or call me and I'll do it for you. There's not a jury in Vermont who would convict either of us."

He turned to Joe. "Do you get the drift?" Joe nodded weakly.

"Now work this out like intelligent human beings. And work it out right now. Don't wait for another time. I don't want to come back here again about this matter." The trooper tipped his hat politely and returned to the car. He made a U-turn in the very driveway in question and nodded in acknowledgment to Magoun's wave as he drove past. His rooster tail of dust had not yet settled when Tina spoke: "I'll make some fresh coffee. Let's sit on the porch and work this out." Stella offered to help. And before the coffee had even been brought out, Bennett and Hoyt had agreed that moving the access a few yards up the road would not kill them. Joe agreed to put in a new gate, and even offered to have the property deed amended, assuring them of a legal right-of-way.

"Naw, never mind," said Bennett. "We've still got the town road. As long as that exists, nothing needs to be changed."

Teresa brought over some cookies, store bought, not homemade, but a good accompaniment nevertheless. By the end of the first cup, the subject had changed, and folks had returned to the timeless Vermont habit of talking about the weather.

Canadians

> "Defending the principle that all men are created
> equal, the early settlers fought to banish Abanakis,
> Yorkers, and Canucks from their midst."
> — ALTON BLANCHARD,
> from *Over Yonder Hill*

> "Vermont is a state of almost no ethnic variety.
> Divisions are so sharp along Chuck/Flatlander lines
> that ethnic heritage is inconsequential. Well, there is
> the occasional French Canadian...."
> — DARWIN HUNTER,
> from *Beyond Yonder*

Nothing unites a nation so quickly as a common enemy. No one gave it much thought when Walt Gunion sold a ten-acre parcel to one Pierre Larriviere of Trois Rivieres, Quebec. Walt was always involved in low-level real estate transactions, most of which collapsed under the weight of their own ill conception. In addition to his local rentals, he sold plots of rough pasture, brush, and woods to starry-eyed Flatlanders who for a few thousand dollars could have a mental escape from lives in the rat race.

Pierre was different, however. He swooped down from the north in his Pontiac Parisienne, hired a backhoe to gouge out a driveway and flatten a site. Within weeks he had hauled in not one but three trailers that he arranged in a semicircular complex opening out to the road. To make matters worse, he painted one trailer electric blue, the second orange, and the third pink. The central courtyard was littered with pink flamingos, glare balls, and other testaments to bad taste. Pierre and a group of friends came down for long weekends and paraded around in bikini bathing suits, swilling American beer to the accompaniment of portable stereos blasting out French crooners. They stayed up late every night, and the drifting sound of their revelry carried into town.

The Stallion, America's last bastion of good taste, was distraught. "I can't believe it," he said one otherwise idyllic evening at Darwin Hunter's as distant strains of a French Sinatra mixed with the sizzling of napalmed chicken on the grill. "Upper Granville is becoming another Old Orchard Beach. We should string up that sleazeball, Walt Gunion." He shook his head, genuinely depressed.

"By the balls," agreed Darwin. "I like tacky stuff, but their taste offends even me. The silver lining is that they're here only during the summer."

"No," countered the Stallion, "the silver lining is that they only put up trailers instead of building houses. If a miracle occurred, they could be gone tomorrow."

The Canadians clashed equally with the Chuck population. They hired Emil Dummerston Weed for odd jobs, then paid him the agreed-upon amount in Canadian dollars, making no compensation for the exchange rate. Emil was less than pleased, especially since they pronounced his name "A-meel." Pierre ran afoul of the Blanchards, as well. He and his friends would drink lots of beer, then get into their cars and turn the dirt road around the valley into a race course. One Saturday afternoon a friend of Pierre's struck and killed a Blanchard heifer. Bennett was livid, but reached new levels of rage when the Quebecois refused to make financial reparation, claiming that Bennett's cow should not have been in the road. They argued that Bennett should pay for damage to the car.

For two summers the residents endured the transformation of their rural hamlet into an unlikely playground. Then, abruptly, the foreigners disappeared. They did not return for a third summer, and even more surprisingly, as soon as the ground was hard enough, a truck came and hauled off the trailers. Save for a few scars on the landscape, the enemy had been vanquished. Pierre Larriviere was never heard from again.

The sudden and mysterious disappearance gave rise to rampant speculation. Perhaps Pierre had taken ill, or died, or simply tired of Upper Granville. It was the summer's favorite topic of conversation, surpassing B.J.'s skinny-dipping in Tomar Brook and the status of vegetable gardens. Finally, the truth was revealed one night when the Clarkes and Hunters were sharing a bottle of Classico Barolo on the latter's front porch. The topic was the disappearance of the Canadians, an event that Darwin likened to "waking up one morning and finding that your cancer has gone away."

The Barolo was a rich wine, full-bodied, dry, overwhelming, and it overwhelmed Sue the Shrew Clarke, who interrupted the speculation on the fate of Pierre by blurting, "I can't stand it anymore. Townshend did it."

"Sue" said Townshend sharply.

"Did what?" asked Sammi.

"Townshend's always 'doing something,'" said Darwin.

"Townshend," Sue addressed him directly, as if she was disciplining one of her children, "we're not keeping this secret any longer." Then to the others: "Townshend bought Pierre Larriviere's place."

"He bought it?" Sammi was amazed.

"He bought it for thousands more than it was worth," Sue continued, "then sold the trailers for a pittance. Pierre Larriviere is probably laughing into his beer at Old Orchard Beach."

"Townshend," Darwin said with warmth, "that's incredible, just unbelievable. The whole community owes you a debt of thanks."

"Terrific," said Sue, who obviously did not share Darwin's admiration of Townshend. "We get a debt of thanks, and meanwhile the guy who thinks that Appalachian living is where it's at still refuses to spend a nickel on making his wife and children more comfortable."

"I like the way we live," Townshend said quietly, but with conviction. "We decided before we got married that we wanted to live uncomplicated lives, close to the land, and close to each other. We wanted to be in control of the process of living."

"Well, wouldn't we be 'in control of the process of living' if we had a car like Darwin and Sammi's or electricity like the rest of the world? Even Emil and the Blanchards think the way we live is primitive. What good is having money if you don't spend any?"

"Let's talk about it later." Townshend and Sue had obviously covered this territory before, but never directly in front of the Hunters.

"No, we'll talk about it now Chucks laugh at us. The twentieth century's passed you by, Townshend, but I'm the one who's suffering. How can you spend thousands of dollars to chase some Frenchman from the neighborhood, while your family dresses in rags and survives on zucchini bread? I'm sick of mason jars and wood stoves and earwigs. Let's spend some money on us instead of trailers that get taken to the dump."

A silence followed. Then Townshend spoke evenly, as if he had heard his wife out but was unmoved from his convictions. "We chose to live this way for a reason. We lack nothing—food, clothing, medical care. That we have money to afford luxury is irrelevant. That's not what our lives are about."

Townshend turned to Darwin, who was taking mental notes of a scene that he was certain had a place in *Beyond Yonder*. "I'd appreciate it if you didn't say anything to anyone about this."

Darwin was not sure if he meant the confrontation between Sue and him or the real estate transaction. Both matters, he decided, were best left as private domains. "My lips are sealed, Townie, but I want you to know, you're a hero to me."

Christmas

> "Christmas gave an ember glow
> to a medieval time of year."
> — ALTON BLANCHARD,
> from *Over Yonder Hill*

> 'In the unforgettable words of Alton Blanchard,
> 'Christmas gave an ember glow
> to a medieval time of year'."
> — DARWIN HUNTER,
> from *Beyond Yonder*

The ritual of Christmas developed its own rhythm.

Soon after Thanksgiving, Bennett Blanchard cuts down a number of spruce trees and, with Emil's help, hauls them down to the front of the Upper Granville Community Church. Three weeks before Christmas, Sammi, Teresa, Sue, Tina, and Martha come over with hammer, nails, ribbon, and wire to make an array of wreaths to hang on the doors, windows, and bell tower. Then, two weeks before Christmas, Darwin and the Stallion go over to set up the tree. A week before Christmas, Stella Blanchard calls each household to coordinate who is to bring what for the social following the service. Then the Saturday before Christmas, B. J. Bosco holds a tree-decorating party with all the neighborhood kids. Joe Pisano assists with the highest decorations and helps keep the kids in line, while Walt Gunion makes yet another surprise appearance as Santa.

Two days before the service, Hoyt fires up the ancient stove, with its stovepipe stretching the entire length of the structure. Only Hoyt has the touch. Let anyone else light the stove and the church fills with smoke, creosote streaming down the sides of the pipe like the runoff from springtime snow. On the afternoon before Christmas Eve, Hoyt lights the lanterns. Just before the service he meets the pastor and the bell ringer (the neighborhood male child closest to puberty) to call the community to the church.

Christmas is always memorable in Upper Granville, but this year especially so. Many relatives were in town. B. J. Bosco's parents were up from Fort Lauderdale to meet her new roommate, Moira Chappee. The meeting was B.J.'s first admission that she was gay. The elder Boscos liked Moira well enough, but their shock in learning of their daughter's sexual ambiguity in combination with the unfamiliar cold weather and the cramped quarters resulted in a reunion more agonizing than sentimental. Mercifully, both parties agreed to postpone hostilities for Christmas.

The Stallion's older brother, a big-shot lawyer from Manhattan, was visiting, too. Their relationship was marked by competitiveness and strife, as genetically identical inclinations toward arrogance and perfection collided. The brother was frustrated by the Stallion's resistance to traditional values, such as worshiping money. Despite his effete tastes, the Stallion had never accepted the basic American work ethic. By Christmas Eve, however, there seemed to be forgiveness, acceptance of a younger brother who chose not to be a lawyer or doctor, but rather an Adonis living a specialized lifestyle in a unique location. Even Emil had family visiting — his younger brother, Dale, came back from work as an oil rig roughneck in Texas for a Vermont Christmas.

Sammi's parents, Tina Pisano's, Joe Pisano's, and Townshend Clarke's were in town, too. The proliferation of children over the past few years had brought generations closer, and even though many of the elders opted for accommodations at the Valley View Inn in Granville, there was a homestead torch passed from one generation to the next.

A light snow fell during the day, painting the town in diamond metalflake. Icicles hanging from rooftops scattered the glint of the colorful lights inside the homes, a heartbeat of flickering warmth to counter winter's stern visage. The Hunters invited everyone for a pre-service spread of eggnog and Christmas cookies. Hiram McBean, Oakley's brother, brought up his team of workhorses and took everyone for sleigh rides up the road that crossed Bear Hill, the road that in Alton Blanchard's history of Upper Granville headed *"Over Yonder Hill."* The children snuggled into the hay beneath heavy wool blankets supplied by Hiram. As the horses pulled the sleigh into the blackness of the woods, Sammi Burger-Hunter led the singing of Christmas carols. Under other conditions the experience might have been frightening, but, everyone agreed, this was a special night. Even the cold and darkness seemed blessed.

At eight o'clock everyone filed into church. Although it was not toasty warm, Hoyt's cranking stove staved off the worst of the chill. Sitting on hard benches in a spare house of worship, decorated with evergreens and lit by the glow of kerosene lamps, even hardened heathens like Darwin, B.J., and the Stallion felt close to a divine presence.

Church, The

The minister, Percival Leach, was new to both parish and state. Teresa Bennett Blanchard, the most active parishioner in town, had been on the selection committee and assured everyone that, although she had not met him personally, she knew Percival Leach to be a dynamic spiritual leader. He did not look dynamic. B.J. described him afterward as looking as if he had been dragged to Vermont behind somebody's car. The Stallion commented that

Percival Leach had "bit the radish."

The carols, accompanied by Stella's sprightly playing on an out-of-tune piano, went well enough. By the time the service started, however, the kids were so wound up that any semblance of serene decorum was shattered. At first Reverend Leach ignored the talking, fidgeting, and muffled reprimands, but when combined outbursts reached bedlam, he became visibly agitated. The coup de grace came when two year old Duane "Duke" Hunter broke loose from his grandmother's grasp and tore across the altar with older brother Darwin junior in noisy pursuit. The Reverend snatched Duke by the arm and said in an all-too-audible whisper, "Listen, you little bugger, this is a house of the Lord, and if you disturb it again I'll rip your little arm from its little socket" The kids quieted down, but the festive mood was, at least temporarily, lost.

After a silent prayer, Reverend Leach asked the congregation if they had anything to share with the others. Silence. The astute person would have moved right along to the next item, but the Reverend would not let it go. "There must be things to share. And in this time of Christmas I think we should open up our hearts and communicate with our fellows." More embarrassing silence, until Stella finally stood and expressed hope that her sister in Burlington, who was in the hospital for this Christmas, would recover. Then B.J.'s father gave simple and sincere thanks that he and his daughter had been able to put aside petty concerns to share in the spirit of the season. Bobby Pisano, this year's bell ringer and Joe and Tina's eleven-year-old, said he was glad neither of his parents had gotten cancer this year.

When the group had been thoroughly milked in terms of participation, Reverend Leach revealed that he had his own message to share. He then told a gruesome story of his own struggle with alcoholism. As a young, virtuous clergyman in east Texas he fell victim to drink. His fall to perdition was swift and sure. Before long he was carrying on with married women, stealing money from the collection plate, and missing Sunday morning services due to Saturday night excesses. From a pillar of the community he degenerated to a honky-tonk regular, and finally a park bench bum. One day in a detox center in Houston, he was reborn with the Holy Spirit. Getting a new job had not been easy, but he wanted to thank the simple country folk of Vermont for giving him this chance. He finished his soul-baring by raising his voice dramatically and saying, "We're all God's children, and I don't care if you're talking east Texas or East Granville. Country folk are the same everywhere. Country is country." The congregation gulped collectively.

The service limped to a close. At the end everyone stood stiffly at the back of the church, where a simple spread had been contributed by community members. They sipped on nonalco-holic eggnog and munched an obligatory piece of Sue Clarke's zucchini bread, while trying to think of something civil to say to Reverend Leach. The Gunions had invited people to their house for a drink, providing a convenient excuse to bid a quick good-night.

"Let me out of here," Darwin Hunter whispered to B.J. on the way out.

"I know what you mean," said B.J. "For the first time in my life I feel like I really need a drink. Do you believe that story about him porking that girl on the church pew?"

Darwin shared her incredulity. "I come to church to hear about Mary, Joseph, and the manger. Instead we get a grisly tale of a guy who spent last Christmas fending off rats in a trash com-pacter in Houston. I never thought I'd say this, but I'm anxious to get to Walt's. Anything to get out of here."

The snow was still falling, everyone remarking that the driving was getting worse. Cars were parked precariously along the steep driveway, conceived and designed by a Flatlander without snowy Christmas Eves in mind. Martha had prepared a spectacular spread—a poached salmon, caviar mousse, baked Brie, a smoked turkey. Walt bought a laser disc player to play the Vienna Boys' Choir. Of course, as with any new toy, he was compelled to play it too loudly, making it seem as if the house was filled with eunuchs.

By now, too much had been packed into the day. Even before all the guests had climbed up the snowy hill, most were suffering from stimulus overload. The kids, having leapt from sleigh ride to Reverend Leach and now to the Vienna Boys' Choir, were ready to let sugarplums dance in their heads. The Pisanos made their excuses after a polite glass of champagne, claiming "Santa work" still to do. When they got to the bottom of the Gunions' steep driveway, Joe found the way blocked by Emil's pickup truck. Even though they were driving Tina's four-wheel-drive Subaru wagon, they avoided collision only by skidding into the ditch.

Emil and his brother, Dale, were angrily spinning their wheels, cursing a blue streak as the depth of their dilemma became more apparent. Joe recognized immediately that both were stinking drunk. He convinced them to stop digging themselves in deeper in favor of alternative means of extrication. He sent Tina back up the hill with the kids to prevent others from following them into the ditch and to send all available bodies down to help. Emil offered to walk to the Blanchards' and come back with the tractor, but Joe nixed that, knowing that Emil would likely wind up with the tractor in the ditch as well. He countered by suggesting they call Bennett or Hoyt, but Emil was not much in the mood for disturbing his employer on Christmas Eve to bring to light his own drunkenness and screwup. They agreed to give it the old manpower try as soon as the others came. It did not promise to be easy, however; the combination of Emil's drunkenness, the size of his truck, and four-wheel drive had wedged the vehicle into a difficult position.

The menfolk came down the hill, doggedly cheerful and determined to do a good deed for Christmas. After a full half hour of pushing and pulling, however, tempers became frayed. Everyone was dressed in his best clothes, wearing shoes that were fine for church but terrible for the realities of Vermont life. Just as it seemed that they were making progress, Emil's truck ran out of gas. As Townshend went back up the hill to get Walt's utility can, the Stallion lashed out at Emil for being drunk, for not having more gas, but mostly for being a Chuck and having caused such an inconvenience. Emil's brother, Dale, interceded loyally, but sloppily, on his brother's behalf, but neither party had enough energy to fight. An awkward silence overtook the group. Everyone was sweaty, tired, and wanting to be somewhere else. Their best clothes had been ruined, their wives and families were waiting impatiently to go home, and there was no solution in' sight. In the back of everyone's mind was the knowledge that if they could not get Emil's truck removed, they would face either Christmas night at the Gunions' or a long, cold walk back to town, carrying sleeping children through the snow.

Darwin Hunter tried to lighten up the situation. "I've got it"

"Whut?" Emil's voice was thick as the crust on homemade bread.

"An artistic inspiration."

"Will it get the truck out?"

"Oh, nothing so mundane, though it will make me immortal, and maybe a millionaire, too." Emil was not sufficiently intrigued to take the bait, so Darwin continued on his own. "What my book needs is a Christmas episode. That way, instead of this being a phenomenal pain in the ass, we can look on this incident as a mere transitory inconvenience that is outweighed by the contribution we are making to literary history."

Emil stared at Darwin with alien contempt, words superfluous to further response.

"I've got an idea," said Joe. "Let's sing a Christmas carol." Several groans were heard, but Emil surprised everyone by snapping his fingers four times and launching into the opening verse of "Jingle Bell Rock."

"PERFECT" screamed Darwin. "The immortal Tommy Helms."

"Tommy Helms was a baseball player," corrected the Stallion. "And he was entirely mortal."

"Bobby Helms. Jerry Helms. Jesse Helms. Gus Helms. Who cares? They were all great"

Darwin joined Emil. The Stallion joined Darwin. Joe Pisano joined the Stallion. Soon there was a ragtag chorus performing an enthusiastic massacre on the Christmas classic. The song ended amid screeched harmonies, with much laughter and back-slapping.

"So Darwin," asked the Stallion, "what are you going to call this Christmas chapter in your book?"

"I've got it covered," said the undaunted Darwin. "It's called 'Away in a Quagmire, No Pills for My Head.'" Laugher reigned, finally dwindling to scattered chuckles and guffaws.

Darwin picked B.J.'s father for some stiff-upper-lip chitchat.

"Whaddya think, Mr. Bosco? You like this Vermont living? I'll bet southern Florida looks pretty good to you right now."

Mr. Bosco's immaculate hair was mussed, his feet were freezing, and the camel-hair topcoat that cost him eight hundred dollars was splattered with debris from Emil's spinning wheels. But his response carried sincerity and dignity: "To be truthful, Darwin, I doubt that in southern Florida I could find this many friends to help me out of trouble. There is no place I'd rather be than here for Christmas." This simple speech, two sentences, was bag balm to chafed nerves.

Townshend could be heard sloshing down the hill with the gas. When the group returned to work it was with cleared minds, a better sense of teamwork, and a quiet commitment to getting the job done. Emil's truck was levitated from its position. Joe Pisano's Subaru proved a piece of cake, and before long, everyone was snug and safe in his own bed. A cold front moved in during the night and by morning it was twenty below zero. No one left the snugness of home or the comfort of the wood stove. It was the best Christmas ever.

Community Events

> 'Above all, Upper Granvillites value privacy.
> Community events are reserved for
> brief and formal ceremonial occasions,
> such as weddings and funerals."
> — ALTON BLANCHARD,
> from *Over Yonder Hill*

> "Caligula would have felt right at home at the party
> following Moira's and Benny's wedding."
> — DARWIN HUNTER,
> from *Beyond Yonder*

Moira Chappee was never a full-fledged community member, yet she played the pivotal role in one of the more bizarre local events. After the obligatory year in the Cowdrey Place, she moved into B. J. Bosco's schoolhouse—initially as a roommate, but pretenses were quickly dropped, and she and B.J. freely admitted to being lovers. For the valley dwellers, this was terrific grist for the mill. Imagine, homosexual lovers in their own little town. Everyone was either too liberal or too conservative to cluck tongues. The lingering values of the cultural revolution of the 1960s allowed, even commanded, each individual to "do his own thing." B.J. had gained acceptance in the community. Her strong personality held enough exotic twists that her sexual predilections were unquestioned, despite apparent contradictions. The Tina Pisanos and Sue Clarkes of the world could not understand how B.J. could bed down a biker from the Tunbridge Fair one night and a feminine lover the next. They were too intimidated by the forceful side of B.J. to ever risk "girl talk" with her. Indeed, B.J. was more comfortable with the men of the valley, enjoying equal fluency on the topics of tractor maintenance (Emil), proper techniques of wooden hand planes (the Stallion), or the merits of Budweiser versus Miller (Darwin).

Although the Flatlanders found the match of B.J. and Moira easy enough to digest, the Chucks had mixed feelings. Bennett and Hoyt professed no interest in B.J.'s private life and accorded her general respect for her mastery of masculine domains. The Chuck women, especially Bennett's wife, Teresa, could not abide B.J., however, and lost no opportunity to decry her lack of traditional femininity, calling her "common harlot," "tramp," and "bull dyke."

The most diehard critic of the B.J.-Moira relationship was Emil Dummerston Weed. He and B.J. had enjoyed an illogical intimacy from her first day in town. In the fall B.J. and Emil went deer hunting at dawn, before she had to go off to work. In the winter he took her deep into the woods with his Arctic Cat. Emil said he never met a girl who could drive moguls like B.J. In the spring on the first warm days right after daylight savings, he and B.J. cruised the dirt roads in Emil's International, looking for woodchucks to blast with .22's. Then on warm summer nights, B.J. would stop by the front porch of Emil's shack to share his quart of Genesee and listen to the Red Sox or country music on his crackly radio. It was the most unlikely match, a beach girl with a Radcliffe education and a misfit from Appalachia, his teeth as yellow as her hair; but whatever bond existed was broken once Moira entered the scene. His dream demolished, Emil's features turned craggier, his teeth more yellow, and his perpetual stubble more gray. He railed against B.J., ranting in lurid terms about the "lezzies" poisoning the community. The more disdainful he appeared, the more his hurt showed.

For nearly two years B.J. and Moira continued a happy-go-lucky relationship that had as its glue nonstop partying. They participated fully in Upper Granville events; they mixed with a high-flying crowd that B.J. knew from the Green Mountain Stove Company; they were regulars at Nino's Lounge in Granville; and they would drive off to Burlington, Montreal, or Boston at a moment's notice to catch a concert or to relieve the boredom of rural life. Their frequent companion who shared their passions for loud music, fast living, and late nights was Benny Malone, the disheveled photographer of the Granville Clarion who had succeeded Moira as the resident of the Cowdrey Place. Benny Malone's entire life was a study in disarray.

Increasingly, the Malone vehicles—first the Torino, then the Cordoba, and finally, the Cadillac—could be seen outside the schoolhouse on the off nights, when no formal partying was scheduled. Benny, B.J., and Moira stayed up late, drank beer, listened to music, and maybe smoked a joint. Gradually, B.J. began to cater to the dictates of common sense and impending middle age by going to bed earlier than the others. Then one afternoon in May, just as the world was turning green, Moira shocked B.J. by telling her she had fallen in love with Benny. Moreover, they were planning their lives together. They would be getting married in the summer, then moving to Burlington, where Benny's chances to begin a semblance of a legitimate career would be better.

B.J. was hurt, but too tough to show vulnerability. She considered herself unlucky in love; this merely confirmed it. If only she had not been so blissfully unaware of Moira and Benny's growing enchantment! How could Moira love such a slob?

B.J., playing the good sport, assumed responsibility for planning the July wedding. Neighborly help was solicited and received. Teresa Bennett Blanchard arranged for a lay minister to perform the service. (No one wanted to risk having Reverend Percival Leach launch into his south Texas tales of woe and perdition.) Sammi and Sue would handle catering; Francoise, flowers; Tina Pisano, the wedding gown; and Darwin, beer and champagne. With the assistance of the Stallion and Joe, he promised the ingredients for a complete blowout after the reception. Even stick-in-the-mud Bennett Blanchard came up with the inspiration of a horse-drawn carriage to spirit away the bride and groom, just as had been done at his own marriage to Teresa ten years earlier. The community breathed a collective sigh of relief as the confused and tangled relationship headed for a normal, happy, heterosexual ending.

The wedding day was as beautiful as a bride's dream. Sometimes nature focuses the actions of man into perfect harmony. The service, mostly from the pen of B.J., who also served as maid of honor, was simple and sweet. Benny and Moira looked young, fresh, and radiant. They left amidst a shower of flower petals into the waiting carriage for a tour of the valley, and the guests meandered over to the Hunters' backyard, where the reception was to take place. B.J. had arranged for chilled Dom Perignon. Everything was falling into place.

The afternoon flowed into an evening equal to the day. The mosquitoes kept a respectful distance, and Bennett and Hoyt refrained from spreading manure. The guests, who all looked beautiful, congratulated each other on the happiness collectively achieved. As darkness descended, the classical music gave way to rock and roll. The older folks and out-of-towners offered final congratulations and vacated, leaving the serious partygoers. Benny turned up the music, and Darwin tapped another keg. The energy that had built up in recent weeks came spilling out in a frenzy of "throbulating" bodies.

B.J. danced with Benny, she danced with Moira, she was a dancing fool. If there were hard feelings, they were well obscured. But on this night adrenaline gushed. Even though the hour was well past the normal northern bedtime (ten o'clock), the crowd caught a second wind.

The worst of the mess had been cleaned up. Sammi brewed coffee, Darwin opened a round of beers, and the Stallion brought out another bottle of Korbel Brut. The crowd gathered in the kitchen, where for once the Dauntless wood stove sat dormant, an unlikely pedestal for an arrangement of wildflowers. This was not just the standard group of locals, but rather the special occasion set, including many of Moira's friends from fast-living haunts. Several of the girls were dancing topless, formalwear having long since been exchanged for jeans and tee shirts, and recreational drugs were used openly.

The locals were too cool to admit their lack of degenerate experience, but Sammi Burger-Hunter blew fifty dollars of coke onto the floor before getting any up her nose. Then she persisted in claiming that she "didn't feel a thing," all the while pestering for more. Several joints of Sensimilla Stupor, an exotic, Vermont-grown marijuana guaranteed to remove the last strains of decorum made the rounds. With both the marijuana and the alcohol, the combined IQ of the partygoers was reduced to below one hundred.

The tableau had Sue Clarke latched onto the Stallion, openly trying to seduce him in front of Francoise. Townshend and B.J. were demonstrating long forgotten dances such as the Locomotion, the Mashed Potatoes, the Freddie, and the Bristol Stomp, while Darwin supplied the music a cappella. Tina Pisano had gone outside to throw up, and Joe was staring contentedly at a recipe for bearnaise sauce pinned on the refrigerator. Sammi was making up an impromptu dessert consisting of vanilla ice cream, Kahlua, peanut butter, and blueberries.

"This is nuts," Darwin said to no one in particular, then went outside where the cool evening air gave the situation a veneer of reality. He took a long leak against a maple in the front yard. Soon the guests staggered out. The Stallion and Francoise were first.

"Oh," said Darwin, feigning surprise, to Bruce, "going home alone?"

Francoise replied for him. "I thought she would try to rape him on the kitchen floor." Her deadpan counterpointed the night, capturing the absurdity.

"Can you blame the poor girl, darling? You know I only have eyes for you." Despite the Stallion's obsequious tone, he was obviously enjoying his role as the center of attention. Sue's head popped out of the kitchen door. "Bruce, want to dance?"

"Let me answer for him," said Darwin. "No. Now get back inside before you get in trouble."

Only a hard core remained. Besides the nuptial trio, the Upper Granvillites maintaining the revelry were reduced to Darwin and the Stallion, who somehow managed to outlast both his wife and Sue. Finally, as fingers of dawn spread over the eastern hillside, the party ended. B.J., the Stallion, and Darwin stood in the shambles of the Hunter kitchen.

"So this is what they mean by the 'cold light of dawn'," said the Stallion.

"I remember when I liked doing this," added Darwin.

The Stallion looked at his watch. "Five a.m. This is crazy. It's time to get up to go running. What am I doing here? It's all the fault of those degenerate friends of yours, B.J."

"At least none of them tried to drag you into the bushes," replied B.J., obviously referring to the Shrew.

The Stallion was nonchalant. "That's the price of being born too good looking."

This was the juncture where normally B.J. would have had an ego-shattering retort for the Stallion. Tonight it was all she could do to mutter "Pig." She had run out of gas.

Bruce bid goodnight, or good morning, and marched triumphantly into the dawn. A moment of silence passed. The first silence in hours. Darwin's ears were ringing with the music, his head throbbed with the initial onset of a hangover, and his body ached with fatigue. He heard a sound that, at first, he could not identify. He looked up to see B.J. sobbing softly. He had never seen her cry. He tried to comfort her, but the sobs only became more violent. He walked her back to the schoolhouse, where the sobs grew to wails of anguish. She did not talk; she was completely passive; he had never seen anyone so distraught.

Wordlessly, he helped her undress and put her into bed. He sat in her room until he was sure she was asleep. Then he went home.

Critters

"Due to its northerly clime and latitude Vermont is
relatively free of the nuisance and pestilence that
affect the rest of the world."
— ALTON BLANCHARD,
from *Over Yonder Hill*

"Ringworm, head lice, coyote, weasels, black flies,
rats, earwigs, skunks, porcupines ... living in Vermont
means living with critters."
— DARWIN HUNTER,
from *Beyond Yonder*

In the North one learns to live harmoniously with critters, or one
leaves. Darwin Hunter discovered this on his first night in his new
home. Upon investigating a commotion in his kitchen, he discovered a nine-hundred pound raccoon nonchalantly munching on
his garbage. He went upstairs, stopping to tell Sammi that the situation was well in hand, and got his .22 rifle. His first shot into
the coon did not even affect the creature's appetite. Three shots
later the beast became severely agitated and charged. Darwin
backpedaled frantically, shooting as he went. By the time he managed to kill the raccoon, his kitchen looked like the set for The
Texas Chain Saw Massacre.

The clinching blow for many a would-be ruralite is the confrontation with a swarm of black flies or finding the small city of
earwigs in the joints of the picnic table. Here is a glossary of critters in the pristine North

Skunks
After B. J. Bosco's noble golden retriever, General
Beauregard, was sprayed by a skunk for the third consecutive
night, she knew the problem could no longer be ignored. She
bought a Havahart cage, baited it with a can of sardines, and
caught the culprit.

She released it on the hillside above the Gunions'. That night
General Beau got hit again. Must be more than one skunk. Sure

enough, another can of sardines caught a second, then a third, and a fourth. She became suspicious that the skunks were willing to trade a few hours of captivity and some exercise for a free meal. Emil confirmed that skunks would travel miles for a free meal of sardines. If B.J. wanted the stench to stop, she would have to kill.

She considered the options. Although she had no objection to shooting animals in the pursuit of the hunt, she refused to shoot a defenseless animal and felt compelled to devise an execution that made clear the skunk's offenses against society. She wanted to be humane, but more important, she did not want to get sprayed. Hanging seemed ludicrous. She considered electrocution using jumper cables but was afraid she might fry herself in the process. Finally, she enclosed the caged skunk in a large cardboard box into which was vented the exhaust pipe of her Volkswagen. Just to be sure, she ran the car for a half hour, long enough, she calculated to provide enough carbon monoxide to kill the entire town, let alone a critter. She removed the box to find an enraged black and white mammal that promptly sprayed her. B.J., in turn, dragged the Havahart over to Tomar Brook, where she screamed epithets during every agonizing, twitching moment of that skunk's demise.

Rats

Nice people don't have rats in their homes. Also, rats are city creatures found in ghettos and along wharves. They do not exist in the country.

Martha Gunion labored under such misconceptions, until it became obvious that the creature they were trying to combat with mousetraps was laughing at them. She and Walt talked in hushed tones about this Godzilla without once mentioning the dreaded word "rat." Then one night Walt heard a noise in the kitchen and found himself face to face with the haughty creature. He even managed a healthy swipe with a poker. The rat smirked and ambled off.

Walt dared not mention that he had seen a rat in their space-age kitchen, but the next day he bought some packets of rodent poison. He set them strategically, taking care to place them where they would be inaccessible to Martha's pet Yorkies. The next day he was pleased to see that the poison had been greedily consumed. What he did not know was that the poison dehydrates its victims, making them ravenous for water. Had he known, he might have prevented Martha's shock the next morning when she discovered a bloated rat floating in the toilet.

Matters went from bad to worse when a second rat stumbled onto the cellar floor, where it promptly ran afoul of the feisty terriers. A day later, the two dehydrated Yorkies succumbed. In hindsight Walt realized it had been easier living with the rat.

Black Flies

A popular local tee shirt says it all: "Black flies don't bite, they suck!

Black flies appear to be harmless gnats. Their bite, however, packs a venomous punch that belies their insignificant size. Ask Sammi Burger-Hunter.

As a local activist in all liberal causes, Sammi was on the committee to welcome Gary Hart to Granville during his campaign for the Democratic presidential nomination in 1984. Despite his underdog status, a visit by a nationally prominent figure was a rarity in central Vermont. Preparations were suitably elaborate. The day before his arrival Sammi did some work in the garden, where she swatted away the black flies as she put in the lettuce. She was bitten in several places, including around the eyes.

She thought little of it until the next morning, when, to her great dismay, both eyes were swollen shut. Darwin could prescribe nothing to help, so she gamely proceeded with the day's plans despite her unsightly disfigurement. Senator Hart was gracious and charming, but Sammi was crushed when one of his aides referred to her as looking "as if she just came through the eighth round with Boom Boom Mancini."

Common Houseflies

The common housefly has been raised to an art form in Vermont. Whether a function of the proximity to dairy farms, the climate, or the leakiness of houses, the North breeds more and hardier flies than anywhere else in the world. The natives handle the situation with ease, perfecting at early ages a lazy hand movement that brushes away the creatures with a nonchalance that approximates the flick of a horse's tail. Diehards do not even bother, but ignore flies on the face, something no Flatlander can do. Townshend Clarke has been trying for years, but after a few seconds his face begins involuntary twitching.

For preventive measures, the Chuck favors strips of flypaper that go up in June and come down in October. Flatlanders prefer violent techniques. Joe Pisano uses a rubber band. Darwin has a spring-powered gun that he bought at the Miami airport. The Stallion favors sucking flies into the vacuum cleaner.

Visiting Flatlanders, especially, have trouble with houseflies. When Sammi Burger-Hunter's parents visited from Cincinnati, the progression was typical. On the first day her mother commented on the flies and gently admonished the children to keep the screen doors tightly closed. On the second day she purchased a can of Raid, which she depleted in two hours. On the third day Darwin gave her a flyswatter. Thereafter most of her waking hours were spent stalking flies in the kitchen, sometimes squealing with glee after a satisfying kill. By the fifth day she was banging away at any semblance of a black spot, babbling about her desire to wreak vengeance on the little black bastards. She began drinking heavily, starting with two martinis at lunch. Her husband recognized danger signals and cut short their vacation. Once safely back in Cincinnati, she regained her sanity, but vowed never again to return to Vermont during fly season.

Mosquitoes

Northland mosquitoes are probably no more prevalent or venomous than New Jersey, Minnesota, or Louisiana mosquitoes. They are, however, more noticeable, because people take less effort to prevent them. Spraying of breeding grounds is unknown, and the short summer season means that people do not bother with such things as screens. A status item in Chuckdom is the blue-violet bug zapper that crackles regularly in executionary frenzy.

Earwigs

Earwigs are flat, oblong beetles with fearsome pincers as tails.
Their pinching qualities pale alongside their ability to produce
cardiac arrest by hiding inside every nook and crevice during late
summer and appearing when one least expects them. After brushing your teeth, for instance, you might be prepared for the final
rinse when you catch a fleeting glimpse of the earwigs just as you
tip the bathroom glass to your lips. These insects are better able
to elicit screams than any other insect known to man.

Head Lice

There are bugs and there are bugs; then again, there are vermin
with which civilized Flatlanders cannot cope. The closest the
Clarkes ever came to abandoning Vermont came when their oldest
boy, Duncan, was sent home from kindergarten with head lice.
Sue went to pick him up from the nurse's office filled with indig-
nation, and left groveling. Even after scouring every inch of the
home and each family member's body, she felt unclean for months
afterward. "Lice!" she kept telling herself. 'Americans don't get
lice!" The stigma lingered until the next September, when Sammi
Burger-Hunter received an identical call regarding her darling little Lisa. If a doctor's child can get lice, Sue reasoned, it was
acceptable for her kid, too.

Giardia

The spring of 1982 was long and wet. By May there still had
not been a day that could be called spring. Everyone was
sniffly, and sickly, and generally at each other's throats. Then, to
make matters worse, everyone's bowels turned to stinky liquid.
Darwin took one of his own stool samples into the hospital for
analysis and found that he had giardia, an internal parasite found
in contaminated water.

One by one the Upper Granville residents brought in their
stool samples and received similar diagnoses. The cure was simple
enough—two weeks of medication—but the uncertainty of the situation caused emotions to run high. What had caused the con-
tamination? The Stallion, of course, blamed the Chucks, specifically the manure spread constantly on their fields. The Blanchards

blamed the Gunions for the change in the drainage when they built their pond. Darwin pointed an accusing finger at Townshend Clarke's goats. Townshend, in turn, blamed the Blanchard dairy farm. Walt Gunion fueled the fires by telling everyone that real estate prices were already plunging, and unless they solved the problem immediately, Upper Granville would become a ghost town.

The state health department was called in; the wells were tested; confusion reigned. In an attempt to rekindle the quickly flagging community spirit, the Hunters invited everyone to a potluck. The sober mood was furthered by the fact that most of the attendees were on medication and could not drink. The evening limped along until Darwin asked if anyone would like a nightcap of bottled water.

"This is ridiculous," said B.J. defiantly. No one had the presence of mind to ask her what was ridiculous; they watched incredulously as she marched over to the kitchen sink, drew herself a large glass of water, and downed it as fast as a draft at a fraternity chugging contest. It had been over a month since any of them had drunk any water, and most now refused to even bathe in it.

"I agree," echoed Bennett. "I've lived here all my life and there ain't nothing wrong with the water." He chugged a glass, too.

"Here's to Upper Granville," said the Stallion, taking a rare position on the same side as a Blanchard and downing his glass as well. "This water tastes great to me. Not as good as beer, but almost."

The giardia episode ended at that point. No one ever found out the cause or the cure. It disappeared as quickly as it came, and by the Fourth of July memories were sufficiently distant to make the topic of Upper Granville's water supply good for endless banter at any town gathering.

Deer Hunting

"Game was plentiful and provided
an important source of protein."
— ALTON BLANCHARD,
from *Over Yonder Hill*

"One November a man from New Jersey brought a
particularly large doe to the weigh station at
Oakley McBean's Granville Store. After
admiring the man's prize Oakley congratulated
him on bagging the season's first mule."
— DARWIN HUNTER,
from *Beyond Yonder*

Bennett Blanchard and Emil Dummerston Weed never missed a chance to talk about deer hunting in front of Sue the Shrew Clarke. The other Flatlander women Tina Pisano, Sammi Burger-Hunter, and even old Martha Gunion—were good audiences as well, but for pure reaction, one could not beat the Shrew. That she could give as well as take also made her fair game. Bennett and Emil rehearsed their routines during the late night milking, then they would corner her at a social gathering and block off her escape routes.

BENNETT: So Emil, done any deer hunting?

EMIL: Got my first buck first day of the season.

BENNETT: So how'd you get him?

EMIL: Baited him with apples for a month. He was coming and eatin' those apples real regular right before dawn. Tame, he was. The morning we was hunting he was feeding on those apples all dumb and happy. I walked right up to him and shot him from about six inches.

BENNETT: When was this?

EMIL: Day before yesterday.

This was the point where Sue was pushed over the brink. Even with the full realization that she was being set up, she would respond emotionally, usually starting with a technicality.

SUE: Day before yesterday? But hunting season doesn't start until next week.

EMIL: Well, I'm not going to wait for hunting season. Someone else might shoot my buck.

BENNETT. Man'd be a fool to let a Flatlander take his buck.

EMIL: 'Specially after feeding it so long.

SUE: And you call this a sport, and yourselves sportsmen?

EMIL: 'Yuh, I reckon you'd have to call us sportsmen, right Bennett?

BENNETT: Eyuh.

SUE. And shooting an unsuspecting beast at point-blank range is your idea of sport?

BENNET: No, if you want sport, you can't beat hunting fawn with a .22.

EMIL: That's so. Them buggers bounce around like the tits on a lady jogger.

SUE: You men are sick. Perverted and sick.

BENNETT: That's not fair, Sue. I'm what you call a humanitarian hunter. I always kill anything I wound.

EMIL: Like that spring you came across that baby fawn sucking on its mother? You killed both of 'em even though the mother was barely wounded. Shame about all that meat going to waste, though.

BENNETT: I didn't want the warden to find me with a freezer of meat in May. Kind of hard to explain.

EMIL: Did you at least get to eat the heart?

BENNETT: Oh sure. I cut it up and split it with my dog.

They would continue along these lines until Sue stalked off in a huff, muttering angrily about the low level of humanity present. Bennett and Emil laughed hysterically, repeating to each other the same lines without the deadpan. Occasionally, B.J. joined them. The language became earthier, the stories more vivid, with no letup until Sue began turning green.

B.J. was consistently the valley's most successful hunter, a fact unattributable to her rearing in southern Florida, where the only hunting was for the perfect wave or perfect tan. Once hunting season began in the drabness of November, within a few days a gutted buck would hang from the tree next to the schoolhouse.

Deer season was the only excuse Bennett, Emil, and Hoyt found for taking a break from farming. They headed up to a small camp on Bailey's Peak for a weekend, returning home sometimes successful but always grizzled. The Flatlander men never hunted, and took care not to even go outside during the season. During his most fanatical days as a would be marathoner, Darwin Hunter wore a fluorescent orange hat for his training runs. After a few catcalls from hunters, however, he decided it was not worth the aggravation.

Teresa Bennett Blanchard was the swing person on the subject of deer hunting. Not a hunter herself, she considered the sport a divine right of manhood. Sue Clarke, who thought herself a totally liberated woman in that she controlled Townshend like a yo-yo, regarded Teresa as the most backward of repressed females. Teresa was securely blissful in her repressed, exploited state, a fact that tormented Sue, who could not understand why Teresa did not want to be miserably liberated, too.

The two clashed within seconds of being in each other's company. One summer evening Sue and Teresa were walking their respective small infants when they met at the bridge crossing Tomar Brook. It was a beautiful evening, warm and still. They greeted each other and exchanged pleasantries about the weather. Teresa mentioned that Bennett and Emil were enjoying the evening by scouting a buck that Bennett planned on bagging during the season. Instantly the languid setting transformed into a field of combat, as customary hostilities were resumed.

"You know," started Sue, "your husband and Emil want that creature to live just so they can kill it. Isn't that ironic?"

"You eat your sheep, don't you?"

"That's different and you know it. Hunters don't kill for the meat, they do it for the kill."

"I think hunting is good for them. It takes them outdoors, keeps them close to nature, provides meat. I think it makes a lot more sense than all your jogging."

'At least joggers only kill themselves." Sue said sarcastically. "Hunting shows mankind at its sickest. The menfolk go off in a little cabin, drink themselves silly, fart, and have fantasies about how women love getting raped."

"How can you have such strong opinions when you're so ignorant?"

Each charge provoked a countercharge, and eventually a challenge was issued and accepted. Sue and Teresa committed the sensitive, caring, non-carnivore men of the valley to go off to deer camp with the disgusting, blood-thirsty drek. Joe agreed to go, if the others did. Townshend had no choice. Darwin said, "I'm game."

Only the Stallion flatly refused: "Me and the boys from *Deliverance* in a cabin out in the middle of nowhere? With liquor and guns? No way."

The first controversy started when Darwin, on his own, invited B.J. to join them. This time it was Teresa Bennett Blanchard and Sammi Burger-Hunter who raised the strongest objections. Teresa slammed the door rather effectively by saying, "I don't care if she is the best hunter. Deer camp's no place for a woman. If it is, then I'm going too." B.J. gracefully declined the invitation, lest she be the cause of yet another rural roar.

The men left on a Friday afternoon. Deer season opened at five o'clock the following morning. Although their destination was no more than four miles from the village, there was a sense of a major expedition getting underway. Hoyt looked strange in his hunting togs as opposed to his coveralls. Darwin had outfitted himself from the Orvis catalog. Townshend tried to look grizzled, but failed. Joe wore a down parka that promised to keep him warm but clearly marked him as a rank novice.

They reconnoitered by the church. The wives and children came to bid adieu to their warriors. B.J. wished them luck. Even the Stallion and Francoise came by in their matching running suits for a little last-minute ragging: "So Darwin, now that you're a redneck, does it mean that you're going to harass us Martians?"

"Better wear your fluorescent hat if you go running tomorrow," returned Darwin, deadpan.

"I'm beginning to see antlers on everything," added Joe.

At camp the men fell quickly to work. Emil and Darwin gathered and cut firewood, Hoyt and Joe fired up the old potbelly stove, Townshend started dinner, and Bennett started drinking. Although not normally a drinking man, Bennett was making up for lost time. The group had come up in two vehicles, Emil's truck and Bennett's old wagon. Both had been stacked high with gear. It seemed excessive until one realized that the bottom tier of both vehicles consisted of cases of beer. Bennett also had a fifth of Mr. Boston Peppermint Schnapps that he claimed was necessary to ward off the cold.

Townshend did a good job with his baked bean and hot dog dinner, and there must have been fifty comments about how the menu selection would necessitate the opening of windows later on. The "psshht" of beer cans was ever present, as was Bennett's bottle of schnapps. The few times Darwin went outside to take a leak and to get a breath of fresh air, he marveled at the solitude of the surroundings compared to the friendly life inside the cabin.

"There's got to be a chapter in here somewhere," he told himself.

The talk was mostly of adventures of past camps. The novices were given sage advice by the veterans, and the topographical maps were pored over to discover routes for the next day. Joe returned from a pit stop reporting that a light snow was falling. "Good!" Hoyt exclaimed. Tracking would be perfect by morning.

The men retired early, comfortably drunk, but each one tingling with a boy's anticipation of adventure. Morning came soon. By three-thirty Townshend, already the unofficial camp cook, was rustling among the pots and pans, brewing up the strongest coffee known to man. By four they were powering down a hearty feed of eggs, beans, bacon, and brown bread. Forty-five minutes later they were heading into the darkness. Even though traces of hangover remained, the crispness of the air, the crunch of the snow underfoot, and the fantasies of what the day held had the adrenalin flowing.

Townshend remained behind, ostensibly to clean up dishes and prepare for dinner, the only other meal planned for the day. His real intention, however, was to spend most of the day in the cabin, keeping comfortable, and maybe going for a walk in the woods later on. Killing a deer held little interest, although he was definitely affected by the enthusiasm of the others. After washing the breakfast dishes he took a nap, then brewed a fresh pot of coffee, brought in a day's worth of wood, and even picked up the beer cans from the night before. Around ten o'clock he could avoid it no longer. He donned his togs, picked up his gun, and took to the woods. He preferred to leave the gun in the cabin, but the thought of having to explain his defenselessness to the others deterred him.

It was a perfect day to be in the woods. Although the sky was gray, the snow whitewashed the ground. Townshend heard a few muted shots, but was unable to judge direction or distance. Once he thought he heard shouting, but encountered no one.

The plan was to return to the camp by dark. Townshend thoroughly enjoyed the peacefulness of the woods. He daydreamed about what he might do if, under the rarest of circumstances, he encountered a deer. He imagined himself stalking it, drawing a bead with his rifle. But he always stopped at that point, standing, waving, shouting, or otherwise sending the deer on its free and wild way.

He did not want to be the first one back to camp, because that would cause others to question whether he had actually gone hunting. He waited until sundown was imminent, yet when he arrived at camp he was the first returnee. As he entered the camp clearing, a movement caused him instinctively to freeze. Fifty yards to his left, grazing obliviously, was a deer, a buck. Townshend knelt slowly and purposefully. His mind was clear. His mind was blank. His eyes were riveted on the deer, while his hands eased off the safety on his gun. He drew a bead, aiming just behind the front foreleg at the heart, following Hoyt's advice of the night before. The buck sensed trouble, but as he stiffened to run, Townshend squeezed off his shot.

The animal dropped immediately. Townshend found himself running, his heart in his throat. It was a clean kill. He knew it. Now he was standing over the animal, still quivering in the hindquarters. For a moment there was silence, although Townshend's heart beat with the jackhammer violence of Emil's truck pounding over the washboard dirt road leading up to Upper Granville. He stood motionless, unsure as to what to do next. Then there were footsteps behind him.

"You got him! Good shot, Townshend. You got your buck!" It was Darwin.

"I killed him," Townshend babbled, "I killed him."

"I know! I can see. Good shot, buddy."

The others converged quickly, drawn by the shot. Townshend's buck had six points and was estimated by Bennett to weigh just over two hundred pounds. Hoyt dressed it out, and they hauled it over to the deer stand to tie it up. No one else had bagged a deer that day, so Townshend's received all the attention. Joe and Emil cooked dinner; Darwin and Bennett cleaned up. They had steaks and baked potatoes cooked in the stove, and, of course, more baked beans. By the second beer, Townshend had repeated the details of his buck kill several times over. Once or twice during the evening he went outside to admire it. After repeated beers and nips of schnapps, the others were good-naturedly telling him to shut up, that they could already repeat the details of the sighting and killing in their sleep.

A tired group crashed early. The next day they got out a little later and returned a little earlier. Hoyt got a small buck, but the rest were skunked. They hauled their bounty, not to mention a small fortune in returnable beer cans, down to the weighing station at the Granville General Store. Townshend watched proudly as his buck tipped the scales at two hundred five pounds. It was the largest reported to date, and the only six pointer, Oakley McBean told him. Townshend beamed, basking in the admiration of the other hunters. He was sad when they put it back in the truck. But he still could look forward to the look on Sue's face when she saw his buck. Deer camp, thought Townshend, was a marvelous institution.

Dogs

> "Dogs provided the early settlers with security, protection, and companionship, ranking just behind the horse as the most valuable domestic animal."
> — ALTON BLANCHARD,
> from *Over Yonder Hill*

> "The twentieth-century dog contributes fleas and liability to his household, little more."
> — DARWIN HUNTER,
> from *Beyond Yonder*

Dogs are the only subject on which Bennett Blanchard and Bruce "the Stowe Stallion" Liebermann agree. Both feel that the only good dog is a dead one, Bennett because canines serve no useful purpose on a dairy farm, and Bruce because of a traumatic experience with a German shepherd when he was young. There are other dog haters in town—in fact, supporters are hard to find—and yet every household has its own flea-bitten version of man's best friend.

At the bottom of the totem pole is Maggie May, a woebegone hound/ shepherd mongrel belonging to Emil Dummerston Weed. This mangy cur is relatively harmless and completely useless. Emil does not believe that dogs need much care or feeding. Maggie May's staple diet is deer entrails. One winter Emil horrified the community by giving his mutt a horse's head to gnaw on for her month's food supply. The dog lay for hours in front of Emil's house scraping and pulling at the pink orb of flesh and bone. Everyone in town was disgusted. B.J. finally took action by bagging the horse head in a Hefty trash bag and delivering to Emil a fifty-pound sack of dried food.

Every spring Maggie May gets knocked up, usually by an equally derelict junkyard dog, and the "free puppies" sign goes up in front of Emil's. There have been lookers, but rarely any takers. The sight of Maggie with distended teats and matted fur is not the image of cuddliness. One day the "free puppies" sign goes down, and no one ever asks Emil questions as to the puppies' fate.

The Hunters have owned a series of upwardly mobile dogs. Bingley, a sprightly Airedale with the bearing of a German military officer, was great with kids, did not chase cars, but was lethal with cats and chickens. When Bingley showed up during the middle of a barbeque with Sue Clarke's limp Siamese held proudly in his mouth, it was bye-bye Bingley.

Bingley was replaced with Morgan, an English setter with the lowest IQ ever recorded in a mammal. The dog was a constant nuisance, always into garbage, porcupines, and skunks, but at least with the redeeming quality of looking terrific lying next to the Dauntless wood stove. Morgan's end came on an icy morning when she chased Joe Pisano's van. Normally she charged the road, then veered at the last moment, parallel to the vehicle, barking and snapping at the front wheel. This day, however, Morgan hit an icy patch just at the veer point and zipped right under the back wheels of the truck.

B. J. Bosco's noble golden retriever, General Beauregard, is the neighborhood's most loved pooch. She bought him as a pup. Although prone to slobbering and humping houseguests, he comes closest of all Upper Granville dogs to representing man's best friend. The worst thing anyone can say about General Beau is that beneath his dignified exterior he has consorted with Maggie May more than once. Emil keeps admonishing the General to "keep it in his pants," but he is blinded by love.

General Beau's closest brush with death came on a Sunday afternoon in August. For no apparent reason he lost all motor control. B.J. panicked and called Darwin, whose ophthalmological training proved of little help. Finally they got Hoyt Blanchard, who was locally renowned for his ability to cure ailments in animals.

Hoyt muttered and yipped, checked old Beau's gums and eyes, and tried without success to get him to stand.

"Has he reached the end?" asked B.J. Hoyt did not answer, but continued poking and prodding the dog. B.J. said in an aside to Darwin, "If his time has come, it will kill me, but I'd rather shoot him than have some strange veterinarian shoot him full of poison. I can't stand seeing him suffer like this." They waited silently for Hoyt's verdict. Finally he stood up, removed his battered John Deere hat, and scratched the back of his neck.

"This a drinkin' dog?" B.J.'s response was a grunt of puzzlement. "'Cuz the only time I ever saw anything like this was when Oakley McBean's pig got into fermented apples and got so pie-eyed it near drowned in the trough. Don't shoot the dog yet. See if he's better in the morning."

"Hoyt left. B.J. looked at Darwin, then her jaw dropped and she said a moaning "Oh-h-—I-— god-d-d" before racing into the kitchen. She came back with an empty mixing bowl.

"This is what's left," she, beamed.

"Left of what?"

"My marijuana brownies. I left the batter on the floor by the stove to keep warm. General Beau ate it all. Poor baby." She knelt down and began stroking his noble, numb head.

"Poor baby?" said Darwin. "The dog must be somewhere out in the stratosphere. Hey, let's put on some loud music and leave him with some potato chips in case he gets the munchies."

General Beauregard

Townshend Clarke's choice of dogs is as eclectic as everything else about his farm. Townshend has never decided whether he is a sheep farmer, vegetable farmer, carpenter, or forester. His choice of dogs reflects the same lack of focus. At one point he thought that raising huskies would be a good income source. He bought several pups, built a pen, made a sled, and read every book in existence on the subject of dogsledding. At the same time, in the manner of so many Flatlander pseudofarmers, Townshend kept several goats tethered in his front yard to keep down weeds and to provide an appropriately rural look. One night the dogs tunneled out of the pen, and Sue came down in the morning to find two gory skeletons tethered to stakes in their front yard. Thus ended Townshend's plans for raising huskies.

Next came Magoo, an exotic white sheepdog, specifically a Kormondor that Townshend bought for five hundred dollars from a breeder in Massachusetts. These dogs reputedly have the genetic programming to make them the consummate sheep herders. Magoo, however, despite months of training, avoided sheep like the plague. The only penchant for herding he demonstrated was with the cars and trucks that passed the Clarkes' home. He would chase a slow moving vehicle ten miles. Townshend finally took him to Massachusetts and gave him back to the breeder. Magoo was not a bad dog, but a daily reminder of how Townshend's best-laid plans went awry. To serve that purpose, Townshend already had Sue.

The most star-crossed dog lovers in Upper Granville are the Gunions. They keep a consistent roster of two or three frivolous lap dogs, and scarcely a season passes without one meeting a grisly death through an untimely confrontation with Vermont elements. The community regards Martha Gunion as psychotic (and Walt not much better) where her dogs are concerned. Their undisciplined dogs are given the run of the house. As a result, the furniture is covered with dog hairs, and an overwhelming odor of urine predominates. Martha and Walt, being childless, fondle the dogs intimately and talk to them directly, referring to themselves as "Mommy" and "Daddy." Moreover, as opposed to the utter lack of pretension demonstrated by Hoyt and Stella Blanchard, who named their collie/shepherd cross "Mutt," the Gunions come up with cutesy names such as Phineas T. Blusterhound and Throckmorton Paddiddlehop.

The Chucks regard the Gunions as aberrant. Their fellow Flatlanders, however, are harsher in their assessment. Only the new and creative demises of the dogs salvage a situation that otherwise ranks clearly in the lunatic fringe. When one of the dogs dies, Martha goes into mourning.

Walt buys a child's coffin from Mortimer and Sons funeral parlor in Montpelier and buries it in a backyard plot complete with markers. Suspicions are that maudlin services are conducted as well, but no one has had the courage to ask, lest their perceived interest result in an invitation to attend the next burial.

Two of the Gunion dogs were run over, the bulldog by Walt in the Ninety-eight, and a poodle by B.J. during their annual summer pond party. The latter incident caused Martha to become hysterical, and everyone left early. A Lhasa apso, thought to have been stolen, was found during the spring thaw to have been plowed into a snowbank. A Yorkshire terrier bit the dust while playing with a poodle when the poodle's teeth caught in the Yorkie's collar and strangled him. The poodle later died of heartworm. A Pekingese took on a porcupine and succumbed when the embedded quills became infected. A miniature collie ran afoul of a bear and ended up a few scattered bits of fur in the woods. A Chihuahua named Senorita met her doom one summer afternoon when the Stallion stepped on it while making a circus save in a volleyball game.

"Gee, I'm sorry, Martha," the Stallion said to the distraught "Mommy," "but that's the only way I know how to play the game."

Martha took each of the deaths hard, but soon Walt would come home with a new yapping, peeing, crapping puppy, and she would become herself, at least until the next tragedy.

Darwin Hunter best summarized the community attitude toward the Gunions one day while jogging when he said to the Stallion, "If dogs are a man's best friend, then those poor bastards are the world's most hurting puppies."

Drunk Driving

"After one memorable evening of merriment my
father fell asleep at the reins of his wagon.
When he awoke at dawn, he was
on the outskirts of Burlington."
— ALTON BLANCHARD,
from *Over Yonder Hill*

> "The most lethal natural hazard of
> Northland living is the drunk driver."
> — DARWIN HUNTER,
> from *Beyond Yonder*

Drunk driving is bad stuff. Both Chucks and Flatlanders know that. And yet, toward the end of a long winter when cabin fever rages like a smallpox epidemic, Vermonters of all ilk are prone to getting liquored up, driving cars recklessly on muddy back roads, and leaving bodies and vehicles draped ingloriously around trees. No one is immune. Whoever lives in the Cowdrey Place finds their way into a ditch four or five times a year. Joe Pisano has a few too many beers at a horseshoe match and runs over his own mailbox. Teresa Bennett Blanchard goes to her high school reunion and misses the entrance of their garage by almost a foot, one inch for each glass of champagne. Two incidents, however, stand out.

Oakley McBean is loved by Chuck and Flatlander alike, both groups depending on the merchandise he sells in his store, the credit he extends, and the wise advice he judiciously tenders, never without being asked. He sucks thoughtfully on his pipe, fills the store with the comfortable odor of Cherry Blend, and mutters aphorisms straight from the heart of his Yankee heritage. Oakley, say the locals, is a regional treasure.

Even regional treasures have flaws. Oakley's is that once a year he drinks too much. "Oakley's toots," they are called, and whenever one begins, the word spreads quickly through the town. "Oakley's on his toot," they will say. "Lock the doors and hide under the bed, 'cause there's no telling what he'll do next."

Oakley's toots begin harmlessly enough, perhaps at Nino's Lounge, around a keg after a softball game, at a wedding. They always end up absurd. He is not a violent or malicious drunk, but the combination of his hardscrabble personality and alcohol lead to the unexpected. Locals talk about the time he walked down Main Street buck naked, or the time he shot out all the windows in his modest home. Another time he gave away all the beer in stock at his store, and once he jumped off a church spire into a hay wagon. He had never mixed drinking and driving, however, until the Fourth of July in 1982.

The Granville Fourth of July parade is held in late morning. A popular pastime for people on the parade route is to invite friends over to watch the spectacle, followed by a potluck lunch, volleyball (Flatlanders), horseshoes (Chucks), and a keg of beer (universal). It is possible for a popular fellow like Oakley to be offered ten beers within a hundred-yard stretch, precisely what happened on this day. By the time he reached the end of Main Street word spread back to his first stop, "Oakley's on a toot."

By midafternoon Oakley commandeered a police car. He had not driven it anywhere, but he successfully locked himself inside, babbling nonsense on the radio and leaning on the horn. Police Chief Magoun put up with the silliness for a while, then created a stalemate by deflating the car's tires. This only angered Oakley, who countered by driving away on the limp rubber and rims. After a quarter mile he abandoned the police car in favor of Linwood Salls's dump truck. Like all good Vermonters, Linwood never bothered to remove the keys, let alone lock the truck. Oakley took off at the breakneck speed of approximately ten miles per hour. He even took time to stop for a six-pack at Ernie and Shirley's Quick Stop before continuing leisurely onto Route 100 toward Upper Granville. The state police caught up with him as he was turning onto the dirt road leading to Upper Granville. Every time one of the cruisers tried to pass him, Oakley slowly swerved, blocking the road and thwarting the authorities' efforts at apprehension. He circled the entire Upper Granville valley at this leisurely pace, blissfully defiant of the flashing beacons and wailing in his wake.

The story limps gracefully to a conclusion. After circumventing the Upper Granville valley, Oakley headed back into Granville, where he retraced the parade route, waving to the cheering patrons lining the route. Word of his toot had preceded him. Upon reaching the center of town, having exhausted his six-pack of beer, Oakley surrendered peacefully to the frustrated police, whose military entourage had been trailing as a useless appendage. His license was suspended, but most people gave him high marks for providing healthy family entertainment on a national holiday.

The second drunk-driving incident in Upper Granville had more lasting ramifications. Sammi Burger-Hunter was an active supporter of every organization (no matter how ill conceived) having a charter to relieve pain and suffering. She helped feed Ethiopians, Eskimos, Biafrans, and anorexics. She stood in solidarity with women, homosexuals, women homosexuals, Democrats, blacks, and American Indians. She fought to protect whales, baby seals, sticklebacks, and whooping cranes.

She also supported MADD (Mothers Against Drunk Driving), SADD (Students Against Drunk Driving), BADD (Blacks Against Drunk Driving), CADD (Caucasians Against Drunk Driving), GADD (Gays Against Drunk Driving), and FADD (Females Against Drunk Driving).

Although his own consumption habits bordered on excessive, Darwin was supportive of Sammi's social activism, even when it involved a neoProhibition movement to which he was violently opposed. He made a conscientious effort to avoid conflict between his own love of drinking and need for vehicular transportation. The worse conflict came on the day of Walt and Martha Gunion's annual summer pond party. It was a terrible party, as usual, and Darwin compensated by matching beers with B.J. When it was time to leave, Darwin insisted, against Sammi's advice, on driving the Saab the one mile home. The sun and white wine had fanned her stubbornness as well. There followed an alcohol-clouded argument, neither side able to compromise. Finally, Darwin drove while Sammi and the kids walked. In a major escalation, however, prior to leaving, Sammi called Chief Magoun and turned Darwin in. The police car arrived long after Darwin had arrived home and settled into watching a baseball game on television. Magoun was sheepish, saying he had an obligation to follow up all citizens' complaints. Darwin voluntarily took a breathalyzer test, squeaking under the legal limit. Magoun apologized and bid an awkward good day.

At first Darwin calmly tried to point out to Sammi how a DUI (Driving Under the Influence of Alcohol) would ruin him professionally and remove from them their only means of livelihood. Sammi responded only that he had broken the law and should be punished accordingly. "What if you had run over a child?"

"Driving on a dirt road out in the middle of Appalachia? Not likely."

"So laws don't apply to you?"

"Wait a minute. I took the test. I'm innocent!"

"If Magoun had got here sooner, you might have been over."

"That would have made you happy, wouldn't it? You wanted me to be caught. But if we're talking laws, let's talk vows. I remember something about 'love, honor, and obey.'"

"Right. In sickness and in health. And you're sick! Maybe being caught is what will help you get better."

One of the great domestic battles in the history of the Flatlander Valley had begun. The shouting, charges, and counter-charges continued into the evening. That night Darwin slept on the couch. For the remaining weeks of summer Darwin slept outside in the kids' tent. The community was polarized, with the Stallion, Sue Clarke, Joe Pisano, Teresa Bennett Blanchard, and B.J. aligning themselves with Darwin, and Martha Gunion, Townshend Clarke, and Bennett Blanchard siding with Sammi. It was a stalemate, often argued but never resolved, the issue more important than the incident. To whom is one's responsibility greater, to one's spouse or to society? Eventually people in Upper Granville turned their attention to other subjects. Darwin and Sammi resumed a conjugal bedroom, but the question remained.

Dump, The

> "Every item was used and reused
> until its usefulness had completely expired."
> — ALTON BLANCHARD,
> from *Over Yonder Hill*

> 'A trip to the dump can be good for the soul"
> — DARWIN HUNTER,
> from *Beyond Yonder*

To raise money for a formal dance associated with an end of the summer celebration, the community held a yard sale. Francoise

Liebermann and Tina Pisano were the elected chiefs, and they organized the event as if it was the landing of the allied forces on D-day. B.J. did posters as well as an ad for the *Granville Clarion* that oversold the event just enough to ensure success. Francoise and Tina collected contributions throughout the week and stored them in the Hunters' barn in anticipation of the sale, scheduled to begin at nine o'clock in the morning on Saturday. They planned to come down a half hour early to make sure everything was ready.

By eight o'clock there were four antique dealers parked on the Hunter front lawn, none willing to wait for the official opening. One of the dealers, a fat lady with a Bronx accent, said repeatedly, "The early worm doesn't come to sit on his tush, dearie." Sammi, trying to deal with the impatient dealers, panicked. She called Tina, who had no advice more useful than "do the best you can," then Francoise, who said that she would be down as soon as she had prepared her darling's morning coffee and croissants. Knowing that Francoise had never been less than two hours late for anything in her life, Sammi prevailed on Darwin to help.

Darwin let the dealers into the barn, then grabbed money as they carted merchandise out. No prices were marked, so he did what he did best, improvised, discovering later that he had sold a footstool worth $100 for $5, and a $35 reproduction copper for $125.

When the others arrived and criticized his negotiating, Darwin sniffed, "If you don't like it, you should have been here to prevent it." The goods were hauled out to the front yard and "merchandised," as Francoise described it later, meaning that little pieces of masking tape were put on each item with a price scrawled on. As the various paraphernalia were brought out, the most frequently heard comment was "Omigod, look at this!"

A few more cars arrived, but their occupants had to compete with the locals, who pored over the goods like rats in a cheese factory. Bartering and bickering went on simultaneously in three or four places, and poor Tina Pisano, the money collector, furiously recorded transactions in a spiral-bound notebook.

By noon, anything vaguely resembling an antique was long gone. What remained was a museum to the changing fashions and mores of the previous ten years. There were:

~• Three copies of Euell Gibbons' *Stalking the Wild Asparagus*, four copies of *Let's Eat Right to Keep Fit* by Adele Davis, two *Whole Earth Catalogue*s, and enough tomes of self-sufficiency to stock a college library. "Looks like the 'Me' Generation has had the radish," said the Stallion, leafing through the pages of Gail Sheehy's *Passages*.

~• A collection of records that could be labeled "A Testament to a Dead Era." Any early stuff by the Beatles, Rolling Stones, or Doors was snapped up early. Joe Pisano's collection of 45's sparked a bidding war between two Granville residents. Townshend ran out an extension cord so he could plug in the KLH stereo that B.J. was trying to sell. After thirty seconds of "The Best of Led Zeppelin," the Stallion commented, "My father was right. This stuff sucks."

~• Clothes, ranging from tie-dyed tee shirts to hip huggers. By late morning when the traffic had slowed down, people got into trying on their own monstrosities. Fit was no problem since nearly everyone was slimmer now than they had been a decade earlier. "How's this for a blast from the past?" asked Sammi, modeling a leather miniskirt, fringe vest, and braided headband.

"Don't make fun," warned Darwin. "That's what you were wearing when I fell in love with you."

"Hey," screamed Townshend at Sue, "you can't throw these away!" He gathered up a pair of Frye boots. "I promised these boots I'd never throw them out, no matter what."

`And how about the suede Earth shoes?" returned Sue. "I suppose those can't be sold?"

"What's the matter, Shrew?" It was the Stallion, cocking a grin. "You have something against `negative gravity'? I bet you were a vision in peasant blouse, long skirt, and hiking boots. Did you shave your legs and pits in those days?"

~• Household goods. B.J.'s lava lamp said it all. "You can't imagine," she reminisced, "how the best years of my life were frittered away stoned, staring at this thing, munching on peanut butter and marshmallow sandwiches in my dorm room at the 'cliffe. I had some of the greatest artistic visions of all times staring at this thing."

"Problem was," added Darwin, "you couldn't remember them five minutes later."

"Five minutes! Try five seconds. So one time I decided to write down these great thoughts. I sat in front of the lava lamp, pad and pen in hand, was struck by inspiration, stopped for a little snack, and forgot about the pad. The next morning I found what I had written: 'The problem with society is'."

"Is what?" asked Sammi.

"Well, we'll never know. Got lost in the purple haze, I guess."

↬ Grand schemes. The shattered ruins of Townshend's planned solar greenhouse made it to the yard sale, as well as Joe Pisano's never-restored riding lawnmower, the Stallion's aborted gazebo, and Teresa Bennett Blanchard's antique bottle collection. All had seemed like good ideas at the time.

At three-thirty the plan was to load everything that remained into Emil's truck and take it to the dump. Darwin and the Stallion were the designated drivers. They went on a body-toning run while the others filled the truck. Upon their return they hopped in and headed off. Just as they were approaching the entrance of the Granville Sanitary Landfill, Bruce said, "Uh-oh. Did you bring any money?"

"No," said Darwin. "I'm not in the habit of carrying my wallet when I run."

"It costs two bucks to get into the dump."

"Hey, this is Vermont. The guy will trust us."

"Famous last words," said the Stallion as they approached the small guardhouse by the dump entrance. Its occupant was Shorty Weed, who looked like an older, more weasly, miniature version of his cousin Emil.

"How ya doin'?" said the Stallion amiably.

"Emil sell his truck?" said Shorty inquisitively.

"Nope. Just loaned it to us. We're neighbors of his up in Upper Granville."

"Upper Granville, now there's a place."

"Now there's a statement," muttered Darwin.

"Yup."

"Eyuh. That'll be two dollars."

"Yes, well...." The Stallion's stalling tactics were obvious. "See, we forgot our wallets. How about we drop the stuff now and pay you Monday?"

"Mister," said Shorty, "do you know how many times on a Saturday someone says that to me? And do you know how many of those people get amnesia before Monday?"

"Oh, c'mon," pleaded Bruce. "We're not going to stiff you. Besides, it will cost us five bucks in gas to go back to Upper Granville in this hog, and you'll be closed by the time we get back."

Shorty was unmoved. "The Town of Granville pays me to collect two dollars from anyone who wants to use the Sanitary Landfill. That's my job, and I'm going to do it."

"Oh yeah?" The Stallion was losing control now. "I'm a taxpayer who pays your salary, who lives in town, and who knows your cousin, and you should be able to tell that we're not going to stiff you for two fucking bucks."

Immediately, a new battle line had been drawn. Shorty drew up. Clearly there was a side of him relishing the confrontation with a Flatlander: "Cursing now, are we? They pay me to keep the trash out of the Sanitary Landfill, not to listen to the profanity of welfare cases." He turned back toward his shack.

"Oh great," muttered Darwin. "What now?"

"Let's just drive in and dump the stuff"

"No. He'll lock the gate on us for sure. I've got an idea." Darwin climbed out of the passenger side and into the back of the pickup.

"Hey, Shorty. We just figured out where we can get the two bucks."

Shorty turned. He maintained his indignant pose, although the quickness of his response showed that he clearly enjoyed his position of power.

"I don't care where you get the money, only that you pay the same rates as everyone else."

"Let's make a little deal here," began Darwin. `About half this

stuff is junk for the dump, but the other half is what we've collected for the yard sale we're having up in Upper Granville tomorrow. How about we find something that's of interest to you in
here? Save you a trip to the yard sale tomorrow."

"Going' fishin' tomorrow," grumbled Shorty, but the lure had
attracted him and he returned to the truck to see the goods.

"How about this lamp? You need a lamp? Works good. Look,
it even has the price marked on it. Ten bucks! Tell you what. Let's
just give it to you for two bucks and call it even. What am I,
crazy? I can't give the lamp away for two bucks. Forget it. Eight
bucks for the lamp."

"You said two."

"Two? I know I did, but I didn't know the real value. You
can't hold me to something like that."

"You said it."

`All right, all right, all right. Hold me to it, you shrewd son-of-
a-gun. Two bucks."

"How much for the painting?" Shorty gestured to an unbelievably tacky painting of a clown with sad eyes given the Pisanos
as a wedding present and hidden in their barn ever since.

"The painting? I can't sell the painting. It's too sentimental.
You know what it's like. You can't put a price on feelings."

"I'll give you five." During the day the price on the painting
had gone from fifteen dollars to fifty cents.

"Five dollars!" exclaimed Darwin. "Shorty, you're merciless.
You're a thief. But you're a nice guy. You'll appreciate the painting. Okay, five bucks."

Shorty cast some bait of his own. "You boys like wicker?"

"Wicker? What do you mean?"

"Wicker. You folks from the Flatlands always like wicker, and
I've got some stuff out back that a lady from South Granville was
going to throw away this morning."

"Hey, Francoise has been looking for wicker," said the
Stallion, who had now returned to normal. The Flatlanders followed the Woodchuck to the wicker, which needed repair, but the
Stallion snapped it up greedily. Darwin noticed a wood furnace
that looked intact. Shorty offered it at a reasonable price, payable
in more goods in the pickup.

Before long the Stallion and Darwin were heading back to Upper Granville, ecstatic about their new acquisitions. Five pieces of slightly damaged wicker furniture, a wood furnace, and railroad ties. And all it had cost them was the truckload of junk they were planning to throw out anyway. They chortled at how they had bamboozled the dump master. As they pulled up in front of the Hunters, most of the yard sale crowd was still lounging, gossiping, and soaking up the remainder of a lazy summer afternoon.

"Wait'll we tell them this story," guffawed the Stallion.

"They won't believe the deals we made," added Darwin. He prepared to launch into the story, but Sammi caught him short by asking, "What's the matter? Was the dump closed?"

Fourth of July

"The community celebrated the nation's
independence with flag displays, gunshots,
and solemn demonstrations of defiance."
— ALTON BLANCHARD,
from *Over Yonder Hill*

"For some reason the Fourth of July stands
unparalleled as an occasion of frivolous festivity."
— DARWIN HUNTER,
from *Beyond Yonder*

The severe Vermont weather is a bottomless mine of material for local conversation. But the Fourth of July is always beautiful. Perhaps the state has made a deal with the devil. Give us a beautiful Fourth, then have your will for the rest of the year. Freeze us into icy suspension, slather us with mud, flog us with sleet and snow . . . just make sure on the morning of the Fourth the sky is blue, the air is warm, and the concept of the perfect day has been redefined and elevated.

The first event is the race, a ten-kilometer run that finishes with all the town residents clapping their support. Darwin and the Stallion deny pretensions of serious competition, but come the last mile down Main Street, they are always huffing, puffing, and trying to gain a minor edge on each other. Being the first Upper Granville finisher is at least worth bragging rights for the year.

Next comes the parade. The residents of Upper Granville have a tradition of a town float that is locally renowned for its sharp wit and even sharper execution. Each year a theme is announced by the parade committee on Memorial Day. Upper Granville's own float committee then launches into action. The chairperson changes each year. The unwritten rule is that although others may contribute ideas, the chairperson has absolute power. The participants must do as they are told without question. Refusals of cooperation result in the offending party's permanent removal from the town float. There have been close calls, but so far no one has tested the absolute powers of the chairperson. In 1983 it was the Stallion's turn to chair the town float. The theme of the parade was "Our Precious Past," and Bruce shocked everyone by announcing that Upper Granville's float would be a tribute to the Blanchard family. To outward appearances the long-standing, bitterest feud in the Chuck/Flatlander War had ended.

Alas, the fires were fanned anew, as Bruce revealed the real theme to be incest and intermarriage. Townspeople were dressed in matching checkered shirts and coveralls, with hair frosted red and garish freckles drawn on their cheeks. Everyone gathered into a hay wagon to be dragged through the village behind Bennett's John Deere. The satire was lost on most of the townfolk, but not on the Blanchards, whose grim visages were parroted by the Flatlanders for every step of the parade route.

In some measure "Our Precious Past" was an element of revenge for the previous year's representation of "Farms of the Future," mounted under the direction of Bennett Blanchard. In this extravaganza Hoyt Blanchard, resplendent in the attire of a Wall Street businessman, was seated in front of a home computer terminal. Beside him was a cow hooked up to an automatic milker that took the raw product from the udder directly to its bottled form without the intervention of a dairy. All the while Hoyt studied the Wall Street Journal, pausing only to punch up the latest grain futures prices. The float was pulled by a team of Flatlander joggers. In the rear, cleaning up the cowplop, was a woebegone

Stallion. The locals loved the float, awarding it the blue ribbon for
"best in show." A picture of it appeared on the front page of the
newspaper, and Bennett, as creative genius, was interviewed. He
made a point of citing the symbolism of the Stallion's position,
claiming, "No matter how modern the farm becomes, there will
always need to be someone to clean up the cowpies." Score one
for the Chucks.

Joe Pisano's turn came when the theme was "Winter in
Summer." He designed an elaborate superstructure to fit over his
van, upon which was mounted a motorized bathtub. The bathtub
had wheels that spun as if the vehicle was stuck on ice. Shaved ice
went spraying out as the driver, B. J. Bosco, pushed the rpm's
higher and higher. As the motorized whine reached a frenzied
pitch, the pipes burst, dousing the onlookers with water. The concept was slightly muddled, but the pyrotechnics were unexcelled,
and Joe won an honorable mention.

The first community entry still stands out in many minds as
the best, even though it was too aberrant to win the favor of the
judges. The parade theme was "The Year of the Child." B.J. hon-
ored it with the Marching Toddlers Precision Drill Team. The
men of the valley were outfitted in diapers and bonnets. (Darwin
even stuffed a cowpie in the rear of his.) They carried guns cut
out of plywood and painted silver. Emil Dummerston Weed, the
only one of the contingent with any military experience, played
the snarling drill instructor, barking out a nonstop series of com-
mands as they marched. None of the men shaved for the week
before the parade to ensure the proper juxtaposition of innocence
and grizzliness. What made the presentation so effective was the
precise execution of the drill routines. For the month before the
holiday, the men gathered at the Hunters' on weekday evenings.
After bolstering from several pitchers of beer, B.J. outlined the
maneuvers she wanted to practice. The aesthetic balance she
sought was midway between West Point and the Three Stooges.
The effect of grim-faced men in diapers and baby bonnets marching in close order drill upon the parade watchers was devastating.
They left in their wake a universal question: "Huh?"

Each year, after the race and parade, the Upper Granvillites
return to their valley, where a potluck picnic is held in the

Hunters' backyard. Volleyball and croquet follow. By midafternoon everyone is stuffed, slightly drunk, sunburned, and exhausted. Some people opt for a nap. Hoyt and Bennett, after whipping everyone at horseshoes, go back to work the farm. B.J. heads off with anyone who cares to come along to find a swimming hole, and Sammi and Sue take the kids down to Oakley's store for ice cream.

Then the Fourth of July ends. Two months of "damn poor sleddin'" follow, then Labor Day, the Tunbridge Fair, and another winter. It all happens so fast.

Haying

> "The poor man is the one who knows in November
> that his hay will not last the winter."
> — ALTON BLANCHARD,
> from *Over Yonder Hill*

> "The cultural void between Flatlander and Chuck is
> never so great as at haying time."
> — DARWIN HUNTER,
> from *Beyond Yonder*

Darwin and the Stallion returned from a Sunday training run dripping with sweat. It was a sultry summer afternoon, seldom encountered this far north. They took a seat on the Hunter porch and sipped on Darwin's famous postrun elixir, an equal mixture of orange juice and beer. "Doesn't seem like Vermont today," said the Stallion.

"Hot town," nodded Darwin. "Summer in the city."

"Right. It feels more like a Sunday afternoon at Jones Beach. The heat and humidity has been building up all weekend and you know it's going to explode any moment."

"Back of my neck getting dirty and gritty."

"A catharsis. Like getting sick when you're drunk. The purge."

"I think I can hear distant thunder."

Their relaxation was interrupted by a grim Bennett Blanchard, who drove by on his green John Deere at flank speed. He neither waved nor wavered. "What's with him?" mused Darwin.

"He's panicking," said the Stallion with confidence, but also with sympathy. "He cut his hay yesterday, and now it's going to get soaked. Half its nutritional value will leach back into the fields."

"What can he do?" Knowledge of farm techniques was not among Darwin's strongest suits.

"Work like a bastard and pray the rain holds off long enough to get some of the hay under cover." Darwin stood to get a better view of the field. Hoyt was pulling the baler; Bennett was hitching up the hay wagon; Emil and even Teresa were wrestling bales into three-sided teepees. Beneath the blackening sky their efforts seemed insignificant.

"You know," said Darwin, "when I was in my rock 'n' roll band, I once tried to write a song about haying. It was called 'My Grain,' and it was about a farmer whose struggle to bring in the crops resulted in migraine headaches. In terms of sheer stupidity, it's the dumbest song ever written."

"I'm glad I missed it," replied the Stallion.

Stella Blanchard turned onto the road in the family station wagon. The Stallion launched out of his seat and flagged her down. "I can't stop," she said to Bruce. "It looks like a storm."

"I know, that's why I stopped you. Can you use some help?"

Stella took a deep breath, but needed only a moment to decide. "Put on a long-sleeved shirt," she said, then drove off.

"Let's go, Darwin. Let me borrow one of yours. Tell Sammi to call Joe, Townshend, B.J., and even Benny Malone. The more the merrier on something like this. But tell them to hustle."

Darwin did as he was told. Within minutes he and the Stallion were reporting for duty wearing their unlikely uniforms of long-sleeved shirts, nylon shorts, and running shoes. Hoyt assigned them to Emil's truck, now a makeshift hay wagon. If Bennett even noticed the newcomers, he did not show it; he was completely absorbed in his own task. The others showed up and were immediately assigned tasks. The thunder continued and the winds began to swirl, but the rains mercifully held off.

Work continued at a feverish pace throughout the late afternoon and early evening. Sweat and hay dust parched throats and
clogged pores, but no one dared suggest a break. It was just past
the summer solstice, so the light stayed with them. The ominous
sky remained, but the look on Stella Blanchard's face, even in the
twilight, evidenced obvious relief when she approached Darwin
and the Stallion. "Make that the last load, boys. We'll clean up the
rest. It's been our lucky day, and you've been a big help."

"How did you convince that rain to hold off?" asked Darwin.

"Must be clean living," she said. "Someone's looking out for
us."

The Flatlanders bid goodnight. Emil and Hoyt waved their
thanks, a small gesture, but one that conveyed immense gratitude.
Only Bennett held true to character, remaining self-absorbed so
that he appeared oblivious to the presence of new hands. After
the Flatlander crew adjourned to the Hunters', where Sammi,
Sue, and Tina had prepared a late supper, Stella approached
Bennett. Reluctantly, he put the tractor into neutral and slowed
the idle.

"Bennett, you should say something to them."

"Neighbors are supposed to help out, Ma."

"We put up a lot of dry hay because of them."

"I know. Might not rain anyway."

"That's not the point, Bennett. They helped, without us even
asking. You should thank them."

"Okay."

"Okay, what?" She spoke as if addressing a schoolchild.

"I'll thank them."

Meanwhile at the Hunters' a tired but fulfilled crew was settling into lounge chairs watching a flashing, rumbling sky while
sipping well-deserved beers and munching on summer salads.

"It's going to take a heap of beer to lubricate this throat,"
gasped Joe Pisano. "I thought I was in decent shape, but I'm
bushed."

"We'll feel it tomorrow," added B.J. "I don't know which
appeals more, a hot shower or a dip in the brook." She opted for
the latter.

"I hope it rains," exclaimed Darwin. "I hope it pours."

Townshend babbled excitedly about the farmer's "oneness" with nature and how exciting it had been for him to have been so involved in a race with the Elements. The Stallion did not share in the euphoria, but instead adopted a more philosophical outlook. He sank into one of the Hunters' lawn chairs and watched the pyrotechnics in the westward sky. "It's just heat lightning. This sky is as constipated as Bennett Blanchard. Can you believe that after all that work, the guy could not even bring himself to say thank you." There was no rancor in the Stallion's normally caustic tone, only resignation.

`And the irony is, he would love to. He's dying to, but he doesn't know how."

Just then the sky let loose, as if someone had slit it with a knife. Everyone stayed outside long enough to get palpably wet. All night long it poured. The next day Teresa Bennett Blanchard came to the Hunters' with a small cake from a box mix, covered with canned frosting. She presented it to Darwin, saying, "Bennett wants everyone to know that we appreciate your help getting in the hay. Make sure everyone gets a piece."

How-Not-To Guide

"The early settler was by necessity a cooper,
carpenter, and tailor. If ye could not do,
ye did without."

— ALTON BLANCHARD,
from *Over Yonder Hill*

"The service economy has reached the
northern antipodes. In 1985 the first
balloon-o-gram came to Upper Granville."
— DARWIN HUNTER,
from *Beyond Yonder*

Early in his career as a rural Vermonter, Joe Pisano's pipes froze, a common experience for anyone living in an uninsulated old farmhouse. Joe was unemployed, an exile from his family, wandering through life trying to provide comfort to a pampered wife and his young son. Because of his soft-spoken, genial yet industrious nature, Joe is most observers a working-class hero, the salt of the earth. A worker without work, however, is as useful as "tits on a boar hog" (Emil Dummerston Weed).

Now the goddamn pipes were frozen. First he had to dig through the snow to access the crawl space. Then he squeezed through an opening with a flashlight and propane torch. He noticed animal turds. Too large for a rat. Probably a skunk or a porcupine. There was less than two feet of clearance. This did not promise to be fun.

Joe wriggled under the pipes. The crawl space was cold, dark, and dusty. Every time he maneuvered, his shoulder brushed a pipe or part of the floor above, bringing a shower of grit cascading onto his face. He managed to light the torch. During the next hour he had ample time to think about his position in life. What had he accomplished? Not a lot, that's for sure. Lying on his back in the tomb of a crawl space, living in a hovel in the northern extremities of society, without electricity—Joe could not imagine a crueler life. Of most immediate concern was his lack of income. Without work he felt deprived of pride, of basic human dignity.

"This sucks," he said aloud, as if the sound of his own voice could provide the company he needed. "This positively bites the big one. I hate this. I hate where I am. I hate what I'm doing. I hate who I am. And I would pay someone a million bucks to make these frozen pipes work again."

This rare emotional outburst from a shy and quiet man was followed by silence, then inspiration. His calling in life would be the dirty jobs. He would fix the fuck-ups. He would be the "how to" person. Before him, in his darkest hour, lay the pathway to success. Pisanos Plumbing and Heating (and anything else your heart desires), thus, was born. "We Fix Fuck-ups" was his unofficial slogan.

Joe's ignominy was turned to benefit, but his was the exception to prove the rule. Vermonters of both persuasions (Chuck and Flatlander) are an independent lot. They make their own mistakes. The Joe Pisanos of the world are called in when the quest for independence is governed by incompetence, resulting in disaster. A catalog:

- ❧ Bennett Blanchard's temper got the best of him when a boisterous young bull escaped through the fence for the third time in a day. The charge in the electric fence didn't faze the youngster. Bennett decided to teach him a lesson and wired the fence directly to the service in the barn. Twenty minutes later he went out and found his electrocuted bull lying dead next to the fence.

- ❧ Darwin Hunter was named "Farmer of the Year" after he tapped several ash trees, thinking they were sugar maples. The humiliating part was that he was exposed by Hoyt Blanchard, the farmer's farmer. Hoyt noticed the taps set as he drove his tractor by the Hunters' brick colonial on a Saturday morning. Darwin was raking the thatch from his recently exposed front lawn when Hoyt stopped. In the manner of a true Vermonter, Hoyt took an oblique tack. "How's sap runnin'?"

"It's gushing," replied Darwin, pleased to be discussing an agrarian subject as a peer with an old timer. I'll have to write a chapter about this in *Beyond Yonder*, he thought.

"You boiling inside or out?"

"Out. I've rigged up a little arch over there. I'll be firing it up this afternoon. How's your operation going?"

"Syrup's just a mite dark, but there'll be lots of it if this weather holds."

"Good," said Darwin. "Sounds like you'll make some money."

"Hope so," replied Hoyt. At this point the conversation reached its natural end. The pleasantries had been exchanged, farmer to farmer. Hoyt should have started up the tractor and left Darwin to his raking, but offered instead some neighborly advice. "If you want to borrow my hydrometer, just holler."

"What's a hydrometer?"

"Measures the dissolved sugar in your syrup."

"Well thanks, Hoyt. But I don't think we'll need it. We're just making up a few gallons for our own use. We'll just go by the taste."

"Eyuh, might be a problem."

"Why's that?"

"Because you're boiling ash sap. Maple works a sight better." Hoyt started up the tractor, leaving Darwin to stew in his own humiliation.

❧ The Stallion, who had a fixation on owning the best of everything, bought a Swedish chain saw, the choice of knowledgeable loggers everywhere. For months he bored the neighborhood with wondrous tales of his chain saw. This was the sharpest, safest, quietest piece of equipment ever created. Moreover, it was easy to service, a fact that he demonstrated by giving it a tune-up himself. Problem was, afterward the saw could not cut through a zucchini squash. Not willing to admit failure, the Stallion pored over the instruction manuals, reconfirming every step. Convinced of the thoroughness of his work, he returned to the place of purchase, a Chuck stronghold called Donnie's Saws 'N Stuff. There, emboldened by the fervor of rectitude, he lambasted an unsuspecting sales clerk for selling shoddy, foreign merchandise. After the hapless clerk was raked over the coals, Donnie himself was called in. A grizzled veteran of the woods, he, too, endured a verbal assault, then inspected the saw for one nanosecond and calmly informed the Stallion that some ignorant dolt had put the chain on backward. Actually, the word he used was "asshole" Such an individual, said Donnie, using the same descriptive phrase, should not be allowed north of Short Hairs, New Jersey, mythical home of all Flatlanders, let alone own a chain saw. The Stallion smiled meekly and tried to make himself disappear. Neighbors were spared further wonders of his saw.

❧ Townshend Clarke, a trust fund hippie and practitioner of the rural arts, should have been capable of keeping sheep fenced. Prompted by the constant complaints of neighbors, Townshend finally invested in an electric fence. At this time the Clarkes were still living without electricity. No problem. Townshend had the power company run service to the barn so that the fence could be operative. Problem solved. Well, not quite. When Sue realized that

Townshend had wired the barn while she was still muck-
ing around with kerosene lamps, she threw what the
Stallion described as a "shit fit." Townshend was dragged,
lambasted, tortured, and abused, but he clung gamely to
his resolve to live a lifestyle bereft of modern convenience.
He did, however, compromise by agreeing to send Sue for
two weeks each winter to the Caribbean island of her
choice. Darwin Hunter pointed out later that Townshend
could have more reasonably controlled his sheep had he
sent them to a Swiss finishing school.

 ᕦ Bennett Blanchard. One of the characteristics of a
 Vermont farmer is independence. Another is stubbornness. Mix the two and you come up with Bennett
 Blanchard's beloved John Deere tractor stuck precariously
 on a hillside. Had he not been blinded by pride, Bennett
 could have banded together the menfolk and extricated it.
 Instead, however, he and Emil went up with another tractor and used the hydraulic winch to send the John Deere
 end over end down the hillside. Besides incurring more
 than ten thousand dollars' worth of damage to the tractor,
 Bennett had to go to the hospital with a broken toe after
 kicking the fallen tractor. Even Chucks can demonstrate
 how-not-to.

The stories go on. Walt Gunion mistakes a bull for a heifer
and endures a year of bull-milking jokes. Townshend's turkey
chicks die when Sue leaves them too close to the stove. The
Pisanos give up goat farming when, in a single afternoon, their pet
Nubian ravages the neighborhood vegetable gardens. Sammi
Burger-Hunter plants a grove of exotic, and expensive, fruit tress
that cannot withstand Vermont winters. In the spring she has a
row of expensive, exotic sticks stuck in the ground.

The stories are limited only by ignorance, a quality that in
Vermont is as exposed as the north-facing hills. There are no
innate abilities of the human species; no one has an exclusive on
the ways how-not-to survive.

Ice Dams

> "The lazy man who failed to keep his roof free of ice and snow often paid dearly during thaws."
> — ALTON BLANCHARD,
> from *Over Yonder Hill*

> "The Flatlander who decries metal roofs has never chopped off ice accumulations at thirty below."
> — DARWIN HUNTER,
> from *Beyond Yonder*

Townshend Clarke awoke to the steady plop, plop of dripping water. His thoughts were of spring. He lay in bed imagining the first unmistakably warm day, when the radiation of brilliant sunshine reduces the snow on the roof to a watery whimper. But, he reminded himself without even opening his eyes, it was still February, in the midst of one of the snowiest winters of the past decade. Besides, this was a different sound from the blip-blip-blip-blip of melting snow.

"Townshend!"

He bolted awake from the shrill cry of his wife.

"We're leaking!" He looked over to the windows, which revealed both a gray February morning and the beginnings of an aquarium as the space between the outer and inner windowpanes was filling with water. The audible dripping was coming from the windowsill to the floor. A brown water stain could be seen spreading on the ceiling like some evil, all-devouring fungus from a grade-B horror movie.

Townshend's response was a muttered curse. Next he ordered Sue to get some buckets, sponges, and towels that he used to fix the immediate problem of the filled window casings. The influx of water continued, however, a fact apparent from the continual dripping sounds as well as Townshend's unintelligible epithets. After the immediate crisis was over, he joined Sue in the kitchen, where she had fixed coffee. She was dressed in her fashionable best. He remembered that she and Sammi Burger-Hunter were planning a morning excursion to Montpelier for an aerobics class.

"Townshend, where's the water coming from?" It was obvious from the tone of her voice that she had thought the situation through logically and been unable to come up with an answer.

"Ice dams! Goddamn ice dams!"

"What are ice dams?" She brought Townshend a cup of coffee, which he spooned honey into, then cradled in his intertwined fingers before responding.

"In weather like this, when it's cold and there's a lot of snow on the roof, heat loss through the roof melts the bottom layer of snow. The melted snow runs down the roof, and when it meets the air again it freezes. That's what causes icicles."

"I still don't see where the water in the windows comes from."

"Ice builds up along the edge of the roof, and the water builds up behind it. Since the water is just standing there it seeps up under the shingles, then down the walls, window casings, anywhere, everywhere!" Townshend's voice contained at least a touch of panic.

"Sounds disgusting."

"It's a pain in the ass, is what it is."

"You're the one who wants to live in northern Appalachia. People in real houses don't worry about ice dams. How do we make them go away?"

"We make them go away by me climbing onto the roof and chopping the ice off with an ax." Townshend's sarcasm was not lost on Sue.

"Well, you know how much I'd love to help you, but here comes Sammi right now, so I'll just grab my leotard and run. Want anything from Montpelier?"

"How about a book on the joys of condominium living?"

"Now you're talking."

"When will you be back?"

"By lunchtime. Don't forget to feed the animals, and have fun on the roof. Ta-ta."

"Ta-ta," he replied, mocking her carefree tone. He decided to have a leisurely second cup of coffee before tackling the elements and the ice dams.

The thermometer outside read twelve degrees when

Townshend headed out to the barn. It was a day utterly without redeeming qualities, gray and lifeless, a perfect day for chopping ice off the roof. Townshend dressed meticulously, wanting at the very least to be dry. He fed the animals, then dragged the extension ladder over to the house. Everything moved in slow motion; the combination of deep snow and heavy clothing contributed an additional dimension of reluctance to what was already a dreaded task.

By the time he was on the roof it was spitting snow. Townshend surveyed the situation carefully. He was astounded at the amount of snow on the roof. Each step brought the white fluffiness well over his knees. After he solved the ice dam problem he would have to do some shoveling. The trick for now was to chop enough ice to release the water without damaging either the roof or his feet. The Northland abounds with horror stories of axes glancing off ice and going directly to the bone. Townshend shoveled the edge to expose the ice, then planted the shovel in favor of the ax. Before taking his first swing he reflected briefly on a comfortable childhood within the womb of civilization. "Real people don't worry about frozen pipes, jumper cables, and overflowing cesspools," he thought to himself. "Real people have never heard of 'ice dams: " He permitted himself a final thought of life in Mashpaug. Open screen doors, warm breezes, freedom from clothes or responsibility. Summertime, when the living is easy....

The Clarke roof is asphalt shingled with tin flashing at the edges. The tin is supposed to prevent the accumulation of ice, but it is obviously an imperfect system. Townshend chopped tentatively at first, but with more abandon as his frustration level grew. After twenty minutes he had accomplished almost nothing, save the creation of a few V-shaped wedges in the ice ridge. He paused for a moment to catch his breath and to reappraise his situation. He looked across the Upper Granville valley into the swirling whiteness of the flurries. He could barely make out the outline of the Blanchard barn, its red expanse turned gray by the intervening snow. Townshend felt very alone and isolated on the roof. He briefly considered going inside for another cup of coffee, but he knew he would never again be able to drag himself back onto the rooftop. No, the situation was clearly a confrontation between Man and the Elements. His home was being assaulted by winter, and winter up to this point was clearly dominating. He could accept the ineffectiveness of his efforts, or he could fight back.

Something happened to Townshend at that moment, something that had happened to him only three or four times in his entire life. He lost his temper. He seized the ax with a new sense of purpose, and fueled by an infusion of superhuman strength, he began whacking at the ice with maniacal vengeance, without regard for the protection of house or body.

For about a minute the ice chips flew. Then there was a mighty swing of the ax, a slight rumble, a sense of the earth moving, and the entire roof-ful of ice and snow let go all at once. Townshend felt his feet go out from under him and had the presence of mind to throw the ax clear. He pinwheeled down in a cloud of whiteness, landing in a cushiony clump. He lay still, trying to assess damage. Was he alive? Yes. Any broken bones or other injuries? Apparently not. He tried to comprehend what had happened. Silence had enveloped the valley. Seconds ago his system had been racing to express every frustration in his life, via an ax, to an unwitting ice ridge. Then the ice ridge struck back, and Townshend was completely buried in a snow pile, still breathing heavily from his own frantic assault. He waited for his pulse to return to normal before trying to move. As he feared, he was completely stuck, enough so that he knew it was useless to waste energy struggling. He began laughing uncontrollably. He had won after all. The roof had been cleared in one fell swoop. He was comfortable, and warm, and although temporarily pinioned by the snow, Sue would be back soon. People just do not freeze to death in their own backyards. The thought of his own silence-shattering laughter emerging from a snowbank sent him further into cathartic sobs of mirth. Once he finally calmed down, Townshend felt better than he had at any other time in his life.

He knew it would be hard to gauge the passage of time. He calculated that it would be an hour before Sue returned home. No problem, he would relax and enjoy the solitude. Several times he heard a car passing and he would time a shout appropriately, but he knew that his wife would be his savior.

What Townshend did not know is that following the aerobics class, Sue had suggested to Sammi a quick trip to the Capezio store to look for a new leotard. This led to some poking around in a few other clothing stores, bringing them to lunchtime and the decision to stop at a Mexican restaurant for a taco salad and bottle of Dos Equis. Townshend had not let his perception of time fool him. In fact he calculated the first hour very conservatively. Each time a car passed, he waited for the telltale slam of a door. At the time he expected Sue to pull in, however, she was pulling out the MasterCard while sipping on a cup of Spanish coffee. Chinks in his mental armor began to appear. Maybe he could freeze to death in perfect health within ten feet of his own back door.

Finally it came, the car that stopped, the slam of the door. Townshend yelled with all his might. What sounded thunderous to him, however, was in reality a muffled whimper. Sue went inside without noticing it. She let the dog out, turned on the radio, and thought little of ice dams or her husband's whereabouts. The dog, Magoo, came over to sniff the snowbank and even to pee on it, but he was unresponsive to his master's pleas for help. Townshend's exhilarated confidence was a faint memory. He was now despondent, certain he was doomed to die a futile death.

The story ends happily, however. After an hour around the house, Sue noticed that Townshend had not hauled the weekly allotment of wood into the shed. This made her mad. It was bad enough that she had to put up with Townshend's persistent denial of his civilized roots, not to mention the trust fund at his disposal. It was bad enough that their lifestyle remained far closer to "Appalachian" than "chic." It was bad enough that they still survived on home-canned tomatoes and lamb they slaughtered themselves. And it was bad enough that they depended on a Dauntless wood stove for heat. The least he could do was perform his weekly chore of bringing wood into the shed. She started to call around, and no one had seen her husband. She looked around the house, in the barn, then outside. When she saw the ladder still leaning on the house, and the enormous pile of snow with a shovel sticking blade up from the pile, she began to sense something amiss.

"Townshend?" she called out tentatively.
"Help!" came the listless reply.
"Where are you?"
"Under the snow!"
"How did you get there?"
"Get me out of here!"

She dug him out, then helped him into the house. Even before it was firmly established that there would be no ill effects from the experience, she began to admonish him for not having been more careful. Didn't he know how worried she was? And didn't he know how much she hated not having wood convenient to the stove?

Townshend was too weak to protest. He sipped some strong tea with lots of honey and listened to his beratement. Next he climbed into a hot bath and listened further as Sue recounted her husband's misadventures via telephone to Sammi, then Tina Pisano and even Martha Gunion. Sue even managed to organize an impromptu Saturday night get-together where she recounted Townshend's confrontation with the ice dam yet another time. He smiled a wan little smile and told himself that eventually he would understand the humor of the episode.

Mud Season

'A fifth season, between winter and spring, makes
outdoor tasks impossible just when the need
to escape the shackles becomes acute.
The results can be chaotic and calamitous."
— ALTON BLANCHARD,
from *Over Yonder Hill*

"Divorces, suicides, murders, genocide spouse beating, sodomy, drunkenness, and mud, mud, mud, mud. Pity the poor soul who has not the means for a Caribbean getaway."
— DARWIN HUNTER,
from *Beyond Yonder*

Vermonters wear Mud Season like a badge. It is the final indignity after a season of endurance. Many a newcomer has survived winter's icy blasts, only to come undone as the expected transition into spring becomes instead a torturous slide into mud. There is no redemption.

The natives have individual means of coping. Sugaring is less a financially viable part of farming than a drug that allows the farmer to swaddle himself in a warm, sweet cloud until the ordeal is over. The nonfarmers have an even more effective way to cope. They leave. The Flatlanders of Upper Granville learned early on that if you can afford the trip to southern climes, save it for March or April when the mud reigns.

One year Sammi Burger-Hunter and Sue Clarke arranged to spend a week at Townshend's parents' condominium in Clearwater, Florida. Due to a variety of logistical and personal considerations, the men stayed home and worked. For months preceding the trip, Darwin and Townshend joked about how they would use the brief interlude of bachelorhood to cut a wide swath through the female population of central Vermont. When the time finally came, however, they opted instead for working late, eating their own bad cooking, and drinking an extra beer in the evening.

The week passed. The families were to return home on Sunday, and now it was Saturday, a miserable day in the Mud Season tradition. Within the previous twenty-four hours it had rained, snowed, and sleeted. At one point there had been some crud falling from the sky that Darwin could not identify. He called Townshend. "Tonight's the night."

"I'll bite. Night for what?"

"To howl, good buddy. To show the women of central Vermont what the meaning of studliness is."

"You're desperate, huh?"

"Going out of my goddamn mind."

"Some day, wasn't it?"

"Unbelievable. The worst."

"So what do you want to do?"

"Get out of this place."

"What's the plan?"

"I figured we could call B.J. to see if she and Moira are going out. We can tag along with them. Sound good?"

"You're on."

B.J. and her roommate/lover, Moira Chappee, were planning a Saturday night of aimless debauchery. This was during their blissful pre—Benny Malone period, and they jumped at the chance to be accompanied by two nonthreatening men. This way they would have dancing partners who would not be slopping and drooling over them all night. Such a momentous occasion called for something more exotic than Granville, so they decided to go to Killington, the ski area that had as many pub and restaurant choices as ski trails.

At Townshend's insistence they took two cars. He was convinced that the girls would want to stay and party long past the time that he and Darwin turned into pumpkins. Rather than jeopardize his beauty sleep, he wanted the option of a quick escape.

The mood of the group was buoyant. They had a nice dinner at a pretentious little bistro. Townshend was particularly voluble, treating the ladies with great chivalry and insisting on a second bottle of Gamay Beaujolais plus a round of dessert coffees.

Then they hit the clubs, three in rapid succession. Each was mobbed with Flatlander hedonists, swilling liquor and dancing to loud rock and roll. Townshend really got into it, but the others found the scene too manic for their simple country tastes. Yes, they wanted contrast to the grays of the skies and the browns of the mud, but this was more than the deprived senses of an Upper Granvillite could cope with. B.J. had a solution. They could head back to Granville, stopping for a nightcap at the Club Casablanca.

Club Casablanca

Darwin had heard of the Casablanca but had never been there. It was a squalid little place just south of town on Route 100, favored by the locals. The crowd was generally Chuck, with occasional crossover from whomever was still up late on Saturday night. Darwin agreed to go so long as B.J. guaranteed that he would not get beat up.

B.J. and Darwin went in her Volkswagen; Moira and Townshend took his old Volvo. The Casablanca was hopping by the time they arrived, and so was Townshend.

"What happened to him?" asked Darwin as they found an open table in the dim and cramped quarters of the smoky club. Townshend had sat down for .0005 seconds before jumping up and dragging B.J. onto the dance floor to groove to the country and western trio trying to muddle through "Light My Fire."

"I wanted to wake him up for the drive," said Moira, "so we did a couple of lines of coke before leaving Killington."

"Aha," said Darwin, enlightened. "The real thing. I don't imagine the regulars at the Casablanca are much into that type of thing."

"You'd be surprised," said the comely Moira, her own eyes dancing. "But the house drug here is Schlitz."

The band gave up on "Light My Fire" and tried an upbeat country version of "The Battle Hymn of the Republic." It was awful, but Darwin and Moira had fun doing a two-step on the crowded floor. Then Darwin and B.J. danced to "Don't It Make My Brown Eyes Blue." The Casablanca had a comfortable feeling, although the mood was a little paranoid even for Darwin, who knew how quickly rumors of a carousing doctor could spread through a rural area. After another beer and a dance or two, Darwin decided that his wild night on the town had come to an end. Townshend, meanwhile, was dancing up a storm with every woman in the place.

Darwin found him at a table with two highly painted ladies with bee-hive hairdos of a type not seen in public since the late 1950s. Townshend howled with protest at the suggestion of leaving. Not a chance, he said. The night was young, and wasn't this the greatest band in the history of the world?

B.J. and Moira decided to call it a night as well. Darwin tried one last time to get Townshend to go home, but he refused, promising that he would leave as soon as the band finished the next set.

The three laughed about Townshend's bon vivant transformation on the way back to Upper Granville.

"No fool like an old fool," said Darwin.

"Did you see those girls he was with? Good thing his vision was blurred."

"They looked like a mother-daughter combination to me"

"I just hope he never has to see them under anything but the dim light of the Casablanca."

Unlike most nights during Mud Season, when it turns colder at night and the roads harden up, this night had stayed mild, leaving the roads as soft and unmanageable as they had been during the day. Darwin gave a passing thought to Townshend's ability to handle the driving. He had seemed okay when they left, high-spirited but not drunk. As long as he did not stay too late at the Casablanca, he would be all right.

Darwin did not give Townshend's welfare another thought until the next morning when he was awakened by the telephone. Instinctively he checked his watch: twenty past seven. Gray streaks of dawn were well established in the eastern sky.

"Hello, I mean hello." Darwin had to clear a few frogs from his throat before making his voice audible. The person on the other end was whispering. Darwin had to go through a series of "What's?" and "Who is this?" before he recognized Townshend's voice.

"Townshend! What's going on? Where are you?"

"In a trailer."

"What are you doing in a trailer?"

"That's a long story. Oh Darwin, I am a hurting puppy."

"What's the matter?"

"I'll tell you later. Can you come get me?"

"Where's your car?"

"I don't know."

"You don't know?"

"I know it's in a ditch somewhere, but I don't know where."

"Where are you?"

"In a trailer at Heavenly Acres Mobile Home Park. Do you know where it is?"

"Yeah. Why are you whispering?"

"Because she's still asleep."

"Who's she?"

Instead of an answer Townshend just gave a low moan. "Can you come right away? I've really fucked up this time."

Darwin threw on his clothes and drove the ten miles to Heavenly Acres. He realized that he had not gotten any address or identification for the trailer where Townshend had spent the night. No matter though, as he cruised the crusty roads it did not take long to find a woebegone Townshend standing at the front of one. He was disheveled and shivering as he jumped into the front of Darwin's Saab and immediately reached to turn up the heat to maximum. His shirt was stained with dry blood.

"Where's your coat?"

"I'm not sure. Probably at the Casablanca."

"What happened to your forehead?" There were several cuts and abrasions, including one rather nasty one right at the eyebrow. Darwin reached over instinctively to examine it.

"Not now," said Townshend, pulling away. "Just get me out of here!"

The story came out in all its sordid glory as they cruised the back roads between the Casablanca and the Heavenly Acres looking for Townshend's car. Townshend had not kept his promise to leave after the band had finished its next set. In fact the only time he remembered looking at his watch, it was almost one o'clock in the morning.

The confessions came boiling out. "I made such an ass of myself. I was drinking like a fish. Plus Moira left me with some coke for the ride home. I was dancing like a loon, being loud and obnoxious. Then I got into a fight."

"A fight!"

"I was being a total idiot with this one girl, and her husband kept telling me to leave her alone, but would I listen? No. I had to challenge him to a fight. I dragged the guy into the parking lot, where he promptly swept it with my face. The guy could have killed me if he had wanted, but I remember him telling me, 'Just be decent, buddy. No one wants any trouble at the Casablanca.'"

"You'd think I could take a hint and go home. No. I go back inside, whereupon the manager cuts me off. No more drinks. I make a stink about that, telling the whole town how I've got incredible connections that will make them regret this. So they kick me out.

"So outside there's this dumpy girl who I had danced with a few times. She asks if I want to continue the party up at her trailer. Since I'm also the world's greatest lover as well as toughest guy, I say 'sure. 'Follow me,' she says. So I do, down all these strange back roads. The mud was pretty bad; my reflexes were shot; and I ended up catching a soft shoulder. I hit my head on the steering wheel, and blood gushes everywhere.

"Oh, I am such a fool!"

Darwin looked at his friend. His hangdog expression was now one of utter anguish. Even though Darwin was inclined to agree with Townshend's last statement, he knew that further recriminations were superfluous. Instead he fell back on his old reliable, humor: "Did you at least get laid?"

"Who knows? I can't remember a thing after getting to the trailer. I've blotted it all out, but I doubt I was able to fuck anything. Oh-h-h, please God, don't ever make me run into that girl again."

Darwin fell silent. He knew, now, that he should never have left his friend. Finally, they found Townshend's car, luckily not stuck too badly. They had gotten Benny Malone out of worse jams many times.

"Not bad," said Darwin. "Your exhaust system looks pretty rocky."

"That's the least of my problems," moaned Townshend. They returned to the Hunter residence by way of the Casablanca, where they found Townshend's coat hung outside on the doorknob. Darwin put together a passable breakfast of scrambled eggs, toast, and coffee. He also cleaned Townshend's wounds and traded a clean shirt for his bloody one. By this time the world looked bright enough that they could concoct the story to tell Sue. They decided not to hide the evening with B.J. and Moira, just to have it end when it should have ended, when the three of them left. As for the cuts, they came on Sunday morning when Townshend helped Darwin remove some brush and an errant limb smacked Townshend directly in the chops. They burned the bloody shirt and were home free, conspirators in deception.

Before leaving, Townshend stopped to shake Darwin's hand. "Thanks, Darwin."

"Don't mention it. You know, you'll probably get black eyes from that knock you took on the head."

"Goddamn that branch. Don't forget to cut a little brush. Mustn't slip up on the details."

"Okay. Get some sleep."

"Okay. Thanks again." The conversation seemed in need of a punctuation mark.

"What a night."

"Yeah," said Townshend, managing a wan smile. "Goddamn Mud Season."

"Goddamn Mud Season," returned Darwin.

Physical Fitness

> "Life was hard back then, and so were
> the men and women who lived it."
> — ALTON BLANCHARD,
> from *Over Yonder Hill*

> "The absurdity of the fitness movement
> becomes apparent whenever, wearing a
> Gore-tex suit with the Walkman blasting,
> one jogs past Hoyt Blanchard on his tractor."
> — DARWIN HUNTER,
> from *Beyond Yonder*

"Putting on a few pounds, are you, 0 Stud of the Slopes?"

"Yeah, a couple. Just my winter layer," replied the Stowe Stallion to Darwin Hunter's pointed question. "Looks like a diet might be in your future as well."

"I dunno. I like slothfulness, but I tell you, I don't like not being in shape. When I think of some of the things I could do in college, it makes me cry to realize how the ravages of time have conquered my body."

"I'd cry, too, if my body looked like yours." The Stallion demonstrated his trademarked lack of tact. This time, however, he struck a sensitive nerve in Darwin.

"I perceive, hidden beneath that crack, the opinion that you think you might be in better shape than I am?"

"Oh, I'm sure I am." The Stallion's confidence bordered on arrogance and had run afoul of Darwin's competitive instincts.

"Bet you're not."

"Oho, a challenge. Is this a gauntlet you're laying down? Name your weapon, pick your contest. Pushups? Situps? One-on-one basketball? Skiing?"

Darwin rolled the situation around mentally. He had to be careful to pick a situation to his advantage. Although he imagined himself a decent athlete, he wanted to pick a contest where he had a distinct advantage: "Darts."

"Darts," the Stallion fairly spat it out in disbelief. "You think that's a test of conditioning? This is typical, you pick the one area where you can excel simply because you're an alcoholic!"

"Okay, you name a contest."

"Skiing."

"Sure. After you've spent the major part of your adult life being a ski bum. I might as well have picked 'optical surgery'."

"Basketball."

"No fair, I haven't played in years."

"A footrace?"

"Okay, but I get to name the distance."

"Name it."

Darwin paused for a moment. The Stallion was bigger and probably stronger than he. His best chance would be a longer race that brought advantage to his more competitive nature while negating his adversary's innate physical superiority. He answered slowly for dramatic effect: "Around the valley."

The Stallion was stunned. "Around the valley? That's got to be eight miles."

"Sounds right." The Stallion's uncertainty gave Darwin the encouragement to put a little arrogance of his own into the answer.

"You can't run eight miles."

"I didn't say I could. I only said I can cover the distance faster than you."

The Stallion was at a rare loss for words, but he regrouped quickly. "Okay Darwin, you named the contest and the distance. I get to name the date."

"Be my guest. I'm ready to go right now."

"Okay, end of the summer. Labor Day."

"Bruce! Tonight is New Year's Eve!"

"So? Now we've got plenty of time to get in shape."

"Oh," said Darwin derisively. "So you're going to make this into a test of your obviously fragile masculine ego."

"I just want enough time to get properly into shape, because I'm going to kick your ass."

"Don't bet on it, O Marvel of the Mountain. On Labor Day next, the first one to the finish line will be yours truly." The dialogue took place at the Hunters' annual New Year's Eve theme party. This year the theme was "Come As You Were" for the year 1968. The conversation and music seemed to vanish once the challenge was issued. Neither of the promulgators had any idea of the ramifications of their taunts, but their wager set in motion events that would change the course of the Western world. Within three years there would be nary an ounce of fat left in the valley. Cholesterol and cellulite would be distant nightmares. The women would become breastless (except for B. J. Bosco). Training techniques would be more discussed than gardening techniques. The Moss Brown Catalogue would replace the Whole Earth Catalogue, and Nikes would replace hiking boots.

The first escalation occurred shortly after midnight, after the champagne had been popped, the New Year toasted, and all the girls' asses pinched. Darwin, always the one to close out a party, went to bed early because he was "in training." The next morning, which was about twenty below zero, he showed up outside the Stallion's and Francoise's bedroom window at eight o'clock in the morning. He was dressed, or more accurately swaddled, in a sweatsuit over layers of long underwear and turtlenecks.

"Hey, Bruce, Let's go. Great morning. What say, a little jog?"

The Stallion's muted curse and finger gesture were answer enough, but the clarion to battle had been sounded. Bruce and Darwin started training as soon as the weather broke. They were joined even by Townshend on occasion. Bennett, Joe, Hoyt, and every woman in town regarded them as aberrations, but the movement inexorably gathered momentum. There were visible signs of fitness. The runners began losing weight, and claimed enhanced overall healthfulness, encompassing everything from sexuality to bowel regularity.

By summertime the pack of runners had grown to several more, and the contest between the Stallion and Darwin Hunter had become an open race for all of central Vermont. The Boston Marathon was not threatened, but a new community event was born. On Labor Day fourteen local runners set out to circumnavigate the valley, a course more grueling for its hills than its distance. A ringer from Montpelier who worked with Darwin at the hospital walked off with first prize, but the real contest ended in a dead heat, with the Stallion's longer legs triumphing over Darwin's stamina by a handful of yards. There was no winner or loser; each runner recognized in the other the work and sacrifice it had taken to reach this point. The community rallied around the participants, and the event broadened from a footrace to a full-blown celebration with a barbequed lamb, volleyball, a keg of beer, and enough local gossip to tide everyone over until the next gathering.

The event was called the First Running of the Valley (R.O.V.), and its participants "Rovers," commemorated by an aptly designed tee shirt from the pen of B. J. Bosco. Immediately afterward the topic was next year's race and ways it could be made grander. Inspired by the accomplishments of the Stallion, Darwin, et al., other Upper Granvillites vowed to condition themselves. The next summer the dirt roadways of the high valley were dotted with the sneaker-clad, sweating bodies of would-be racers. When the Second Running of the Valley took place on the following Labor Day, the crowd was smaller than the running pack. Francoise Liebermann and Sue Clarke became the first official female Rovers.

Darwin raised the fitness stakes the next summer when he competed in the New York Marathon. The Stallion countered by participating in several triathlons. The others were pulled right behind. By the time the Fifth Running of the Valley took place, the only neighborhood spectators were Walt Gunion (bad back), B. J. Bosco (slothful), Townshend Clarke (anticompetitive), and the Chuck contingent, who were disdainful of Flatlanders padding around the hills.

Training became a local fixation. Conversation focused on stretching techniques, interval training, and diet. Champagne was brought out whenever any community member set a new personal record. Subscriptions to Runners' World and Triathlon magazine were shared freely, and collectively the neighborhood poured thousands of dollars of disposable income into ten-speed bikes, canoes, Nikes, Nordictracks, Lycra shorts, GoreTex running suits, entry fees, and health club memberships. Upper Granville was likely the most physically fit town in America, if not the world. Cheekbones protruded, breasts disappeared, everyone hobbled from shinsplints or stress fractures, and claimed to feel better than ever before.

Through it all Emil, Bennett, and B.J. gracefully slipped toward middle age, their faces uncreased by worries about such things as breaking forty minutes in a 10K. The absurdity was recognized just before the Fifth Running of the Valley, which the neighborhood collectively celebrated with a formal cotillion held the night before. The event had grown to the point where nearly one hundred runners participated. The Fifth Running was significant, and the locals had collected money to do it up right—outdoor tent, live band, fancy hors d'oeuvres, and formal dress. Even Emil wore a tie! And shaved! Bennett had found a tux at the neighborhood thrift store and looked far more dashing than when he wore his ball cap on his John Deere. Hoyt wore the suit Stella bought him to wear to the funerals of his farmer friends, and she wore a dress that had last been seen at her grandson's christening.

Everyone looked sleek and civilized. Only the late summer chill (you could see your breath by nine o'clock) and the odor of manure betrayed the location as the hills of Vermont. Aside from people staying up too late, drinking too much, and eating excessively, a good time was had by all. The late crowd, the diehards, gathered in the Hunters' kitchen, where they moaned in advance about the pain to which in a few short hours they would subject their bodies. For the first time, Darwin perceived that he had now passed over the horizon glimpsed on the New Year's Eve more than five years earlier. Time to move on to the next phase.

"You know something, Master of the Moguls, this will be our fifth Labor Day race. You've won two, and I've won two. Let's say it's winner-take-all tomorrow, then call it quits. It's time we portrayed something a bit more requiring in finesse and strategy.

Something like golf. I bet I can whip your ass in golf."

The Stallion did not bother to check whether or not the bait concealed a hook. He charged the wriggling worm like a large-mouth bass, mouth agape. The veins on his temples bulged ever so slightly. "Golf? You're out of your mind. I grew up at the country club. I almost quit college to turn pro. I took lessons for years. I can annihilate you at golf."

Darwin acted unconcerned. The game was now afoot, with the ball in his court, just where he wanted it. "Maybe we should name some stakes."

Potluck

> "Just before marriage a bride was given
> the family recipes. These were treated
> as great treasures, preserved in secrecy
> from generation to generation."
> — ALTON BLANCHARD,
> from *Over Yonder Hill*

> "The arrivals of Gourmet and Bon Appetit
> magazines were significant events, since
> they contained recipes that might establish
> culinary dominance at the next potluck."
> — DARWIN HUNTER,
> from *Beyond Yonder*

The state cuisine of Vermont is the potluck dinner. Although attempts are made to portray the Northland as a cornucopia of delicacies such as cheddar cheese, maple syrup, native brook trout, and venison, the truth is that good cheddar cheese is available anywhere, real Vermonters sell their syrup to Flatlanders and prefer Log Cabin themselves, the brook trout have been washed away by acid rain, and the enlightened transplants don't eat red meat, let alone shoot deer.

Moreover, the IGA supermarket in Granville is, by civilized standards, a relic, a squalid relic. Its owners have not heard about the explosion in gourmet foods. One of the most prevalent laments in Upper Granville is the lack of a decent supermarket, ranking alongside the lack of an ocean as the area's greatest flaw. The residents make the best of the situation by making strategic runs to the Purity Supreme in West Lebanon, New Hampshire, a supermarket so advanced that it even has a Chinese vegetable section. An alternative trek is to the specialty shops of Burlington, from which are brought freezable quantities of bagels, smoked fish, and fresh pasta.

The quintessential potluck was held soon after B. J. Bosco moved to town. Townshend Clarke had the inspiration to hold a colonial potluck, featuring the fare that a dweller of 1790 might have expected. The back-to-the-land movement was still strong enough that all attendees took their assignments seriously. The meal was held at the Clarkes', where power and running water were still eschewed as degenerate luxuries. Townshend and Sue served a dish that they read about in *Over Yonder Hill*. It consisted of a hollowed-out pumpkin into which was poured two quarts of raw milk. After baking, it was served as a stringy soup of little flavor and repulsive consistency.

The other contributions were equally unpalatable. B.J. characterized the entire meal as "a study in swill" and scoured the house for junk food. The only successful dish was Darwin Hunter's Flip, a beverage of beer, eggs, brandy, gin, and spices into which was thrust a hot poker. The resulting foamy, heady liquor was a handy refuge from the food offerings. Because everyone was drinking on an empty stomach, everyone got roaring drunk by midevening, and a good time ended up being had by all.

Despite the limitations of their Appalachian surroundings, however, the residents of the Flatlander valley eat well and appreciate good food. Several of the dishes that typically appear at a summertime potluck have achieved legendary status:

Dr. Darwin Hunter's Napalm Chicken

Dr. Darwin's chicken involves very substantial amounts of ritual. The marinade is made in the morning and allowed to mellow. It consists of the following:

- Two tablespoons frozen orange juice concentrate
- One cup beer, preferably St. Pauli Girl
- Two tablespoons maple syrup

- One half cup tomato catsup
- One large onion, finely chopped
- Six pressed garlic cloves
- Oodles of cayenne pepper or tabasco sauce
- A little bit of everything in Sammi's spice rack

Two hours before the chicken is to be cooked, the first treatment of sauce is administered, and Darwin always opens his first beer of the day to commemorate the start of the barbeque. One hour before, he starts the fire, using only a nonchemical firestarter and real hardwood charcoal imported from Canada, with mesquite chips from Texas added for a certain "je ne sais quoit"

By the time guests arrive the fire is perfect. Darwin is working on his fourth beer by now and gets heavily into greeting people and being the perfect host. An hour later Sammi admonishes Darwin for not having already begun the chicken. He refuels the fire with half a bag of briquettes, squirts on a pint of charcoal lighter, and ignites the mound by throwing on a match from five feet away. The chicken is thrown on hastily moments later and is soon a smoky inferno. By the time Darwin has officially killed his first six-pack, the chicken is completely black on the outside, raw on the inside, with petroleum as the only identifiable spice.

Francoise Liebermann's Instant Pasta Salad

Francoise Liebermann arrives at the gathering fashionably late but looking fabulous. She is carrying a wooden bowl and a jar. The other guests have begun eating. One of them asks Francoise what she brought as her contribution.

"My pasta salad. My darling loves my pasta salad." Her darling, the Stowe Stallion, beams. Instructions:

- Ask the hostess if she has any pasta.
- Spend the next hour asking for a succession of exotic ingredients and kitchen utensils, expressing great dismay when sun-dried tomatoes or the right brand of capers is not available.
- Place the completed salad in the refrigerator, removing all other items to make room. Spend the chilling time making excuses about how the salad might not taste right due to the absence of proper ingredients or utensils. Describe work conditions in the hostess's kitchen as comparable to camping out.

❧ Serve with appropriate flourish just as everyone is finishing their desserts. Spoon out separate platefuls, using clean china, of course, and never paper plates, to each of the men present. They will follow the Stallion's lead of wolfing down the first few mouthfuls, blurting out an enthusiastic compliment, then putting the rest politely aside.

❧ Under no circumstances wash a dish, not even the wooden bowl or jar you brought that contained an obscure type of olive oil you doubted the hostess would have. Politely protest that you have an allergy to dishwashing liquid.

Marshmallow Mold a la Teresa

This dish is most remarkable for the fact that it survives every potluck dinner completely intact. The base is green and the top is red, with a separating layer of cottage cheese and an assortment of floating fruit and vegetable chunks throughout. The crowning glory is a package and a half of Kraft Marshmallow Miniatures bobbing on the surface like so many sailors drowning in a sea of blood.

The key to success is in creating the expectations. Teresa always brings it forth with an air of "you're really going to love this." Afterward she never expresses disappointment at her dish's lack of popularity, but instead comments that her kids will be thrilled that so much is left over.

B. J. Bosco's Goat Food Delight

B.J.'s real forte is junk food, and everyone breathes a sigh of relief when they see her arrive with the supereconomy bags of Wise Potato Chips and Doritos. Too frequently, however, some ancient animal instinct overwhelms her and she feels compelled to retreat to the kitchen.

Someone once made the mistake of complimenting B.J. on her tabouli. Now, tabouli in the right hands can be a tangy, wonderfully refreshing summer salad with accents of mint, parsley, and lemon to carry the blandness of the bulgur wheat base. In the hands of B.J., however, it becomes a random collection of food chunks in a desert of bulgur. The ingredients vary from time to time, but the result is inevitably the same.

❧ Make the equivalent of a bucket of tabouli, figuring roughly on a pound per person. B.J. brings an enormous serving bowl and returns with an almost equal amount. She once horrified town residents by revealing that she actually made twice the amount that she brought and often ate tabouli every meal for the week following a potluck.

❧ Cut vegetables, including squash, raw potato, onion, and celery, into one-inch chunks. Add to tabouli.

❧ Add squares of tofu, cheese, and other ingredients never before seen in tabouli.

❧ Stir, making sure not to add any sauce or moisturizing element that might bind the concoction together.

The typical feel of B.J.:s tabouli in the mouth is that of a mouthful of cracker crumbs. At one dinner B.J. and Joe Pisano were standing together when he took a bite of B.J.'s creation. "Who brings this shit?" he asked innocently in his most conspiratorial tone. When B.J. informed him that she did, he adroitly took another big mouthful and covered up by adding, "Ummm. I love this good shit." Little bits of bulgur flew as he spoke.

Finally, after B.J. had brought tabouli to potlucks for more than two years, Darwin Hunter, emboldened by a few drinks, could contain himself no longer. "B.J., you're about the most talented person I know. How can you make such godawful tabouli and repeatedly inflict it on us, your good friends, at these social gatherings?" B.J. smiled and accepted the comment in the spirit with which it was given. At the next neighborhood dinner she brought a new dish, wild rice salad. Dr. Darwin made an elaborate ceremony of taking the first helping. After the first bite he pleaded with her to go back to the tabouli.

Skiers

"In winter the children used the snow
for recreational purposes, but
not until all chores were done."
— ALTON BLANCHARD,
from *Over Yonder Hill*

"Nothing strikes a Chuck as more absurd than

> sliding down a hill with boards on your feet;
> unless, that is, it is running through
> the woods with boards on your feet."
> — DARWIN HUNTER,
> from *Beyond Yonder*

Harry Harwell is a bear of a man whom history will remember as the founder of the Green Mountain Stove Company, makers of the Dauntless wood stove. Harwell was a contemporary of the Stallion's from his Stowe days, when both men spent their days in search of perfect snow and their nights in search of romantic novelty. They found plenty of both.

The men were respectful rivals. Their styles were so different that they rarely found themselves in direct competition. The Stallion was an artist, with fine features, a rapierlike wit, dancing eyes, and sleazy charm. Harwell's charm was in his straightforward approach to life. A burly man with an unkempt beard and rosy cheeks, he liked laughing loudly, drinking too much, and making love. His boldness stood him in good stead when he became involved in business in the days when Vermont perched on the vanguard of the energy movement. Harwell designed a wood stove that combined the looks of a Franklin stove with the airtight efficiency of the contemporary Scandinavian models. Then he adopted a business philosophy of "don't look back." When the energy crisis eased and the demand for stoves slowed, Harwell had the good sense to realize that his "damn the torpedoes" approach would quickly sink the ship, and he turned the company over to professional managers experienced in meeting the demands of a declining market. Harwell attended monthly meetings, collected weekly checks, and generally played the role of a beneficent chairman of the board. The time and energy that he had spent building the company now went where it had gone before the company existed—into having a good time.

When Walt and Martha Gunion took a winter off to go on an around-the-world cruise, they put their house up for rent. This was not, Walt claimed, because they cared about money, but rather because they would rest easier knowing the house was lived in. Certainly it was not because of the consistently terrible experiences they had with tenants in the Cowdrey Place. Greed apparently was a more significant factor than Walt let on, because he advertised the house exclusively in the ski areas, ostensibly to reach "a better class of people." Harwell, who wanted a retreat within easy reach of both his company and the slopes, rented it.

"Walt's going to regret this," predicted the Stallion. "Harwell is a first-class party person. Plus he's a slob. He'll wreck the place." B.J., who knew Harwell through her employment, concurred.

Harwell liked to surround himself with humanity. Thus, each weekend saw an influx of cars with New York and Massachusetts license plates and ski racks on the back. At night the music blasted, and by morning someone had inevitably failed to negotiate Walt's steep driveway and needed help from the ditch. Emil developed a nice sideline pulling BMW's, Peugeots, and Audis out of ditches that winter.

The Hunters took a chance and invited Harwell to their New Year's Eve party, an annual event with a different theme each year. This year's was "High Tack, a celebration of tastelessness." Darwin wore a sharkskin suit from the thrift shop over a slinky, polyester body shirt slashed to the navel, and lots of gold chains. B.J. made a dress out of old curtains and looked like the grand dame of the pauper's ball. Benny Malone wore a Hawaiian shirt and sunglasses, sucked on a toothpick, and looked exactly like himself. Sammi served hors d'oeuvres of Cheese Whiz in the aerosol cans and Spam cubes on Ritz crackers.

The evening was off to a fast start. Everyone was grooving to the tacky music (Barry Manilow), admiring each other's costumes, and sipping on highballs, universally regarded as a tacky drink. Darwin mentioned to the Stallion that he had sent an invitation to Harwell. His response was vintage Stallion, a study in opinionated, ill-informed authority: "He'll never come. He would rather have the flu than come to an event like this. You've got to understand what a guy like Harwell is all about. First of all, he lost his ability to relate on any kind of a human level when he was about twelve. He surrounds himself with weaklings who won't threaten him, and vacant women who will mindlessly adore him. He thinks that just because he's rich, he's a genius, which couldn't be farther from the truth. The guy has the intelligence of a Chuck. You did-n't have to be much of a genius to make money selling wood stoves when the Arabs were driving the price of oil through the roof."

He paused only for a moment, long enough to draw a few more people into the performance. "I tell you, it was a riot when we both were at Stowe. He was on the ski patrol, even though he couldn't get out of his own way. He was a joke. No one would invite him to their home because he has the manners of an orang-utan. He drinks like a fish, talks like a sailor, and will fuck any-thing on two legs."

At this juncture the doorbell rang. Darwin opened it and admitted Harry Harwell, dressed in a blue leisure suit over a gray athletic shirt for the South Carolina Gamecocks bearing an expectedly lewd exhortation. His companion had on a bathrobe and pink floppy slippers, her hair up in curlers, and an unlit ciga-rette dangling from her lips. Despite it all, she looked smashing. Harwell brought a house present of a six-pack of generic beer and a bottle of Boone's Farm Apple Wine with the price tag still attached. He had not even had a chance to introduce himself to Darwin when Bruce, with scarcely a missed beat from his mono-logue, boomed, "The Bear!"

Harwell looked up to see the source. He blinked his eyes in mock disbelief. "I don't believe it. The Stallion!"

"The Bear!!" Bruce repeated in a lower, guttural register.

"The Stallion!!" echoed Harwell in the same tone.

They shook hands, they embraced, they slapped each other's back, they held each other at arm's length and said such things as "Let me get a good look at you," and "So how have you been, really," and "I can't believe it's really you." For the rest of the night they were inseparable, trading anecdotes about the good old days. Sure, they did not have a pot to piss in back then, but the freedom! The lifestyle! The girls! Ah youth.

It was a terrific party. The energy of the Stallion and the Bear's reunion provided the wave that pulled everyone else along. The men drank oceans of beer, then went outside and exchanged shrewd insights as they pissed long and hard into the snow. At midnight the champagne corks erupted like shooting stars.

Everyone kissed everyone else's spouses, and maybe snuck in a pinch on the ass. B.J. went over and rang the school bell. The peals carried through the still winter air, echoing off the upper ridge of Bear Hill, then were swallowed by the night. Let the New Year begin.

Bruce and Harry made elaborate pretenses of wanting to get together after the party, but they never did. Throughout the winter the cars streamed up to the Gunions' and got stuck coming down the driveway. Everyone seemed to be having a hell of a good time.

In mid-March Darwin received a letter from Walt, who was writing from the Hilton Hotel in Bali. His rental agreement with Harwell ended on April 1, and he wanted Darwin to check out the place before Harwell left, to make sure there was no damage.

Darwin mentioned it on a Sunday afternoon when he and the Stallion were going for an early season run. Exercise at this time of year needs a purpose so that one does not have to confront directly the absurdity of the process. Checking out the Gunions' sufficed.

As the duo ran up the steep Gunion driveway, they heard what sounded like shots. This was not cause for great alarm in central Vermont, since there is always some hunting season in progress. Next there was the sound of tinkling glass. "Uh-oh," said Darwin cresting the hill, for the telltale bullet holes could be seen in the tall windows that faced the south side of the Gunion home.

"What's going on?" Darwin asked no one in particular.

"I'll tell you what's going on. The Bear is berserk," said the Stallion with his usual complete confidence.

They approached the door and knocked tentatively. A muffled voice bade them to enter. The place was chaos. Beer cans and bottles were littered everywhere. Ashtrays overflowed. The all-pervasive smell was of stale booze and garbage. Harry Harwell was sprawled in the Gunions' "conversation pit," a collection of overstuffed sofa components. At his side was a half-filled bottle of Courvoisier. In his hand was the proverbial smoking gun. He looked up and waved them over with the revolver.

"Hey guys, good to see you. Come on over and have a drink."

He took a swig of cognac, then pointed the revolver at the window, fired two shots, then clicked repeatedly on the empty chamber. He tossed the gun onto the couch and held out the bottle to the newcomers.

"I don't usually drink when I run," answered Bruce, his answer sufficing for both.

"What are you doing?" asked Darwin. "This place looks as if a bomb exploded."

"Just a great party," answered Harwell. He reached over, picked up the pistol, and heaved it through one of the picture windows.

"What are you doing?" repeated Darwin.

"Having a good time," said Harwell with a shrug. He took a hit off the Courvoisier bottle. "Don't you know how to have a good time?" He held out the bottle again.

"Harry, listen." Darwin tried to sound clinical. It was the same tone he used whenever he had to tell a patient that he had a dread disease. "Walt and Martha come back here in two weeks. This place is a wreck. You've got to fix it up."

Harwell surveyed the Armageddon surrounding him. "Shit," he hissed, "this is going to cost me a fortune, isn't it?"

"Yes."

"Well." Harwell hit the Courvoisier yet again. "It's been a great winter, I think. I only remember about a third of it. You know, the best time was New Year's Eve at your house. That was a blast." There was only silence following. Harwell sensed that the conversation had reached its natural end. "Don't worry, you guys. I know you're being good neighbors. This place will look as good as new when I leave. Better. Just don't worry."

The runners left quietly. Once padding in their rhythm on the road, it was the Stallion who spoke. "I told you he was a slob."

"Do you think he'll fix the place up?"

"Not a chance."

"What do we tell Walt?" asked Darwin.

"That we're not his real estate assistants," said the Stallion.

Harwell left the place a mess. Walt Gunion went berserk upon his return, but Harwell quickly pacified him by sending a sum of money to cover the extensive damage. It must have been an adequate settlement, because Walt Gunion never complained. He did resolve never again to rent his house to skiers for the winter.

Thunder Road

> "The Abanakis tried to learn the ways
> of the settlers, but after a while
> they gave up and went north."
> — ALTON BLANCHARD,
> from *Over Yonder Hill*

> "Sometimes the cultural void between
> Chucks and Flatlanders is a Grand Canyon,
> other times a spring freshlet."
> — DARWIN HUNTER,
> from *Beyond Yonder*

Darwin Hunter had a million-dollar idea. Instead of people flying across the oceans to experience cultural diversity, why not explore the cultural diversity under their national noses? Why, for instance, go to India or Africa when a tour of the South Bronx will provide an exposure to an equally broad spectrum of the human experience?

True to his own theory, Darwin saw cultural stimulation under his own nose with the Chucks. Moreover, he suspected they were as curious about him as he about them. Thus he made the following proposal to Bennett Blanchard: we'll do something you like with you, and then you do something we like with us.

Bennett was immediately suspicious. Darwin must have something up his sleeve. Or else he was planning to make fun of him.

Nothing could be further from the truth, Darwin assured him. In fact, he claimed a profound respect for the lifestyles of others. That is why he wanted to learn more about the native Vermonters and their attitudes toward life. Bennett tried to figure every possible unscrupulous motive, and only when he was convinced that the doctor's curiosity was real and nonmalicious did he agree to discuss some possibilities.

Bennett wanted Darwin to be the first to reveal the events he had in mind. Darwin suggested cross-country skiing. Bennett countered with snowmobiling. Next Darwin suggested a Mozart Festival up in Burlington. Bennett thought long and hard, then came back with Thunder Road, the local stock car racetrack.

Cross-country skiing was first, and almost last. Sammi, Darwin, the Stallion, and Francoise planned an outing that combined the finest in local scenery and aerobic conditioning. Sammi mixed up some gorp, the high-energy food mix favored by cross-country skiers; the Stallion brought a flask of brandy; and Darwin gave a quick lesson in waxing. The Chuck contingent consisted of Teresa and Bennett Blanchard, Emil Dummerston Weed, and B. J. Bosco, who as Emil's companion was nominally a Chuck for the day. The route followed a logging trail up Granville Ridge to a cabin where Darwin thought they could have lunch. The Stallion, resplendent in one-piece Lycra racing tights, Francoise in tow, went zinging up the trail, leaving those in his wake feeling oafish and unfit. Darwin stayed with the pack, none of whom, with the exception of Sammi, was more than a rank novice on skis. Darwin tried to encourage them, but this was not a group that appreciated the rigors of exercise. It was a two-mile climb up a fairly steep hill to the cabin, and Emil must have asked fifteen times why they didn't just use a machine invented to take man up snowy trails. Darwin smiled wanly, then demonstrated herringboning techniques to help them climb hills.

The cabin was reached after an agonizing climb, during which the Chuck contingent had not stopped complaining. Lunch was served, as Sammi brought out the plastic bag of gorp, took a handful, then passed the bag to Bennett. "What's this?" he asked disdainfully, eyeing the mixture of dried fruit, nuts, chocolate bits, and sesame sticks.

"Lunch," answered Sammi.

"Gorp," said Darwin.

Bennett picked out a few peanuts, then passed the bag to Teresa. "Here, have some rabbit food."

"Stupid us," said the Stallion in a tone of impending insult. "We should have thought to bring some Wonder Bread so that you could have a Velveeta sandwich. God forbid you try something new."

"I could have walked over to the barn if I wanted a handful of grain. Not dragged my butt up a mountain."

"Oh, quiet you two." interjected Darwin. "Look, I brought some crackers and cheese, too. You can have that." He unwrapped packages of Norwegian flatbread and Brie, put a slice and wedge together, and handed it to Bennett.

"What's this?" Bennett wore a pained expression, as if he had been asked to eat a dead slug on an asphalt shingle.

"Oh, stupid us!" said the Stallion. "We forgot that cheese to the Chucks are yellow, plastic squares that come individually wrapped in a package that says 'Kraft Singles.' And crackers come in a red, yellow, and blue box that says `Ritz. "

The farmer sniffed his Brie cautiously, uttered a small groan, then bade the others in the group to do the same. "Smell that," he commanded Teresa, then Emil, and finally B.J. "Am I wrong, or does that smell like an outhouse?" They all agreed.

"It's just a little ripe," said Sammi. "It tastes great." She took the cheese from Bennett and ate it, much to his horror.

"I wouldn't care what it tastes like," drawled Emil. "If I want to eat something that tastes like an outhouse, I'll just stick my head down the hole in the johnny."

The downhill was a little better. B.J. enjoyed getting completely out of control and crashing into the woods. Bennett was actually heard whooping at one point, and everyone shared a hearty laugh when the Stallion started showing off and did a face plant in three feet of powder.

A moderately successful beginning.

The snowmobiling was, surprisingly, an unqualified success. Darwin, Townshend, and Joe Pisano joined Emil, Bennett, and Emil's brother, Dale, for a thirty-mile tour of the woods. Without the tension of the Stallion's constant sarcasm, the mood was more relaxed. The Chucks delighted in taking their Flatlander brethren onto harrowing trails that challenged their newly acquired skills. Also, as opposed to the skiing excursion, when Bennett had refused even a nip of brandy because of Teresa's presence, on this occasion he was into the peppermint schnapps as soon as they were out of sight of the house.

The Flatlander men were game with both machines and schnapps. Before long the combination of frigid air, exhilaration, and alcohol had placed everything in a pleasant white blur. They arrived back in Upper Granville as the afternoon shadows were disappearing, tired, hung over, and spent from the day's buffeting.

The Mozart Festival portended well. Teresa Bennett Blanchard loved the idea of dressing up and going out for "culture." Bennett, however, was sullen, as if the entire evening was an insult to his position in life. He chafed in his jacket and tie. He smirked at the luxury of Darwin's Saab. He recoiled at the small portions of pretentious food served at the bistro selected for a preconcert repast. He slept through the concert. So did Teresa. So did Darwin. All in all, a bad time was had by all.

The final event of the cultural exchange was a men's trip up to Thunder Road. They rode up in Dale's "Heavy Chevy," a 1975 Nova with fat tires and the rear end jacked up. Flames were painted on the side, along with the car's name, "Li'l Devil."

When the Stallion saw the car idling in its jet engine glory, he tried to back out of the evening. Joe Pisano and Darwin would not let him slip away, however, and soon the three were sandwiched in the back seat along with a cooler jammed with frigid Budweiser. Dale had the radio at ninety-eight decibels tuned to the local country and western station. When a certain Crystal Gayle song came on, he turned to the group in the back, trying to be friendly, and said to the Stallion, "I could fuck this song."

The Stallion was equal to the task. "I could fuck the whole album," he replied, his face a study in distaste.

"I could fuck the radio," Darwin added.

The beers were popping with regularity as the "Heavy Chevy" lurched along the back roads of central Vermont. Joe needed to make a pit stop, but the front seat denizens just laughed and told him to go in an empty can.

"Just don't tip it over in the back seat of my car," warned Dale. Joe protested weakly, but was informed that this was standard procedure for trips to Thunder Road. He held it for a while, then succumbed. "I haven't done this since high school," he muttered, `and I didn't like it then, either.

"This is ridiculous," said the Stallion.

"It's supposed to be ridiculous. Just relax. Think of it as reliving your youth," whispered Darwin.

Emil asked for another beer. The Stallion rattled the cover of the cooler, said "Here, let me open it for you." opened a beer, then grabbed the can of urine from Joe and passed it to Emil. The others in the backseat froze. This was going too far! The great Chuck/Flatlander War would break out as soon as Emil took his first sip. Joe and Darwin were horror-struck. The Stallion could barely contain himself.

Emil was singing to the radio. For what seemed the longest time, he idly fingered his beer can, turning it slowly and aimlessly. Finally, he went to take a draft. Darwin felt his stomach rise to his throat. Then Emil stopped and made a comment to Dale about a certain "ping" he could hear in the engine. Then he put the can right to his lips, turned at the last second, and drawled, "You turkeys ought to know that you have to ice down the can if you expect that one to work, you sons 'a bitches!'"

He was laughing. The backseat started laughing, as much out of relief as good humor. In between guffaws, Emil explained to Dale and Bennett what had happened. "These bastards tried to get me with the oldest one in the book, a can of pee. When's the last time you went to Thunder Road that somebody didn't try the can-of-pee trick?" Then they, too, joined in the laughter. Fresh beers all around. Emil told a few boorish, simpleton jokes. Everyone, especially the Stallion, laughed giddily. Soon all were dredging up inanities from their formative years.

At the racetrack the senses were bombarded with tangibles of the motorhead mentality. The smell of gasoline permeated the air, pierced by the whine of grinding gears and the screech of brakes. They did not sit in the grandstand, but up on the hill where the crowd was more casual and the mood more festive. The race was no more than a backdrop for a nostalgic trip back into adolescence. The cars drove around the track. Someone won, and more people lost, but no one seemed to care. By the time it was time to go, the collective mood was as mellow as the summer night. Upon leaving they found themselves trapped in a traffic jam with all of Vermont's other motorheads. Dale related a story about the crowd once getting so rowdy that they set a pickup truck on fire. Bennett one-upped him by claiming that one night back in his day they had set a police car on fire. His story was confirmed by Emil, who that same night had found himself learning the facts of life in the back of a Pontiac Catalina from a girl who now is married to a banker in town.

Bennett immediately began guessing to whom Emil was referring. Within thirty seconds, by process of elimination, the girl's identity had been revealed through inductive reasoning. He and Dale hooted and hollered in lascivious delight at a minor sexual conquest that had taken place eighteen years before.

Darwin related some of his own exploits, all of them abortive, as a member of Cincinnati's hottest rock-and-roll teen band of 1966. The Stallion waxed lyrical about the Studebaker Golden Hawk he had known and loved and foolishly sold for a pittance. Joe related stories of road trips he and his friends made down to the Jersey shore in search of exotic and wild women from Asbury Park and Manahawkin. The results were never quite as planned, and after the search for women had proven in vain, the boys settled for simple troublemaking, such as yelling obscenities at pedestrians.

"The favorite yell, the one guaranteed to get any Jerseyite's blood boiling, was 'Scumbag!'"

"'Scumbag?'" asked Dale querulously.

"Yeah," said Joe. "The key was not so much in the word as the delivery." Emil asked for a demonstration. Joe cleared his throat, took a hit of beer, leaned out the window toward the pickup next to them, and screamed, "SCUMBAGGG!!!!"

The occupants of the pickup next to them in the traffic jam, a boy of about seventeen and his girlfriend, responded by closing their window and turning up the radio. It was enough, however, to send the "Heavy Chevy" occupants into hysterics. Just as things were quieting down, Darwin let out his own bloodcurdling "SCUMBAGGG." This was just as hilarious until the five ornery-looking occupants of the next car over, a hot Plymouth, responded with some nastiness of their own. Masculine honor had now been offended on both sides. Bennett came up with the strategy. As soon as some open road appeared before them, they would let loose with a salvo of "Scumbags," then fire off down the road. The rest agreed to the plan. They waited patiently for the right moment, then on the signal from Bennett let fly: "SCUMBAG!

Scumbag! Scummmmbaggg! SCUMMMMBAGGGGG!!"

Then Dale put the pedal to the metal, and they were off. The Plymouth came in hot pursuit. For fifteen minutes there was a hair-raising chase on back roads as the Chevy and the Plymouth matched recklessness. It was low-grade "Dukes of Hazzard," but it was wild enough to arouse the adrenaline of those involved. The chase ended when Dale wheeled the Chevy onto the entrance ramp for Interstate 89. The Plymouth, which had held its own, decided it was no longer worth the chase. The "Heavy Chevy" occupants were jubilant.

"So long, scumbags!"

"Way to go, Dale."

"Tach it up!"

"Shut them down!!"

The drive back to Upper Granville took the rest of the beers. The next day, in relating the story, however, the complexion of the event changed. Neither group was able to admit that such child-ishness had actually been enjoyable. The Stallion, Joe, and, to a lesser extent, Darwin were unable to portray themselves as any-thing but unwilling participants in an event that could only be described as moronic. Bennett and Emil felt the same. Embarrassed at having found common ground, the cultural exchange ended.

Town Meeting

> "Farming took a backseat to self-government
> on town meeting day"
> — ALTON BLANCHARD,
> from *Over Yonder Hill*

> "If town meeting were held on a warm summer
> day rather than in the midst of Mud Season,
> no one would come."
> — DARWIN HUNTER,
> from *Beyond Yonder*

Town meeting is a Vermont tradition, democracy in action. It takes place the first Tuesday in March, just as the sap starts to flow, the snowbanks melt, and the entire world turns to slop. It comes when cabin fever rages and human contact is reduced to its barest elements.

The Upper Granvillites show up faithfully, sitting on the cold, metal, folding chairs in the gymnasium of the Granville Elementary School to perform civic duty. Usually the town business is routine, but occasionally an issue arises that brings local tensions bubbling to the surface. Battle lines are often drawn strictly along Chuck-Flatlander lines. Examples:

~ The Kindergarten Debate. Flatlanders feel that no amount of money is too great to invest in the education of their young ones. Chucks want to keep taxes affordable, and ever since the population influx of the 1970s, school costs have grown with the wild abandon of zucchini in August. The natives want what is best for their children, too, but feel that too much education, like not enough, is not good.

Stella Blanchard's opinions carry great weight. As a native Vermonter, a lifetime educator, and a farm wife, she has credibility with each segment of the population. When the question of adding a kindergarten program came before the town, Stella found herself in the awkward situation of having to publicly oppose her daughter-in-law, Teresa.

The scrap started between Sammi and Teresa. Sammi had researched other townships in Vermont and compiled an impressive dossier of statistical proof that children with preschool education fared better in later school years. This was pooh-poohed by a sarcastic Teresa, who countered with charges that kindergarten was a disguised form of subsidized day care that enabled uncaring parents like Sammi to avoid parental duties so that they could indulge themselves in aerobics classes, shopping sprees to Burlington, and other hedonistic excesses. Sammi was outraged, immediately losing her professional demeanor and making the fatal mistake of combating Teresa on her own terms. She accused Teresa of not caring about the education of her own children because they would never get off the family farm.

"Oh?" said Teresa, nimbly changing tacks. "So the family farm is something to be ashamed of? Are you saying that people who run family farms are ignorant? That they don't need the skills of a computer programmer? Let me tell you a little bit about the skills needed by the independent farmer."

Once on her soapbox, Teresa was invincible. One imagined the background music (John Philip Sousa) welling up while Old Glory waved proudly in the breeze. The crowd was with her, too, until she fell to the temptation of yet another personal slur: "So while the family farmer puts in his fifteen-hour days to feed America, the educated, such as your doctor husband, are bleeding the common man with extortionary rates to provide simple health-care services. And why? So that you can have charge cards at every store in Burlington, and so that you can work for the election of the bleeding-heart politicians who will support the social welfare policies that ensure that the rest of us can keep you living in style."

Stella Blanchard could take no more. She was recognized by the floor and wasted no time in putting Teresa in place: "Don't be so ignorant, Teresa. You'll give us farm folk a bad name. The world needs farmers just like it needs doctors and teachers. What it doesn't need is squabbling neighbors at town meeting. Now, one party here has presented some carefully prepared documentation of the benefits of preschool education. The other has waved the flag, and shot off fireworks, but offered nothing that helps the average man or woman make an intelligent decision."

Teresa tried repeatedly to remount the soapbox but was prevented by Stella's well-directed parries to produce evidence, not hysteria. The kindergarten was approved. The Blanchards could have charged admission to their family dinner that night.

❧ The Case of the Liquid Manure. A farmer must feed his fields by returning the nourishment that is taken away by grazing animals. On the Blanchard farm this means taking tankful after tankful of liquid manure from the barn to various entry points to the property. For two or three days the valley smells like an outhouse. The locals like to joke about the Blanchards' timing, which always coincides manure spreading with some outside event such as a community barbeque.

Walt Gunion, who is always concerned about real estate values in the valley, became convinced that manure spilled onto the roads was a major drawback to potential home buyers. Thus he petitioned that it become illegal to spill manure onto a public road. He actually managed a hundred signatures, most of them from Granville, where no one had to contend directly with the problem or the neighbors.

Walt presented his petition, and Bennett had to be physically restrained. When the speaker opened the floor to discussion, Hoyt shushed Bennett and stood himself. It simply was not practical, he said, for him to get manure to his fields any other way than over the roads. He was paying to maintain those roads himself, and this was perhaps his greatest need for them. Besides, if Vermont were to disallow manure spreaders on the road, could they allow any other farm vehicles, such as tractors and hay wagons?

Walt blustered about tourism being the state's largest industry, and Hoyt countered that they came to see the beautiful countryside, dotted by Holsteins and silos. The official vote was superfluous, for it was a rout in favor of the farmers.

∽ The Renaming of Tomar Brook. Darwin Hunter surprised everyone by petitioning to have Tomar Brook renamed. He had researched the town's history and discovered that the brook was named for Eben Tomar, who was hung as a deserter of the Revolutionary Army. The ensuing debate was lively. Several residents, familiar with the Hunter sense of humor, questioned the authenticity of the facts, but Darwin's knowledge appeared so encyclopedic that it was hard to undermine his credibility. When asked what he would rename the stream, Darwin said, "Blanchard Brook," drawing howls of protest from the attending Flatlanders, especially the Stallion, who suffered an apoplectic fit. When given his own chance to speak, he suggested the name "Hunter Brook," since Darwin's act of treachery was unmatched by any since the day of Eben Tomar.

A debate seemed about to rage when Stella Blanchard was recognized by the floor. "I'm surprised at you, Darwin. You've contributed so much to the community with your generosity and humor, but now you seem to think town meeting is a forum to indulge your own need for a few laughs. This is government by the people, and you can participate or not participate, but don't waste our time or make fun of us."

A thoroughly chastened Darwin Hunter asked to be recognized and withdrew his petition for the renaming of Tomar Brook. He apologized to the attendees, then sat down, wishing his chair could sink through the gymnasium floor.

Tunbridge World's Fair

"The Tunbridge Fair is appropriately attended with a jug of liquor and another man's wife."
— ALTON BLANCHARD,
from *Over Yonder Hill*

'Although once a raucous affair permitting locals a glimpse of flash and sleaze before winter, the Tunbridge Fair in recent years has become a family affair, characterized by good, clean fun."
— DARWIN HUNTER,
from *Beyond Yonder*

The Tunbridge World's Fair appeals to all. For kids there are rides and junk food, and a guarantee that anyone with five dollars to spend will wind up with a stuffed animal or souvenir trinket. For the motorhead there's a demolition derby, billed as the "world's largest," but more accurately one of the planet's dinkiest. For teenagers there is the glitter of low-level show biz, the romance of the traveling carnies, rock and roll, and fried dough. For the serious ruralite there are ox pulls, livestock competitions, and blue ribbons to be won for the largest pumpkin and best raspberry preserves. And for life's degenerates there is the late-night jalapena pepper eating contest, the mallet where you try to ring the bell, and the beer hall where you get lubricated enough to pick up the mallet. The girlie shows and all-night parking lot revels may be memories of the past, but the tradition of raunchiness hangs as heavily in the air as the smell of fried dough. Why else would Alton Blanchard have described it as correctly attended "with a jug of liquor and another man's wife"?

The juxtaposition of wholesomeness and sleaziness gives the Tunbridge Fair its cachet as much as its timing on the brink of winter's precipice. It is a weekend of bright sunshine and chilly evenings when the stove is fired up for the first time since April. The fair is cotton candy and beer, apple pie and painted ladies, night and day, summer and winter. For whatever reasons, despite offerings that seem meager in an age of Disneyland and video wonders, no one in central Vermont—Chuck or Flatlander—misses the Tunbridge World's Fair.

Darwin Hunter always enjoyed the fair, its raucous atmosphere and nonstop procession of new faces. As a member of the medical community, he volunteered to work one of the Saturday shifts at the Central Vermont Free Blood Pressure Booth. He drew the late shift, from four o'clock to eight in the evening. Sammi and the kids went with him at noon, and the family spent some fun-filled hours touring the midway, hitting the required rides and attractions. Then he kissed them all good-bye and went to perform his civic duty. Fairgoers are not keenly interested in having their blood pressure taken, so traffic at the booth was slow, but being in a fixed spot had the advantage of letting one sit and relax while all the friends and neighbors stopped by. He saw the Stallion and Francoise, Oakley McBean, Walt Gunion, a few of the nurses from the office, Benny Malone, B J. Bosco, Teresa Bennett Blanchard, the Pisanos, and the entire spectrum of central Vermont humanity. Everyone was in a festive mood. B.J. was half loaded and determined to find herself a "farm boy or biker" in the beer hall. Teresa was working the 4-H booth over by the exhibition halls and was flushed with excitement. Benny was his usual "Born to Boogie" squirrelly self, taking nips of Wild Turkey from a silver hip flask. He offered Darwin a hit. Darwin considered briefly his professional ethics, then accepted. What the hell.

This was Tunbridge Fair.

The day turned cold with darkness, and an intermittent drizzle settled over the fairgrounds and green hills. Inclement weather might deter revelers at other fairs, but in Vermont people expect Saturday night in Tunbridge to be cold and raw. They come prepared. This is the last blowout before curling up to the stove for a few months, and they will not be denied. The tradition holds!

Darwin closed down the blood pressure booth early (he had not had a customer in an hour) and went to the beer hall for a quick drink before going home. The beer hall consists of spare wooden tables underneath the grandstand. The servers come out with cases of uncapped beer that they slap down as quickly as dollar bills are thrust at them. Every twenty minutes or so the place is emptied out and a new crowd goes in. The serious partyers go right back in line and wait for their turn to go in again. The trick is to see how many beers you can throw down your throat during a twenty-minute stint.

There was the usual line. Darwin muscled into place alongside Benny and warmed himself with another hit of Wild Turkey. Before long they stampeded into the hall with the rest of the crowd. Although he must have known at least a dozen people, there was no opportunity to arrange seating. But no matter. The randomly selected tablemates inevitably turned out to be good company, fitting components of a tapestry of laughter, smoke, and confusion.

Darwin had a couple of quick beers, and was about to head home when B.J. nailed him to stay for another round. She had in tow a pair of the sleaziest greaseballs of all time, one hanging off each arm. She was wearing a leather cap like the one Marlon Brando wore in *The Wild Ones*. Darwin knew that staying was a bad idea, but thought maybe B.J. was in need of rescue from her chipped-toothed and tattooed companions, who had the fitting names of Motown Eddie and Itch. Nothing could have been further from the truth. As the crowd pushed inside, B.J. nimbly put the biker's hat on Darwin and slipped off, leaving him to spend two beers' worth of time with Motown Eddie and Itch, who, it turns out, were not such bad dudes after all. Darwin ended up inviting them to camp at his house if they could not find a place.

Such is the way of the Tunbridge Fair. Whomever fate dictates to share your table—a farmer, a biker, a doctor, a thief—becomes good company.

Even though it was not yet late, Darwin was starting to get a pretty good buzz on. Now it really was time to go home, but he thought he'd benefit from a little food first. He bought a grilled turkey leg to give himself the appropriate feel of a carnivore, and followed that with a boatload of french fries liberally doused with salt and vinegar. A feminine hand snuck a few from his pile, and he looked up into the smiling face of Teresa Bennett Blanchard. Teresa, along with all the Blanchards, had always regarded Darwin as one of the transient Martians, an invader of her valley. But at the Tunbridge Fair, the territorial stigma was removed. They commiserated about working booths of little interest to Saturday night fairgoers.

When the last of the french fries had been devoured, Teresa made an odd request of Darwin. In her nearly thirty years of fair attendance, said Teresa, she had never once been into the beer hall, and although she was not much of a drinker, it was an experience she thought she should have before she died. She did not dare do it alone, however, so would Darwin accompany her?

Darwin's resolve to leave evaporated in an instant. Teresa Bennett Blanchard in the Tunbridge Fair Beer Hall? This was an experience not to be missed.

Outside in the line they encountered Benny Malone and his ubiquitous, and bottomless, flask. Darwin declined, then winced as Benny offered it to Teresa. To his surprise she seized the flask without hesitation and pointed it skyward. Immediately she protested the strength of the whiskey, but made sure to take another nip before handing the flask back to Benny. She clung to Darwin's arm as the crowd pushed inside, and within moments was exchanging dirty jokes with their tablemates and challenging everyone to liar's poker. Darwin sat back, quietly stunned. This was not like any Teresa Bennett Blanchard he had ever seen. She was outgoing, vivacious, carefree, and uninhibited. And it flattered her. He had never seen such a sparkle in her eye. She told a very funny joke about a French Canadian who tried to get girls by putting a potato in his bikini bathing suit. The table roared with laughter. Teresa grabbed second beers for them, and Darwin told her, "If this is what drinking does to you, Teresa, you should become an alcoholic."

They had hardly been pushed outside when Teresa dragged Darwin back into the beer hall waiting line. He tried a feeble protest, but fell easy victim to her "just once more" plea. After all, Teresa told him, "we may never pass this way again."

By ten o'clock on Saturday night at the Tunbridge World's Fair, no matter how rainy or cold it is, the entire world takes on the rosy hue and roar of the carnival. The senses are as full of lights, voices, and music as the bellies are with turkey legs, french fries, and beer. Strangers become bosom buddies; the world becomes one.

Was it one or two more stints in the beer hall? Darwin was never able to reconstruct it. Teresa continued to be her vivacious self. But as with all good things, even Tunbridge Fairs come to an end. It was not yet late, and the crowd had barely reached the height of revelry, but it had been a long day for the booth workers. Time to go. Teresa asked Darwin to walk her to her car, a reasonable request since the parking lot at the fair is for the rest of the year an unlit pasture. They passed by Darwin's car first. Teresa was clinging to his arm for support, not that he was the Rock of Gibraltar. Then she stopped. "I know what you're going to do."

Darwin was not sure, but he thought she wanted him to kiss her. He thought it better to play dumb than sorry. 'And what's that?" he replied noncommittally.

"You're going to tell me how that front seat of your Saab folds back, and you're going to force me to do terrible things that I would never do if I hadn't drunk all that beer." She was already leading him back toward his car.

"I am?" His response struck him as passive and dumb. Then again, he was in a state of shock.

The front seat of his Saab did indeed fully recline, and within moments Darwin and Teresa were grappling and groping in a way that he had not done since high school. Somehow they managed to remove enough clothing to allow an approximation of sexual intercourse. Teresa muttered obscenities all the while they were making love.

It was over as suddenly as it had begun, a thunderstorm of lust. The dark, drizzly, silent night in central Vermont foretold of the winter to come. Two people, two strangers, were locked in intimate embrace in the middle of a cow pasture against a backdrop of carnival sounds. Teresa opened the door and got out, very businesslike, without delay. In a moment she had reassembled herself. Then she spoke: "Better drive the back roads home. You've had too much to drink."

Then she was gone. His breathing had not yet returned to normal. He felt very alone and very fucked. So that he would not have to worry about being stopped by the police, he drove the back roads home.

Tupperware

> "Each household was equipped with a variety of vessels, pails, containers, and firkins."
> — ALTON BLANCHARD,
> from *Over Yonder Hill*

> "Entrepreneurial opportunities in Upper Granville are both rare and a waste of time."
> — DARWIN HUNTER,
> from *Beyond Yonder*

There are several basic strategies of earning a living in the rural North. In farming, one coaxes a living from an uncooperative and unforgiving earth. The work is hard, the hazards enormous, the rewards small, and the satisfaction infinite. Ask Hoyt Blanchard.

The Flatlander juxtaposes a professional career with a rural lifestyle. Trade-offs in income are made for improvements in lifestyle. Darwin Hunter and B. J. Bosco are rural professionals. A subset of this is the rural entrepreneur—Joe Pisano, who farms the pipes and cesspools of the region, or the Stallion, who supplies glamour and identity to people whose lives are so swaddled in luxury that they are willing to pay a premium for the right kind of discomfort.

"Scraping by" is a strategy practiced by necessity (Emil Dummerston Weed) or by choice (Townshend Clarke). Either way this strategy involves hard, tedious work with little tangible reward. One cuts wood, boils sap, shovels roofs, plows driveways, and gains freedom only from the problems of the world. Emil never gave his lifestyle much thought. Townshend agonized over his for years before and since moving to Vermont.

No matter what one's financial circumstances, in the Flatlander valley poor-mouthing is common. Poor-mouthing occurs whenever someone, for reasons real or imagined, is overcome by a cheap attack and does not participate in an activity, pleading poverty. The classic example is Townshend Clarke, who lives on earned income while his trust fund grows at a daily rate that exceeds Emil Dummerston Weed's net worth.

Darwin Hunter earns the biggest salary in the valley, even though Vermont ophthalmologists rank low among their peers on the national financial scale. He and Sammi have little in the way of assets other than their house and cars. When the end of the month comes, there is little for the savings account. But they live well. And as Darwin points out, when *Beyond Yonder* is a household word, they will be rolling in clover.

The Blanchards, old and young, live at a consistent level of indebtedness. If times are good, they expand the farm. Conversely, if times get bad, a pasture is sold. Little has changed in this regard since Hiram Blanchard came down from Baddeck, Nova Scotia. They live modestly, their main concessions to twentieth-century living being a satellite dish and a radar range.

Emil Dummerston Weed earns little enough to qualify for anyone's poverty list. He has no money, no assets, but, luckily, no expenses either. Many meals are eaten at the Blanchards. Property taxes are minimal, and Bennett allows him to fix his truck on work time. He also lets him cut wood to sell from the upper acreage so long as he provides for the Blanchard firewood as well. Emil is fond of saying that he will leave this world with no more than he came in with.

Oakley McBean could be more prosperous if he could bring himself to steal from the till at the store. His Yankee ethics are so strong, however, that he refuses to do anything that might cheat the government from its rightful taxes. Joe Pisano has a running argument with Oakley on what he calls "the fine art of slippage." Joe maintains that the government expects an individual entrepreneur to steal at least a little bit from a business and sets the tax rates accordingly. In reporting every cent, one is cheating himself. The argument has been going on for nearly five years, with neither side making any concession. Upon paying for anything at the store, Joe leaves Oakley with the advice "stick it in your pocket."

B.J. earns a good salary at the Green Mountain Stove Company. Additionally, her parents have provided her with a modest trust fund. None of her friends, the Moira Chappees and Benny Malones of the world, have the proverbial pot to piss in. They exploit B.J. and her generosity, but in minor and inoffensive ways. She is happy to share the wealth.

Neither of the Gunions have a full grasp of the fortune at their command. It is managed by professionals back in New Jersey who send a check each month, along with various forms to be signed. Occasionally Walt needs money for a land deal or Martha for a car. They ask for it, and a check arrives a few days later. In the meantime Walt attends every Kiwanis, Odd Fellows, Lions, and Chamber of Commerce function, telling himself that it is work when in reality it is no more than an excuse to have another rubber chicken meal and a few drinks.

For the person with no trust fund, minimal education, and some ambition, the North Country offers a dilemma. There is a paucity of goods and services, offering ample opportunity, and yet the market is so slim that even the best-executed venture is doomed to a war of attrition. The situation has been unchanged since Vermont's earliest days, when hard currency was unknown. Farmers have always been cash poor.

Teresa Bennett Blanchard is devoted to the afternoon soap operas. She is bombarded with the commercial messages that accompany them, and has fallen prey to the desire for cosmetics and convenience foods created. Although the Blanchards own several thousand acres, more than a hundred cows, and enough farm equipment to start their own dealership, there is precious little cash for frivolities. To be precise, there is none. Bennett and Teresa have an agreement. If she wants little luxuries, she must earn the money herself. Conversely, if she earns the money, Bennett will not criticize her for how she spends it. Consequently, Teresa is always hustling valley residents for a buck, whether it is maple syrup sales, hand-knit Christmas tree ornaments, Amway products, or Mary Kay cosmetics. They cringe when Teresa approaches, for as Francoise Leibermann says with her Continental lilt, "Ze woman, she is relentless, like ze Scirocco winds."

Thus it was a surprise to no one when Teresa became the local Tupperware representative. The announcement, made one summer evening to a group gathered informally on the bridge over Tomar Brook, was greeted with collectively clenched teeth. They steeled themselves for the bite; they did not have to wait long.

"I have an exciting opportunity for one of you. You can sponsor a Tupperware party in your own home and be eligible for exciting prizes. We women could use a fun occasion, just for us. But only one of you can be the sponsor, and the first one wins."

At this moment Sammi Burger-Hunter and Sue Clarke had exactly the same thought: "What if I jumped off the bridge, right now? Would that get me out of this situation?"

To their amazement and relief, B. J. Bosco volunteered. Teresa's eyes narrowed in suspicion, but she had dug herself in too deeply to do anything but accept gracefully. A date was set, and Teresa left the group to cackle in her aftermath.

"Whatever possessed you?" Sammi asked B.J.

"I'm shocked," added Sue.

'Are you going through with it?" Sammi still appeared stunned.

B.J. nodded cryptically.

"I'm shocked!" said Sue again.

"Don't worry," said B.J., "it will be fun."

There was no love lost between Teresa Bennett Blanchard and B. J. Bosco. Each woman was strong-willed and aggressive, one enslaved to attitudes evolved through generations of life on the farm, the other to her own liberation, a child of television and southern Florida. There are no bounds, no restrictions, and no limits to B.J.

On the night of the party, Teresa Bennett Blanchard arrived to

174

the wail of rock and roll, a house full of valley women, and the whine of the blender as B.J. made nonstop pitchers of frozen strawberry daiquiris. Teresa laid out a display of plastic goodies and tried in vain to command the group's attention. Finally, she isolated B.J. by the blender. "If we don't do the presentation, you won't get your prize."

"Check, roger, wilco," said B.J. "What was that prize, anyway?"

'A kitchen canister set in harvest gold or avocado, but we have to take two hundred dollars in orders."

"Yeah, well, okay, gotcha. Uh, Teresa, listen. Pass that tray of ice cubes, and could you cut up a few more strawberries? I think the best thing is to let everyone get loosened up, you know? That way they'll be a little more free with the purse strings. Know what I mean?" Teresa nodded. B.J. hit the blender switch, and another pitcher of daiquiris was born.

An hour later Teresa was panicking, so B.J. obliged by turning off the music and gathering the group in her living room. Teresa made it through two minutes of her canned presentation, but when she demonstrated how to "burp your food," that is, release the air pressure in a container so that it doesn't explode, she lost control as the group exploded into convulsive laughter. It was ten minutes before a semblance of order was restored. Teresa went on, describing the convenience of individual items in great detail.

Everyone suppressed their giddy snickers until she came to the plastic container especially designed to hold your loaf of Velveeta cheese. This pushed Sue Clarke over the brink. "I can't believe this," she blurted. "A plastic container to hold plastic cheese! I don't even have electricity, and you want me to buy a plastic container to hold something I wouldn't even put in my mouth."

"Tupperware," said Teresa with a tight little smile, "is designed for the modern woman."

"Now maybe if you had something wedge-shaped for Camembert," said Sammi, trying to head off a confrontation.

"I'll make another pitcher," said B.J., trying to create a break in the action.

"'The modern woman;'" repeated Sue, accumulating a full

head of steam. "Look who is lecturing me on 'the modern woman: someone who keeps herself thirty pounds overweight because her husband likes big boobs."

"This is hopeless," whispered Sammi to B.J.

"Yeah, but you have to hand it to Teresa; she's not afraid to take on a whole room of catty, snide bitches. I don't know if I'd have the courage to take on a roomful of Chuck wives."

The confrontation turned quickly from food and Tupperware to lifestyles and social awareness. B.J. reacted quickly and turned on the stereo. Decorum became impossible to maintain, and Sue and Teresa's heated discussion became but one siren song in the din. The party prevailed. Happily, the event was salvaged by B. J. Bosco, who quietly bought two hundred dollars' worth of Velveeta storage containers that, months later, she gave to the women in attendance as Christmas presents. Teresa figured her humiliation was well worth the commission, especially since B.J. told her she could keep the canister set.

Winter Driving

'A blessing of winter was that packed snow on the roads made travel in horse-drawn sleighs a delight compared to the bumps and ruts of clear roads."
— ALTON BLANCHARD,
from *Over Yonder Hill*

"From October through May,
the driving conditions are so variable
that even a trip to the Granville General Store
can be an exercise in survival."
— DARWIN HUNTER,
from *Beyond Yonder*

For the uninitiated, the phrase "winter driving" conjures images of violent snowstorms, whiteouts, and multicar chain collisions. A season in Upper Granville quickly teaches that these are not the most fearsome conditions, because they can be foreseen and avoided. One does not drive over a mountain gap during a snowstorm, or even when there is a threat of one. One stays home. The Vermonter substitutes common sense for bravado, and rarely gets stuck because of it.

Flatlanders and young, male Chucks, however, never dispel their innate disdain of the Elements. Benny Malone, a born and bred Vermonter but without the usual Flatlander phobia, was one of the more colorful residents of the Cowdrey Place. To call Benny irresponsible would have been entirely fair, perhaps even charitable. Although in his early twenties, Benny's body already showed the effects of excess and neglect. He never had enough money to pay Walt the rent or to afford snow tires for the hulking wrecks he drove. He seemed incapable of feeding or clothing himself adequately, and yet his affable nature earned him a niche in the collective community heart.

Benny was driving home from Granville late one evening after his monthly trip to the laundromat. While his clothes were in the dryer, Benny had killed time with the regulars at Nino's Lounge. He had also smoked a joint, so by the time he left town he had reached his nightly level of inebriation.

To add one more ominous variable, this was a wild night when the sane Vermonter curls up in front of the tube and watches the Channel 3 News to see what tortures the night holds in store. Temperatures were already below zero, with sheets of snow blowing from the north with the same relentless fury with which Benny had powered down beers at Nino's. The situation was worsened by Benny's car, a 1977 Ford Torino with bald tires.

As Benny crested the hill into Upper Granville, the road disappeared into whiteness, and the next thing he knew, he was hopelessly mired in the soft shoulder. Although no more than two hundred yards from the Pisanos, he was too disoriented to know his whereabouts. A naturally lazy person, Benny had no trouble convincing himself that physical labors would be fruitless. The gas tank was hovering right on the empty mark (Benny was not too good at advance planning, either), and the chance of someone else being out on such a night was remote. Besides, his usual winter garb was a thin leather jacket over a tee shirt, with old sneakers.

Tonight was no different. The way it was blowing and snowing, to leave the car would have been suicide.

Benny, with the aid of his clouded brain, analyzed his predicament and came to the conclusion that he was about to die. This moment of lucidity then produced the inspiration that saved his life.

Before getting loaded at Nino's, Benny had done his grocery shopping. On his shopping list were Frosted Flakes, frozen pizza, a package of carrots, Joy dishwashing liquid, paper towels, toilet paper, a twelve-pack of Genesee, Kleenex, and a jumbo box of Hefty trash bags. As he munched on handfuls of the Frosted Flakes and sipped a beer, wondering what to do when the gas ran out, he had an idea. He took out the Hefty trash bags and fashioned them loosely around his legs and torso. He then stuffed them with the toilet paper, Kleenex, and crumpled paper towels. When those stuffing materials were exhausted he slit the backseat of the Torino with his pocket knife, no great loss there, and filled the bags with handfuls of the upholstery filling.

When Joe Pisano left for work at seven-thirty the next morning, he saw Benny's car in the ditch and assumed the worst. On other occasions he had found Benny sleeping it off by the roadside. Last night, however, temperatures had fallen well below zero, into the serious survival zone. Joe knew that Benny, although a native Vermonter, was not the swiftest guy in foreseeing or combating the Elements. Joe was not prepared for the sight that met him upon opening the driver's side door—an obese, plastic-swaddled Michelin tire man with Benny Monroe's face sleeping like a baby. At first Joe thought Benny was dead, but after considerable shaking and shouting, he came to recognize the familiar symptoms of a drunk arousing himself from stuporous slumber.

It took Benny a few minutes to remember where he was, then a few minutes more to realize he was still alive. He had been reasonably confident he would, in his own words, "wake up dead." It took two cups of coffee at the Pisanos for him to provide the full details of the Hefty trash bags filled with toilet paper and his Torino's backseat. By that Friday night, when he encountered the rest of the community at a party at B.J.'s, he had transformed his desperate actions into the innovations of pure genius. By the sixth and seventh retelling, Benny's story had attained epic proportions. Amongst themselves, however, community residents were less than impressed.

"Fool!" exclaimed B.J., her tone carrying disdain at Benny's total disregard for the Elements as well as relief for his deliverance. "I'd have been pissed off if that little mother bought the farm. Who would I buy my dope from?"

"Sounds like he wrapped one of those Hefty's a little too tightly around his head," added Darwin.

"That guy's brain is the consistency of that stuffing from his backseat," contributed the Stallion.

"His neocortex is as smooth as his tires." said Sammi.

"Damndest story I ever heard," summarized Oakley McBean.

Every denizen of the North, not just Benny Malone, has a winter driving adventure. The driving conditions most feared by Vermonters are the least foreseeable. Freezing rain is the worst. The water makes contact with the frozen ground and solidifies into an invisible shield. Rain on snow-covered roads is treacherous, as is the haphazard freeze/thaw cycle of Mud Season.

On such occasions the Elements make it questionable whether life in Upper Granville is worth the effort. One such night occurred on a Friday when a warm front moved in following a cold spell. After ten minutes of gentle rain on the snow-covered road the hill between Route 100 and the town became completely impassable. The Clarkes and Pisanos had gone to dinner at Nino's and were the first to try, the first to fail. As they got out to reconnoiter, they found conditions deteriorating so rapidly that it was becoming difficult even to stand. The Stallion and Francoise followed. B.J. and Moira Chappee were right behind, already half lit from an assault on the Club Casablanca, Granville's only pretense of a boite de nuit. Finally, Darwin and Sammi arrived, making it almost a complete neighborhood gathering. The Stallion had a couple of six-packs, so the brainstorming was at least sociable.

"Well," said the Stallion, passing around the beers, "who has a great idea?"

"The only way anyone is going to make it up the hill is with chains," said Townshend.

"That makes it easy," returned the Stallion facetiously, "who's got chains?" The expected silence ensued.

"But you don't understand. We've got to get the baby-sitter home by eleven." Sue Clarke's voice had a whiny edge to it that touched off B.J.

"Oh, do something, someone! The baby-sitter has to get home."

Townshend shared B.J.'s annoyance. "If we get up the hill, you can't possibly think I would go down the hill only to have to come up the hill again."

"But Townie, you know how hard baby-sitters are to find."

"But Townie," echoed B.J.

"So I still haven't heard any great ideas," repeated the Stallion.

"We can walk," began Darwin.

"No we can't," interrupted Francoise. "I have on heels."

"My darling doesn't dress for the weather," said the Stallion, his voice dripping approval.

"Okay, so we forget the walk. We can stay here and wait for the sand truck."

"That could be tomorrow morning!!" Sue was mortified.

"Right! So we could wait for spring."

"We could go down to Oakley's and call one of the selectmen and tell him to get the sand truck out here right away." Townshend was trying to be rational.

"We could finish the beer and die happy."

"You're a big help, Bruce."

"Now, don't get peevish, Shrew, I mean Sue."

Townshend continued, "We could go to Oakley's and call Walt."

"That would help," bubbled B.J. "He could tell us what's happening on 'Dallas' tonight. Don't forget Walt's the guy who once tried to get Darwin's Saab unstuck by putting sand and wood ash under the rear wheels."

"Well, then, we could call Emil."

"Emil doesn't have a phone," B.J. pointed out.

"We could call Bennett. He even has chains for his old station wagon." The group fell silent. The implications of calling Bennett were perfectly clear. The Flatlander contingent would be asking a

Chuck to throw them a lifeline. Bennett would say nothing, but the cliches about Flatlanders being helpless victims of the Elements would be proven.

"Oh lordy, lordy," sighed the Stallion, his tone implying that there was no alternative.

The Stallion, B.J., and Darwin started the half-mile slide down to Oakley's, where, unless struck by inspiration, they would rouse Bennett Blanchard from bed and eat humble pie for the rest of their lives. The rest of the group sat in Townshend's Volvo in the pitch black, listened to the patter of the gentle rain, and reconsidered their decisions to live in the North. After a seeming eternity, headlights approached from the pavement side. The lights were followed by the rumble of a one-ton pickup and the welcome clank of chains.

"We're saved!" They could hear B.J.'s voice over the low-gear whine of the engine. The truck pulled alongside the stuck cars, and the occupants spilled forth into the black night. "Hop in, everyone. Say hi to the savior, Roland Calhoon." The driver had killed the engine and was enjoying his newfound notoriety.

"Rollie!!" said Moira with obvious familiarity. "Long time no see. It must have been at least an hour. What are you doing here?"

"I'm hanging out at the Casablanca," he began thickly, his speaking abilities impaired from excess alcohol. "And there's a call at the bar for me. First time I ever got a call at the bar, 'cept when it's the old lady. And it's B.J. telling me about the party at her house."

"Yeah," interjected B.J., "I told Rollie that he was missing a helluva party, and suggested that he come out here."

"Whoo-eee. Let's party!" whooped Roland.

"Everyone in the back. Moira, why don't you keep Rollie entertained up front. Make sure he stays conscious at least until we get up the hill."

"Nice friends you got, B.J.," said Sue as they lurched up the hill.

"One more complaint and I'll throw you out of the truck, Sue. And don't even think of asking Rollie to take your sitter home. He's too shit-faced." B.J.'s tone carried a finality that Sue challenged by looking to Townshend to come to her defense. He avoided her gaze, however, as if summoning the courage to assist B.J.

"Such a night," sighed Francoise, lightening the mood.

"It's a beautiful night," said the Stallion, and indeed he had a look of contented serenity on his face.

"I wouldn't go that far," said Darwin.

"It's a beautiful night," repeated the Stallion.

"It's cold, dark, rainy. We're all wet, and tired, and our cars are stuck at the bottom of the hill. Why do you call it beautiful?"

"It's beautiful because soon we'll be home in our very own beds and tomorrow we can come down and get the cars. No harm will have been done." As he spoke, the lights of Upper Granville came into view. The Stallion's tone was wistful, whimsical, lacking its usual edge of self-conscious arrogance. "It's beautiful because we didn't have to call Bennett. We may be saved by a Chuck, but at least we're not saved by the Chuck."

Wood Stoves

> "The technological advance that most improved the
> comfort of the colonial settler was when the open
> hearth was replaced by the cast iron parlor stove."
> — ALTON BLANCHARD,
> from *Over Yonder Hill*

> "By mid-January, while one is in the act of digging
> frozen wood from a snow-covered pile, it becomes
> obvious that the greatest genius in the history of man
> was the creator of central heat."
> — DARWIN HUNTER,
> from *Beyond Yonder*

Perhaps the biggest difference between the Flatlanders of Upper Granville and their brethren in civilization is the way they stay warm. The Down-country People get up, go to work, and around October 1 when the temperature plunges they twist the dial on the thermostat up to seventy-two degrees. Then in April or May,

182

they turn it back to "Off."

The Uplander, however, starts the heating year in April, resolving not to make the mistakes of the past winter. Primary among the sins were burning green wood and running out in March. The remedy is simple. Order wood in April and order twice as much as you need. The orders placed, one relaxes and concentrates on springtime projects until July 15, when you realize that the three people you ordered from have yet to deliver a single stick. You call to make sure; after all, you want the wood to dry before you burn it this year. The first tells you his truck has broken, but he expects it back the next week; the second says he hurt his back and is a few weeks behind schedule; the third cannot be reached, and you hear from a friend that he has gone down to Florida to look for a construction job.

Time goes by, and no wood. In late August the first cold evening is accompanied by the first trepidations. You call the first two wood suppliers. The first gives you the same story, verbatim, about his truck, and it sounds as if he has been drinking. The second claims to have never heard of you.

Panic. The posters are now up for the Tunbridge Fair. The tomatoes have bit the dust.

You overreact and call five different people advertising wood in the classifieds of the *Granville Clarion*. For reasons unexplained, they all react instantly and show up on the same day, at the same time. To make things worse, two of the originals show up, too. It's a conspiracy! You explain the predicament, and they all say that they could care less. The wood, all ten cords, is already dropped. You will pay, or they will see that no one in Vermont ever sells you wood again. Thoroughly intimidated, you become the proud owner of a ten-cord mountain of hardwood.

There are a thousand and one stove tales in the Flatlander valley. The ladder blows down while Joe Pisano is cleaning his chimney, and he spends seven hours on his roof. A squirrel gets caught in Walt Gunion's stovepipe. The story ends with a wrench thrown through the picture window, and Walt going to the emergency room. There is the Hunters' New Year's Eve party, when severe down-drafting fills the house with smoke, causing an impromptu shift of venue over to B.J.'s. Townshend Clarke, assisted by Joe

Pisano, rigs up a hot water heater for his stove. It works fine as long as the stove is going. When the Clarkes leave for a weekend, however, and the stove goes out, all the water backs up into the stove. The Clarkes return home to a living room covered in a half inch of wood ash sludge. And finally there is the night the Stallion tries to force a piece of twenty-six-inch wood into a stove that takes twenty-four. He tries jamming it, wedging it, swearing at it, and willing it, but nothing works. He succeeds only in igniting it, meaning that he now has a flaming piece of twenty-six-inch wood and no place to put it.

The Stallion is buck naked, this being the final loading prior to bedtime. He grabs Francoise's nicest potholders, picks up the burning log, and plunges outside, arching the log safely into the snow. For reasons never fully explained, Teresa Bennett Blanchard is taking a late night stroll, and is standing in front of the Liebermann residence when the Stallion makes his fiery appearance. The Stallion briefly considers an explanation, but decides that the cultural gap is unbreachable. Once a Martian, always a Martian. He booms out a passage in Yiddish remembered from his bar mitzvah, then returns inside. Teresa never mentions the incident, although the Stallion relates the story to anyone who will listen.

The valley Flatlanders burn their wood in Dauntless stoves, made by the Green Mountain Stove Company in Granville. There is a certain local pride in owning a Dauntless, although the Chuck population eschews Dauntless stoves in favor of large, nameless box stoves that offer little in the way of pleasing aesthetics, but that take big pieces of wood and heat like sons a' bitches. Bennett made a disparaging remark about "those worthless airtight pieces of junk" at a community gathering on a hot summer afternoon, and touched off a range war with B.J. Bennett made some good basic points about how his own stove had been blasting heat for more than twenty years because there was nothing that could possibly go wrong. A Dauntless, on the other hand, with its automatic thermostat, air bypass dampers, and multiple controls, could be turned into a creosote factory in the hands of the untrained operator.

"What you're saying, Bennett, is that you need an IQ of at

least seventy to operate a Dauntless. Maybe that's the problem."

"Bennett's got an IQ of seventy," interjected Darwin, ever helpful.

"Yeah," added the Stallion. "Luckily, Hoyt was smart enough not to marry his sister."

"Very funny," countered Bennett, who had heard it all before, "and very original. Was it prep school where you both learned to be so witty?"

B.J., fresh from doing all the ads and sales brochures for the Green Mountain Stove Company, was a fountain of facts and figures, quoting BTU outputs, burn times, and grams per hour emission statistics that Bennett was not equipped to combat.

"All I know is that I like my stove," blustered Bennett. "And I wouldn't have one of those pretty boy stoves in my house unless someone gave it to me." B.J. closed in for the kill by proposing that she would give Bennett a Dauntless. He could use it for the winter, and if by the end of the heating season he did not agree that it was an improvement over his present stove, she would take it back. Nothing ventured, nothing gained, but nothing lost. If he did agree that it was an improvement, he would buy it. Terms were settled quickly. For once, each party was willing to put his money where his mouth was.

B.J. brought home the Dauntless, enlisting Emil, Darwin, and Joe to move it into Bennett's and install it. No sooner had the installation been completed than Bennett let out a howl. The Dauntless takes twenty-four inch wood, and Bennett's entire supply was cut to twenty-six. He tried to back out of the deal at that point, but B.J. held him to it. Bennett thought he caught the trace of a snicker from Emil, and snapped, "What are you laughing about? Who do you think is going to cut two inches off every stick in the woodpile, sucker?"

The experiment was not off to a grand start, although Teresa Bennett Blanchard established herself as a surprise Dauntless supporter due to the improvement it made in the appearance of her living room. For once there was an element of looking forward to the heating season. Would the Chuck prefer the Flatlander stove? If so, would he be too stubborn to admit it?

On the third weekend of September, the weekend of the

Tunbridge World's Fair, the temperature dipped into the lower forties. On Sunday morning the community awoke to wisps of smoke curling out of all the town's chimneys, including the Blanchards'. Everyone managed to find an excuse to buttonhole Bennett to ask him how his first night with the Dauntless had gone. He answered each inquiry with a smirk and a mumble; Teresa blew his cover by revealing that he had read the operator's manual from cover to cover the night before. The race was on.

B.J. and her Dauntless established an early lead that grew as the winter progressed. It was a cold winter, and the stove lived up to its name. Bennett took great pains to point out the stove's shortcomings, but by February he was reluctantly admitting that the even heat output, reliable overnight burns, and lower wood consumption were making the Dauntless look like a winner compared to his old box stove. He even made a few statements to the effect that he was starting to save up so that he could afford "the overpriced tin can."

In March there was a thaw. The weather turned mild, the sap began to flow, only to have winter return with a vengeance, as temperatures plunged back into the frigid zone. Bennett filled the stove with the day's garbage after dinner, as was his habit, and settled in with the kids to watch a game show on TV. At the Hunters', Sammi was tucking in her brood when she caught an orange glimmer out the window. She gasped when she looked over to the Blanchard residence to see a fiery plume shooting twenty feet out of the chimney. It looked like the exhaust from a jet engine, and it took several seconds for Sammi to register what was happening.

"Chimney fire!" she screamed to Darwin, who moved immediately to put on his boots and coat. "Should we call the Blanchards?" she asked.

"Bennett's probably in the barn. Call the fire department; tell them to get out here right away!" Darwin had rehearsed the situation with his own house enough to know that when one lives five miles from the nearest hydrant, seconds can mean the difference between saving a house and losing it entirely.

Darwin felt the surge of adrenaline as he dove into the night air. In front of him he saw B.J.'s door fling open. She was pulling on her coat while running with the same urgency. He called out, "We've called the fire department."

"Good! Do you think Bennett's in the barn?"

"Let's check the house first." As they ran toward the Blanchard residence, Darwin was awestruck at the spectacular display issuing forth from the chimney. It was midway between a Fourth of July spark fountain and an erupting volcano. Sparks were settling symmetrically onto the tin roof. In the distance the sound of the fire department sirens could already be heard, along with the crunching footsteps in the snow and the pounding hearts of B.J. and Darwin.

B.J. reached the door first, banging three times, then entering without waiting for a response. She burst into the kitchen, which was empty. There was sound from the living room, and she and Darwin ran toward it, bursting in upon a scene of domestic tranquility. Bennett, still wearing his overalls, but having removed his boots, was roughhousing on the floor with the kids. "Family Feud" was blasting from the television set, and Teresa was comfortably nestled in an easy chair, oblivious to the surrounding chaos. Everyone looked up at the intruders, more in surprise than alarm.

"Chimney fire!" gasped B.J. Bennett responded with a blank stare that suggested that some vital link was still missing. "You're having a chimney fire," she repeated.

"I don't hear anything," said Bennett. B.J. marched over to the television and turned it off. There was a perceptible but distant-sounding dull roar, not the freight-train-in-the-living-room experience that often accompanies chimney fires. "Guess you're right," he said matter-of-factly.

"You should see it," added Darwin. "You've got a real shower of sparks coming down on your roof!"

"Oh, it's a good roof," Bennett was still unconcerned, although he had risen and was pulling on his rubber barn boots. "Should be able to withstand a few sparks."

Outside, the show was still going on, although the shower of sparks had lost a bit of its spectacular arch. Hoyt came puffing up, and the Stallion's pickup screeched to a halt.

"Bruce," called B.J., her voice assuming great authority,

"bring your flashlight so we can check the rafters."

"Oh, don't bother," Bennett seemed almost sheepish. "It's a real good chimney. It'll be all right."

"Don't be crazy. Any weak spot can start a fire. Let's go."

"Let's do it, Bennett," said Darwin sensing Bennett's uneasiness at the situation. "No sense in taking chances; besides, the fire department should be here in a minute."

"Fire department?" Bennett's voice was incredulous. "You didn't call the fire department, did you?"

"Yeah, I did," said Darwin, now sounding defensive. "Better safe than sorry."

"You shouldn't a' done that. You call them right back and tell them not to come." Bennett was suddenly furious, directing all his wrath toward a silent Darwin Hunter. "You've got no right to do that. They'll put it in the newspaper. You call them right now and tell them not to come!"

"Too late for that," said B.J., as the rumble of a truck was heard coming up the last stretch of hill to Upper Granville. "Look. Let's stop arguing about this, and let's start making sure your house doesn't burn down. Let's check the beams and walls to make sure there isn't any problem."

The truck pulled to a stop, and the driver hopped out. The cars of several volunteers were right behind. The chimney spout had died to a wisp. Bennett stomped to the doorway, sputtered a curt "I'll check my own house!" and then slammed the door behind him.

The fireman walked up to Hoyt. "Bennett cleaning his chimney, Hoyt?"

Hoyt chuckled, "It's clean as a whistle now, by jeezum. I reckon this one's under control. Bennett's checking around inside."

"Want us to check from the top?"

"Let's wait to see what Bennett wants to do."

"Ayuh. How's the sap flowin', Hoyt?"

"Oh, middlin. Got to warm up a bit, don't you know." As they listened to the chitchat, Darwin and B.J. felt their adrenaline melting as quickly as a springtime snow. From their roles as heroic house savers, they had now slipped back into the dumb Flatlander category. Bennett reemerged from the house. He was livid, his face red as his neck. "It's the stove! It's that goddamn stove! I never had a chimney fire before."

B.J. tried a rejoinder, but the door had already been slammed, so there was no one to deliver the message to. Everyone thanked the firemen profusely. They did not indicate any annoyance at being called out for a chimney fire, only relief that everything turned out all right. Everyone slunk home into the night. B.J. came over to Darwin's, where they killed about ten beers bemoaning Bennett's lack of appreciation for their sincere efforts.

The next morning, while B.J. was off at work, the Dauntless stove was delivered to her front yard. It sat there, a reminder of her lost bet, gathering rust until later that spring when it was hauled off by Darwin Hunter, who had the brilliant idea of using it as the heat source for a sauna he was building in his backyard.

Zucchini

> "The diet of old-timers was limited to what could be grown and preserved. Come January, families got some sick of pumpkin."
> — ALTON BLANCHARD,
> from *Over Yonder Hill*
> "It is a spiteful God who made the only vegetable ideally suited to Vermont the zucchini squash."
> — DARWIN HUNTER,
> from *Beyond Yonder*

When B. J. Bosco came to town, the two hot subjects among sapient beings were wood heat and gardening, just as a few years earlier the topics had been consciousness and music, and a few years later they would be gourmet food and physical fitness. The Arabs were forcing Western civilization to its knees by withholding oil. Americans blew the clarion call to battle by returning to their pioneer roots. The jettisoned-by-choice, the refugees of the Northland, abandoned the security of civilization for the uncertainty of the Elements. They were heroes, self-sufficient, courageous, close to the earth. Each spring these people set their jaws, hitched up their pants, and started up the Troy-Bilt Rototiller.

The first lesson any Northland gardener learns is that the mind is stronger than the back. Thus the layout that looks terrific on the legal pad in January is four times as large as any couple can sanely work and ten times as large as they need. The rule of thumb is to plan your garden, cut it in half, then cut it in half again. The second lesson is that the growing season is ten weeks long.

By March the Vermont countryside is so dead that it is difficult to imagine it ever returning to lush greenery. All around is addled snow, pock-marked and filthy beyond a teenager's nightmare. As the snow level declines, the sins of the previous months rise day by day, layer by layer— the garbage the dog scattered the night he got into the trash, the toys the kids left out the night before the first snow, the leaf rake, and the many forms, colors, and shapes of four months of frozen dog shit. This is not the Vermont sold to the skiers at Killington or portrayed on the cover of *Vermont Life*. It is, however, the state of the state when the gardens get planned.

Sue Clarke saves her calendar, upon which she records such significant moments of passage as the last snow, date of planting peas, first frost, and number of jars of tomato sauce canned. When the archivists seek the style and character of life in Upper Granville in the 1980s, this will be their most significant document, even more significant than the notes and files for *Beyond Yonder* on Darwin's desk.

The first entry on Sue's calendar is the theme for the Hunters' annual New Year's Eve party and what resolutions she and Townshend made: On January 2 it says, "Seed catalogs arrive!"

The seed catalogs are insidious. The temperature is ten below, with a two-foot snow cover and a north wind; the thought of a garden is someone's idea of a cruel joke. The catalogs are filled with bushes laden with plump fruits, jungles of edible greenery, exotic new varieties of melons that will grow in the tundra. For an evening one can delude oneself that spring really is right around the corner.

But the experienced dweller of the North knows to put aside the catalog until a more reasonable date. Nothing is worse than staring at seed packages when snow covers the ground. The true signal to order seeds is when the dog shit is exposed. The perverse juxtaposition of water and fertilizer cries out, "Garden!!" Checking the catalog order form, you see it says, "Allow six weeks for delivery." Omigod, you say, that takes me into May. "I'm too late!" You forget that your entire garden perished in a frost last June. You also forget that when you ordered last March from this same catalog you had your seeds in time for St. Patrick's Day, when the skiing is still great.

Everyone in Upper Granville has a specialty. Hoyt Blanchard plants rows and rows of peas that the entire family shells for endless hours on the front porch. "Mother doesn't let me up from the table unless I eat my peas," he says with a nod toward Stella. Bennett grows corn and tells the same joke summer after summer. Question: How can you tell if the corn is ripe enough to pick? Answer: It's the day after the raccoons eat it.

Emil does not garden because he does not eat vegetables. Darwin tries for the largest squash at the Tunbridge World's Fair. Sammi grows flowers to dry, and Françoise Liebermann has the best herb garden in town. Stella Blanchard savors her asparagus, although Hoyt won't touch them because they make his pee smell funny. Walt Gunion handles his tomatoes with the same loving devotion a mother shows to a newborn, and Townshend Clarke tries each year to grow an edible watermelon. One year he actually got one the size of a softball that he picked the night before the first frost. It was white and grainy, not at all sweet, but he ate it anyway, figuring this was the closest he might ever come to his goal. The Stallion loves radishes and hot peppers, and plants several varieties, any of which can blow steam out the ears of a normal man.

It's all there on Sue's calendar.

Zucchinis exist to remind all of the sins of seed ordering. Order form in hand, you force your brain back through winter and fall to the previous harvest. You remember vaguely that you had too much zucchini. Now, you don't particularly like zucchini, but they are such a successful crop you order a packet of seeds.

So does everyone else in town.

A packet of zucchini costs less than a dollar and contains forty to fifty seeds, with instructions to plant them three to a mound, with mounds six feet apart. The novice, who has a garden approximately ten times as big as what he needs, plants all his seeds. The veteran, remembering his abundance of zucchini last year, plants only one mound, then puts in one more just to be sure. The native Vermonter, who counts only peas and corn among the vegetables he will eat, thinks that zucchini is a type of pasta and plants none.

The zucchini consumption for the average American is three pounds per year, the equivalent of one medium squash. The average zucchini plant produces fifteen or so fruits that through nourishment, then neglect, grow to forty pounds each. Multiply the variable factors by the number of gardens in town and one can imagine the zucchini glut that hits communities in the northern tier each August.

The natives realize the cruel trick that their memories have played. "I don't mind being stupid," lamented a bitter Darwin Hunter one year as he put a wheelbarrow with a "Take 'Em— Free!" sign by the side of the road, "but I hate being stupid in the exact same way year after year?'

The first year B. J. Bosco planted a garden, Darwin and the Stallion convinced her that she would need at least six mounds to serve her needs. All summer long they admired her crop and smacked their lips at the prospect of zucchini bread, zucchini casserole, zucchini blossom salad, smoked zucchini, stuffed zucchini, fried zucchini skins, and pickled zuke. Then the first time she came over to offer an armload of surplus squash, they laughed in her face. B.J. knew she had been had, but extracted a measure of revenge by filling the trunk of Darwin's Saab Turbo with flaccid squash just after the first heavy frost. By the time he discovered them, they had turned to green slime.

The natives have responded to the zucchini problem in a variety of ways. Philanthropy, as practiced by Darwin with his wheelbarrow of squash, does not work at all. Diligent consumption is equally ineffective. In the early days valley residents made an attempt to eat what they had grown. Sue, Sammi, and Tina got together and made enough zucchini bread to airlift to Biafra. They then put it in the freezer where it sat untouched for a year before being taken out and thrown in the compost. One summer the Stallion came up with the idea of feeding squash to a pig that Emil was raising. After one day not even the pig would touch them. The only usefulness related to zucchini is that valley women have discovered that the prospect of green squash for a fourth consecutive night is a foolproof way to wrangle a dinner out.

Then one year, they all got smart. No, not smart enough to not plant zucchini, but smart enough to not fight it. They organized and held the First Annual Zucchini Festival.

The idea was a Darwin Hunter original. At first, others claimed credit. Later, no one disputed his authorship. The idea was simple. Declare Upper Granville the Zucchini Capital of the world. Put up a few posters, place an ad in the local paper, and have some fun. Seemed like a fantastic idea at the time.

B.J. created awesome posters that exhorted the townfolk to bring their tired and poor zucchini to Upper Granville for all kinds of "squash madness." The Blanchards, although they could not find anything overtly perverted or sacrilegious about a zucchini festival, thought the effort frivolous and, therefore, not worthy of participation. This was strictly a Flatlander effort. Darwin, Joe, Townshend, and the Stallion organized activities. There was a zuke sculpture contest, "name that zuke," zuke football, zuke softball, bobbing for zukes, a zuke toss, a zuke launch, a burning of Zuke of Arc, a singing of "Zuke of Earl," a Miss Zucchini contest—all in addition to the world's largest ever zucchini potluck dinner.

On the day of the festival, the first inkling of trouble came with the arrival of a television crew. Next came a reporter from the Associated Press in Montpelier, then the crowds. More than five hundred squash-laden people showed up. The valley people had prepared for no more than twenty besides themselves. They were woefully unorganized, particularly since the residents had to spend more time giving interviews than dealing with guests. Before long, exuberant chaos reigned, and zucchini squash were flying back and forth across the Hunters' front yard. Paper plates and plastic forks were exhausted within the first half hour. The Hunters' cesspool began overflowing during the second. Before the crowd had finished arriving, others were already leaving in disgust.

The pictures and stories that subsequently appeared disguised reality and painted instead the image of a madcap, zany gathering put on by carefree gnomes in the Green Mountains. The wire services carried a photo of Sammi Burger-Hunter and Sue Clarke munching on a forty-pound zuke as if it were a giant phallus. The accompanying story recommended that anyone with a good recipe or suggestion for next year's festival send it along to good of Darwin Hunter.

The aftermath was as bitter as frostbitten squash. The town was strewn with zucchini bits. B.J:s and the Hunters' front yards were several inches deep in green slime and related trash. The same people claiming credit for the idea only days earlier were now pointing accusing fingers in every direction. For weeks strangers brought surplus zucchini to leave in the front yard of Darwin "the Zuke of Earl" Hunter. By the first snow, however, zucchini was yesterday's problem, and the festival took on the softer glow a memory.

Over the course of the year there were enough inquiries about the next year's festival that Darwin Hunter had the following cards printed up

```
Dear Zucchini Lover:
        There will be no Second Annual
Zucchini Festival due to the fact that the
first one was a complete disaster. Do not —
repeat do not — come to this town with
extra zucchini, because you will not be
welcome. Instead you might try this prize-
winning recipe from last year's contest:
```

Dr. Darwin's Zucchini Flambé

```
* Wash and stack a dozen zucchinis
* Douse with one cup gasoline
* Stand back fifty yards and shoot
  with flaming arrow
* Laugh deliriously
* Serves any number.
```

```
          Remember, don't come!
          Sincerely,
```

Dr. Darwin Hunter

But just to make sure, on the same weekend the next summer, everyone left town.

Over Beyonder

Part Three

❧ ～～～✦⟨◈⟩✦～～～ ❧

The First (Since 1892) Spring Fling

Having established the proper environment for creativity, with pregnant files standing in alphabetical glory, Darwin was poised to work on the masterpiece *Beyond Yonder*. But he knew that one did not simply plunge into writing without a foundation in research. For a year he buried himself in Vermont-related books, especially Alton Blanchard's unheralded classic, *Over Yonder Hill*.

Next he set out to find a publisher. He sent proposals to New York publishers and high-powered Hollywood agents. Darwin was talking major motion pictures, serialization, translation rights, and the cover of *Newsweek*. The responses, alas, were talking rejection. Only semi-daunted, Darwin resolved to publish *Beyond Yonder* himself, earning even greater profits for the select investors he would let in on the deal. When this thrust faltered, Darwin tried selling advance copies of the book to friends and neighbors for a paltry "prepublication special price" of thirty dollars. Amazingly, the only person shrewd and far-sighted enough to jump on the offer was Francoise Liebermann, who bought one as a novelty birthday present for her darling. Darwin guaranteed delivery within six months or double your money back. The Stallion laughed hysterically when Darwin was forced to make good. It was the best investment he had ever made.

Another year passed. Darwin had dubbed around with finances long enough. The time to begin writing was clearly upon him.

But first he had to get in shape.

The community at this time was in the grips of collective fitness hysteria. Darwin convinced himself that an able-bodied writer would be more efficient than the flaccid, armchair variety. His time spent in training would pay off in the long run. A year later he had run his first sub-four hour marathon, but had not yet opened the ream of corrasable bond that was destined to become his book.

Darwin sensed the project bogging down. To make matters worse, B. J. Bosco was doing just fine on the photographic end and had nearly completed her assignment. His commitment needed reaffirmation, a punctuation mark to show the world how dedicated he was to the propagation of Alton Blanchard's efforts. He achieved this by purchasing a twenty five-hundred-dollar word processor and printer. Now truly he was poised, with no further excuses other than the fact that he had not the foggiest idea of how to use the machine. Two manuals, one seminar, a University of Vermont Adult Extension Course, and hours of practice made Darwin as much an authority on word processing as on *Over Yonder Hill*. And still, not another word made it to the page.

"I admit," confided Darwin to Sammi one evening, "I'm off to a slow start; but that's my style. I did this all the time in college. I remember French exams where I didn't crack a book until the night before. Then I aced the test. This is no different."

Encouraged by his own bravado, Darwin marched to the keyboard, turned on the monitor, and sat motionless for three hours.

"Uh-oh," he said to Sammi, who had come to check on progress before going to bed, "writer's block."

"Writer's block? Most people get writer's block after they've written something."

"I'll be all right once I get started."

"But Darwin" — the frustration in her voice was obvious, even though her tone was calm" — it's been more than six years since you started this book. We've owned four cars and had three children, and you still haven't started."

"Has it been six years?" Darwin sounded unimpressed. "Well, *War and Peace* wasn't written overnight."

"It's been more than overnight, and this isn't *War and Peace*. This is a sequel to an obscure book that has been read by fewer than one hundred people."

"That doesn't mean it's not important."

"All I'm saying is that you better hurry up, because we're not going to live here forever."

This brought to the surface one of Darwin's least favorite subjects, the Hunters' future in Upper Granville. With their youngest now out of diapers, Sammi had commenced planning her reentry to the job market; but there was no job market. Also, their oldest child was now in first grade, causing Sammi to bemoan the limitations of rural school systems. Darwin found it difficult to counter his wife's argument that the solution was to move. Moving had never been part of his plan. Besides, he liked Upper Granville too much to consider leaving. Thus far he had been able to parry Sammi by agreeing with her premises while downplaying the need for immediate decisions. The increasing persistence of her statements, he knew, meant that a more definitive resolution of the situation would be needed before long.

"I suppose all artists have to cope with a certain amount of jealous ridicule," he muttered to no one. Sammi took the hint, however, and went to bed.

Alone with his thoughts, Darwin dipped into his single malt collection for the inspiration that only a fingerful of Glenmorangie could provide. As its smoky fire enveloped his palate, he retreated into the ancient world of Upper Granville as depicted by Alton Blanchard in his dog-eared copy of *Over Yonder Hill.*

This night he read about the Spring Fling, an institution greatly celebrated by locals in the 1800s. The winters were just as long back then, and the farmers took their work just as seriously as the modern-day Bennett Blanchard. For one delirious afternoon, the first truly warm day of spring, the chores would be put aside, the church and school bells would ring, and the community residents would gather for a potluck lunch followed by a horseshoes match at the town tavern, now the residence of Darwin and Sammi Hunter. The match was always spirited, encompassing the release from winter's dreary grasp as well as the continuation of well-established rivalries. According to Alton, the Spring Fling was a topic of conversation all year long, but especially in those prolonged final gasps of the eternal winter.

The inspiration fired Darwin as surely as the firewood did his Dauntless and the Glenmorangie his innards. Through the window of his den, he stared through the black void of a starless twenty-below January night. He watched the last light in B.J.'s schoolhouse go out, leaving him alone with his thoughts, alone in the Northland. The idea was so simple. This year they would have a Spring Fling. By two o'clock in the morning, Darwin had all the details figured out.

Horseshoes is a game for midsummer, when the hay is in and the frantic pace of farming can be relaxed "just a mite." The easy rhythms of the game and the graceful arch of the throws are well suited to the lazy feeling of the season and provide fertile backdrop for socialization among the menfolk. Even types as disparate as the Stallion and Bennett Blanchard can suspend hostilities while throwing the 'shoes.

In the weeks preceding the Spring Fling, however, the simple pleasures of summer were transformed into obsessive ends of desire. An official horseshoe amphitheater was built in Darwin Hunter's yard with pits, lights, scoreboard, and bug zapper. His Garden Way cart became a mobile beer wagon, complete with spigot and CO_2 dispenser. Moreover, the competitive fires of the community had been fanned to the brink of a holocaust.

The perpetrator of the excess, "Mr. Instigator" as B.J. called him, was Darwin Hunter. He now channeled the energies that propelled him through medical school, rock and roll, the Zucchini Festival, and the Running of the Valley into a horseshoes binge. Not only had he built the court, but he assembled his team nightly for practice, rules-drilling, and psychological motivation. In the hands of Darwin Hunter, the horseshoes match had become a metaphorical confrontation between the Chucks and the Flatlanders for dominance of the valley, if not rural America.

Everyone had responded positively to the idea of reinstituting the Spring Fling. The realities of twentieth-century life, however, removed some of the spontaneity in favor of being able to assemble all people in the same place at the same time. A likely Sunday in April was set. Teams were established strictly along Chuck/Flatlander pedigree, with B. J. Bosco agreeing to referee. Townshend Clarke and Joe Pisano created an appropriately named trophy for the winners, the Alton Blanchard Cup.

The Chucks were confident. Oakley and Hoyt had spent life-times chucking 'shoes. Surely their experience would come to the fore. The Flatlanders were similarly confident that their meticulous preparation would stand them in good stead. Neither group counted on the weather, which harkened not of spring but winter. Snow swirled chaotically from billowy clouds moving fast enough to reveal periodic sunshine. It was so cold that most players were forced to wear gloves. Darwin built a bonfire in his Weber so that players could thaw between throws. The spectators monitored the match from the Hunter kitchen, over repeated cups of coffee and exclamations about the frailty of the male ego.

Darwin took the game's first throw and immediately buried it in the snowbank surrounding the pit. "Did I kill anyone?" he asked. Indeed, when the wind whipped the flurrying snow, it was impossible to see the opposing stake.

"Play!" commanded B.J.

"Durndest thing I've ever done," chuckled Hoyt, calmly throwing a 'shoe into the whiteness and hearing the reassuring "clang" of contact with the stake. The Chucks jumped to a quick lead that they seemed unwilling to relinquish. The Flatlanders' week of preparation was not enough to combat Oakley's and Hoyt's lifetimes of experience.

If the newcomers were to dominate, they would need strategies that did not rely on skill. Bruce Liebermann protested the weight of the Chucks' horseshoes, making B.J. take them into the house for an official weighing while the participants stayed outside and froze. The Chucks retaliated when the Stallion stepped up to the line. At the height of his backswing, Bennett spoke: "Say, Bruce, you ever had any of them homosexual experiences?"

The throw went wild to the right, and the Stallion launched a loud, immediate, and vociferous protest to B.J.

"Just kibitzin'," said Bennett. "Nothing illegal about kibitzin' in horseshoes. It's part of the game."

Another delay ensued as B.J. consulted Darwin's official rule book. There was nothing in there about kibitzing, so she made the following ruling: "Horseshoes is a social game that tests concentration as well as throwing skill. Kibitzing will be allowed so long as it conforms to the tone of normal conversation."

When Bennett's turn at the line came, he was braced for the insult that the Stallion issued, a comment on the physical resemblance between Bennett and Teresa. He let it pass, but Emil picked up the gauntlet: "You never answered Bennett."

'Answered what?"

"About whether you ever had any of them homosexual experiences."

"What are you talking about?"

Emil picked up the flag and charged. "You know, where you ram it up some other guy's poop chute?"

"No," said the Stallion icily. "At least the sheep and heifers are safe around me."

"By the jumped up jeezum!" exclaimed Emil with seemingly genuine enthusiasm. "If you want a sweet heifer, we'll go over to the barn after the match."

The Stallion was the epitome of supercilious propriety. It was his turn, and he stepped to the line again. "If you don't mind, gentlemen, shut up." He returned his focus to the opposite stake.

Bennett waited until he was at the height of his backswing before speaking. "Just kibitzin'," he said with a tone of mock apology. The Stallion's throw fell way short.

Emil played second banana again: "Jeezum Crow, what's a friendly horseshoe game without kibitzin'? That's half the fun." The Stallion said nothing, but smoldered so smokily that it was obviously just a matter of time before he burst into flames.

"What a revolting development. What are we going to do?" whispered an anxious Darwin to B.J.

"I don't know," she responded. "It seems like a lot of your ideas end up this way, don't you know?"

As the barbs sharpened, so did the competition. Concentration had to be maintained under the psychological barrage and verbal taunts of kibitzin'. Townshend Clarke was called a "trust fund hippie," Hoyt Blanchard an "old coot," Joe Pisano a "Dago thief," and Oakley McBean a "calcified fart." Finally, B.J. stepped forward and put an end to the silliness, ruling kibitzing in any form grounds for forfeiture.

For a few minutes the game was free of rancor. Bennett Blanchard stepped to the line. A ringer would end the match and deliver the Alton Blanchard Cup to the Chucks. His arm drew back, he threw... .

"Foot foul!" said the Stallion authoritatively.

The shoe continued its trajectory. It landed without touching the bar, a perfect ringer.

The Chucks exploded in glee, grown men, hardscrabble Vermonters squealing like schoolchildren over the throwing of a horseshoe.

"FOOT FOUL!" repeated the Stallion, making sure there was no doubt. The revelers quieted.

Bennett turned slowly and narrowed his eyes. "We don't call foot fouls in this town. We decide games on skill."

"No we don't. We call foot fouls," answered the Stallion cheerfully, some would say smugly. "We just did. I just did. You lose your turn. Throw doesn't count."

"Yes it does count," said Bennett in slow, measured tones. "I threw that 'shoe the way I've been throwing them all my life."

"I know. You've been foot-fouling all your life."

"And why didn't you ever call it earlier?"

"Oh, I dunno. Never felt like it until now."

"You're not going to win this match on a chickenshit move like this. I say it counts." Even in the gray light of the afternoon, the red flush to Bennett's face was obvious.

"Let's ask the rules master. And Bennett, you look very macho when' your eyes get so fiery. Must be the Latin in you." The Stallion reached up to pinch his adversary's cheek, only to have his hand slapped away.

He recoiled a step with a ready reply: "Bennett! Just kib-itzin'!" He then looked directly at Emil. "Jeezum Crow! What's horseshoes without a little kibitzin'?"

B.J. consulted the rule book, then suggested a compromise: Bennett should rethrow the 'shoe. Both parties refused. She tried a second compromise, suggesting that the game be replayed. Both parties refused. Then she moved that the entire tournament be replayed. Another refusal. Forced to a decision, B.J. ruled that the foot-foul call, although completely immoral and a chickenshit maneuver of the first magnitude, was technically correct. Both teams had agreed to play by the rules, and this was a rule.

Bennett's throw was null and void.

Bennett's response was spit out from between clenched teeth: "When push comes to shove, you folks from the Flatlands stick together."

"I'm sorry, Bennett, but no one here seems inclined to budge," said B.J. And it was true. The Stallion's teammates tried to get him to withdraw his protest. But he was more than resolute; he was rigid as a stone. Bennett stalked off. Townshend, whose turn came next, refused to throw.

"That means your team forfeits, Townie," said B.J.

"Who cares? If that's the way we have to win, it's not worth it."

Inside the Hunter kitchen, the festive mood had been dampened by word of the petty squabbling. A collective bitter taste prevailed. The group —Chucks and Flatlanders—was united in condemnation of the Stallion, who this day had not even the mindless support of Francoise to buoy him. Bruce sat stubbornly through the abuse, adamant about the correctness of his protest.

The crowd dispersed quickly. Darwin tried to maintain some interest in an official ceremony to present the Alton Blanchard Cup. How about some beer and something to eat? Maybe people would like to see some of the photos B.J. had taken for *Beyond Yonder*? How about a sauna? Darwin had fired it in anticipation of some riotousness. But the neighbors escaped with the ease of small fish through a large net. The Stallion, ironically, was the only one to remain. He accepted Darwin's offer of a sauna.

Darwin's Sauna

Dusk.

Darwin and the Stallion walked out to the shack that housed Darwin's sauna.

"Your craftsmanship never fails to amuse me," said Bruce.

"I thought you liked primitive stuff. This is bona fide Appalachian funk."

"Feels like the ovens at Dachau." The men undressed and climbed onto the wooden benches.

"Ouch. Darwin! Didn't anyone tell you about countersinking the nails?"

"It only burns for a second. Besides, it's hard to recess roofing nails, which is all I had."

"Why didn't you put a light in here?"

"Quit complaining. Why would I want to see you naked, let alone sweating?"

A silence ensued, weighing heavily. Both men were well into their first sweat before Bruce spoke again.

"Go ahead," he commanded.

"Go ahead what?"

"Go ahead and say I'm an asshole. That's what you're thinking."

"I've always thought you were an asshole."

"I mean for ruining the Spring Fling, the Alton Blanchard Cup, and all that."

"Doesn't matter. But what does matter is whatever is bothering you."

The Stallion sat stonily, arms hanging limply, gaze unfocused. His tone was one of resignation. "I don't know. I guess I'm tired of running around with my tongue hanging down to my knees. I'm tired of the pieces of my body falling off like withered skin. I'm tired of saving the world from bad taste. I'm tired of bending over for clients. I'm tired of flattering women."

"Which reminds me," interrupted Darwin, "where's your darling today?"

"Which reminds me," interrupted Darwin, "where's your darling today?"

"Got the flu." The Stallion's speech was continuing. "For once I'd like to be the guy with more money than taste, or even the guy with no money and no taste who wraps his house in plastic and whose biggest concern in life is how to improve his television reception. I want to gain a few pounds, let my skin sag, and walk around with my gut hanging out."

"Well," Darwin feigned great surprise, "that's quite a statement coming from the Winter Wonder himself."

"Darwin, the problem is I'm shooting blanks."

"What are you talking about?"

"I'm not fertile. My sperm's dead. I can't reproduce myself." In all the time of their acquaintance, Bruce Liebermann, a.k.a. the Stowe Stallion, had always maintained a posture of superiority. Now, there was no veneer, and this very real person appeared barely capable of keeping himself from fading into the darkness of the shack.

"How do you know?"

"Francoise and I have been trying to have a kid for the last year."

"No kidding?"

"Very funny."

"Sometimes I can't control my comic genius. Have you been tested?"

"Tested for what?"

"Your sperm count."

"No, I just know."

"Bruce, that's ridiculous. There are a thousand potential impediments to conception, and unless you eliminate some of them you'll never be able to discover what the problem is—if there's a problem. Call me at the office tomorrow. I can set something up for you."

"You're an eye doctor."

"I know, not a real doctor. Anyway, all I'll do is give you the name of a specialist."

"No, it doesn't matter anyway."

"Why are you torturing yourself? Of course, it matters, but

it's not the end of the world."

"It doesn't matter because Francoise is gone." Bruce looked directly at Darwin. "She's left me."

Darwin blustered for a little time to let himself more fully comprehend Bruce's revelation. "It's not unusual for a woman to be very disappointed at an inability to conceive. She's probably blaming herself, not you. She'll come back."

The Stallion shook his head. "She is seriously gone. Packed her bags, renewed her passport, and now is sipping Pernod on the Champs Elysees. She's been gone for more than a week."

"Bruce ... you can't be serious."

"This is not an April Fool's joke."

"She left you because you couldn't conceive?"

Bruce gave a sarcastic half-laugh and stood up. "No, that's not why she left. She left because of Sue."

"Sue Clarke?"

"That's it, `Sue the Shrew: "

"Bruce, there's part of this story that's missing"

"I've been fooling around with Sue." The Stallion paused for dramatic effect. Darwin couldn't tell whether he was embarrassed, bragging, or searching for the next thing to say. The Stallion continued: "It wasn't a real affair. Just the occasional, you know, roll in the hay. Didn't mean anything to me, but it seemed to be the biggest thing in the world to her. I looked on it as kind of a gift. You know what I mean?"

Darwin rolled his answer around carefully. Bruce had not used the word "service" in describing his relationship with Sue, but his trainer would have. "If it was so casual, why was Francoise so upset?"

"It wasn't Sue; she was just the straw that broke the camel's back. The real problem was that I couldn't stop."

"There were others?" The Stallion confirmed it with a nod.

"Oh yeah. Upper Granville, Stowe, Montpelier . . . wherever. I never promised complete fidelity, but my complete lack of it surprises even me. If some chick admires me, I perform. Darwin, what am I going to do?"

"About Francoise?"

"About me! I'll be forty years old next month. I'm not the

stud of the slopes anymore. I don't have a real job. My only friends are in this town, and most of them aren't speaking to me at the moment."

"Whew," said Darwin, "you sure know how to burn bridges. This one's going to be tough to charm your way out of. Let's get some air and think it through."

Outside, the evening brought an unmistakable return to winter. The men stood naked in their boots, shriveled penises exposed to the breeze. The outline of the surrounding hills was as dim as the memory of the Spring Fling.

Epilogue

*B*eyond Yonder was begun in earnest before the buds had yet appeared on the trees. Following the spirited fancies of the Spring Fling, Vermont sank back into the mire of a star-crossed Mud Season. Rather than attempting redemption, the Stallion slipped away. The only local who heard from him directly was Walt Gunion, who put the "For Sale" sign on the Liebermann house. In a typical Stallionesque gesture, a new horseshoes set was, sent to the community, care of Bennett Blanchard. Rumor had the Stallion living with his brother in Manhattan, plying his trade as a restorationist with wealthy clients in the Hamptons and Connecticut suburbs. Supposedly there was a new babe on his arm.

B.J.'s father had a sudden stroke. He was alive, but impaired. Not knowing how long he would live, B.J. responded to the family plea to return home immediately. She promised Darwin she would come back to Vermont, but her timetable was indefinite enough that Walt Gunion could not hold the schoolhouse. Before leaving she gave Darwin the last of the photos for Beyond Yonder. It was all there.

Bad things happen in threes. For the residents of Upper Granville, the third blow came one morning when Emil Dummerston Weed found Oakley McBean face down on his floor, dead as could be. The coroner revealed that he had choked on a piece of ham the size of a pack of cigarettes. Had that not killed him, his blood alcohol level would have. His last toot ended sadly.

Darwin foundered in the sudden void of companionship. He sat in front of his word processor and typed the opening lines of *Beyond Yonder*: "This is not an epic; this is not a saga. This is a description of specific people in a specific place at a specific time. This is how they lived." The words poured out of Darwin as they had out of the Stallion the night after the horseshoes match. This time Darwin's verbosity made it to the paper.

The first and only draft of *Beyond Yonder* was completed before the Hunters' lawn needed its first spring mowing. Darwin delivered the manuscript and B.J.'s photographs to a printer in

Montpelier and was promised a finished book in time for the
Tunbridge Fair. Instead of the normal reactions of exhilaration
and relief, however, Darwin drifted through an aimless summer,
devoid of friends. There was no Upper Granville float in the
Fourth of July parade and only eight runners padded around the
valley in the Sixth Annual Running.

His resistance to Sammi's appeal for cultural stimulation via
geographic relocation weakened as the days grew shorter. If they
were going to make the change, she argued, they might as well do
it before the snow flies.

With a heavy heart, Darwin called Walt Gunion to appraise
their house. His new, charcoal Oldsmobile 98 was a frequent sight
on Upper Granville roads these days. Business had never been so
good. Darwin was standing on his front lawn discussing the
upcoming Tunbridge Fair with Stella Blanchard when Walt
arrived. Darwin's annual attempt to grow the prize-winning
squash had yielded an anemic fifteen pounder, hardly a blue ribbon winner. Stella was concerned that if there were no heavy
autumn rains, wells might run dry during the winter, something
that happens every decade or so.

Gunion powered down the passenger side window and, as
was his custom, yelled across the body of a self-conscious passenger, a thin, sprightly woman with short gray hair.

"Howsa boy?" Another brilliant beginning. Darwin's nod was
enough to prompt him to continue.

"I'm getting rich off this community. Just rented the Cowdrey
Place to a divorcee from Barre. Got a dentist from Massachusetts
looking at Liebermanns', and might just have a new occupant for
the schoolhouse." He gestured with his head toward the woman,
who looked down demurely, obviously uncomfortable with
Gunion's penchant for treating people as commodities. He ram-
bled on: "I told her she'll love the schoolhouse. Great spot for a
single lady. She even jogs, so she can run in your race every summer. Hey, Doc, I got some boxes for you. Now, get a load of this."
Gunion reached down and flipped an automatic trunk release.
The rear hood popped open revealing the red and white "For
Sale" sign, as well as two cardboard boxes.

Gunion chortled through his folded jowls. "Don't have to lift more'n a finger with these new cars. Even got a built-in radar detector. 'Course I always say, if you're serious about real estate, you've got to drive a nice car. No one wants to buy anything from someone who looks like he doesn't have a pot to piss in."

"What's in the boxes?" asked Darwin.

"A guy from a print shop in Montpelier left them at the office. Said he couldn't find your house, but I doubt he even looked."

"My book," said Darwin vacantly. He attacked the cardboard with his penknife.

Gunion purred on, as monotonously as the engine of his 98: "I brought the sign along, in case you decide you'd like to give me the listing right away. You'll be wanting to get the sign up before the leaf peepers invade."

"Darwin," exclaimed Stella, "I didn't know you were leaving."

Darwin looked up from the book. His only response was a tightening of the lips and a firm look into her water-blue eyes, eyes that had seen every valley child in the last half century grow up. Even though the school bus now took the kids into town, he wanted his own children under her watchful eye as well. But, then, there was Sammi's practicality to consider. Never before had Darwin felt so drawn and quartered by his emotions.

"I never figured you for transient," she said. The word "transient" pushed him over the brink of decisiveness.

"It's all a joke, Stella. You know my sense of humor. I thought I would stick the sign on your barn to get a rise out of Bennett." As he spoke he felt a sudden loathing for charcoal Oldsmobiles, for overweight realtors, and for himself at having been weak.

"I dunno," said Stella. "Bennett doesn't have much of a sense of humor to begin with, especially having anything to do with the farm."

"I know. Just a bad idea, like renaming Tomar Brook. For every good one there are about five bad ones. Here, you can be the first in your neighborhood to have an official copy of this long-awaited, soon-to-be best-seller."

He walked to the passenger side window. For a man who seldom took life seriously, Darwin's visage had the humor of a farmer watching a thunderstorm washing away newly planted seed. To the woman in the front seat he spoke softly. "Welcome to

Upper Granville. I'm Darwin Hunter. This is a very special place. Whatever Walt's asking, offer fifty bucks less. And don't budge! Make the deal contingent upon him fixing the leak in the living room. Here's a welcome present." He gave her a copy of *Beyond Yonder*.

To Gunion he spoke directly: "Walt, you're an interesting combination of the grim reaper and the stork."

Gunion's potato puff face screwed into puzzlement. He never knew how to take Darwin. "We don't need any help negotiating, Darwin. Don't you want the `For Sale' sign? Got to put it up soon if you want to catch the leaf peeper traffic."

"Ah yes, the leaf peepers," laughed Darwin. "You see, Walt, my problem is that I just had an attack of sanity. If this is such a great place to live, then maybe I should live here. But it's great to know that, should I decide to move, the services of a well-trained, highly professional realtor are available right here in the community. By the way if you want a book, it's twenty-four dollars."

Gunion beamed like a Holstein in dandelions and reached for his wallet. Darwin spoke in a cryptic aside to the woman in the Ninety-eight: "A trivial victory in a meaningless war."

He smiled, then turned back to Stella to discuss important things, like the weather.

The next week Darwin took the whole family to the Tunbridge World's Fair. For the forty-fifth consecutive year, it rained on Saturday night, but Vermonters are not about to let a little inclement weather ruin a good time. While Sammi and the kids were looking at the prize-winning lambs and bunnies, Darwin found time to sneak off to the beer hall for a quick one. At first he felt "just a mite" lonely, but then an old codger challenged him to a game of liar's poker. Darwin lost three consecutive games, but the man, a weathered logger out for a good time, atoned by buying another round. Anyone you meet in the beer hall turns out to be good company.

Just out of curiosity, Darwin looked for a familiar visage Teresa or B.J., Benny or the Stallion, or even Motown Eddie or Itch. Through the smoke and din, across the sea of smiling faces, with two beers in his belly, he could see them all.

About the Author
Stephen Morris writes about salt water, green mountains, wild turkeys, cluster flies, rock and roll, and Spam (the semi-edible kind). His other novels include *Beyond Yonder* and *Stripah Love*. He lives in the part of Central Vermont that is next to nothing but close to everything, called Beyonder.

The
Public
Press

We are The Public Press.
You are The Public Press.

Corporate media conglomerates continue to consume independents. While ownership consolidates, new book titles, specialized cable channels, and new websites proliferate. Amidst a din of commercial noise the bandwidth and coherence of available information is narrowing. Thoughtful authors find it more difficult to find publishers for sustained, original, and independent ideas at a time when technology is making it easier than ever to disseminate information.

The casualty is free speech.

The Public Press was founded in 2004 to protect freedom of speech "word-by-word." It is a grassroots organization, beholden only to its readers, its authors, and its partners.

The goals of The Public Press are printed opposite:

For more information, and to get a free subscription to the newsletter, The Page, visit: **ThePublicPress.com**.

Empower authors.

The Public Press puts the fewest possible filters or impediments between the creator and audience. The Public does not control the publishing process in the same way that a commercial publisher does. As a result there are stylistic and quality variations from title to title. The resulting books are like hearth-baked bread or handcrafted beer compared to more uniform, but less distinctive, products of commercial counterparts.

Treat authors as partners.

The Public Press is destined to become an author co-operative, where the authors are business partners with the publisher, not licensees paid a small percentage royalty on the sales of books. The Public Press offers an alternative to the traditional author/publisher model.

Leave the lightest possible footprint.

Book publishing, historically, has been a notoriously inefficient industry from the standpoint of resource consumption. A book can travel across the country only to be returned, unsold, to its original point of shipment. The Public Press strives for economies of scale-small scale. New technologies have made available writing and editing tools, print on demand options, improved communications, and new sales outlets that make it possible for publishing to be a model of resource efficiency.

Shout from the highest tree.

The Public Press is comprised of a community of individuals who share certain values (such as an appreciation for independent thought and freedom of speech) but who may not share geography or demography. The success of The Public Press is entirely dependent on our ability to reach these people and to convince them to involve others. As opposed to our namesake counterparts, National Public Radio and Public Television, The Public Press receives no government funding.

What is a "Four-Part Trilogy?"
It is a "Totally Beyondered" Concept.

Life has a way of interfering with art. *Beyond Yonder*, *The King of Vermont*, and *Darwin and the Tunnel of Love* were always intended by the author to be a single work, telling the epic story of the daily lives and times of the inhabitants of the tiny hamlet of Upper Granville, Vermont.

But life intervenes. It happens! Day jobs take priority. Parents grow old. Little publishers sell to big publishers. Editors move on to different jobs. Opportunities knock. Kids leave home. It happens! It happens! And it happens!

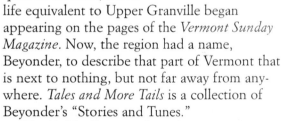

As a result, the epic novel came out in fits and spurts. First, *Beyond Yonder*. That's when the publisher got sold. Then, *King of Vermont*, that's when the editor quit. Meanwhile, a real life equivalent to Upper Granville began appearing on the pages of the *Vermont Sunday Magazine*. Now, the region had a name, Beyonder, to describe that part of Vermont that is next to nothing, but not far away from anywhere. *Tales and More Tails* is a collection of Beyonder's "Stories and Tunes."

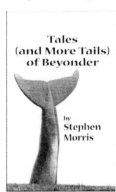

The Public Press is pleased to present Beyonder in its original glory – ficticious and non-ficticious. This is the Director's cut, digitally remastered, and in full Dolby sound. This is Beyonder at the peak of foliage, at the depth of Mud Season despair, in the procreational frenzy of the vernal kaboom, and in the enveloping eternity of an August night watching the meteors shower in a part of the world where you can actually still see them.

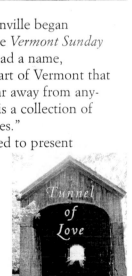

Also from **Stephen Morris:**

Arthur Gordon doesn't get it. After a string of successful films his latest opus is reviled as sexist and politically incorrect. Emotionally wounded, he retreats to the sanctity of a summer cottage where carefree recollections buffer him from his self-inflicted firestorm. Only after running headlong into the realities of changing times does he decide that redemption will be his only if he can catch a big fish on a little feather.